Winner
Takes All

Katie Price is one of the UK's top celebrities. She was formerly the glamour model Jordan and is now a bestselling author, successful business woman and star of her own reality TV show. In 2015, Katie won Celebrity Big Brother. She is a patron of Vision Charity and currently lives in Sussex with her five children.

Also available by Katie Price

Fiction

Angel

Crystal

Angel Uncovered

Sapphire

Paradise

The Come-back Girl

In the Name of Love

He's the One

Make My Wish Come True

Playing With Fire

Non-fiction

Jordan: A Whole New World

Jordan: Pushed to the Limit

You Only Live Once

Love, Lipstick and Lies

Reborn

Katie Price x

Winner Takes All

arrow books

1 3 5 7 9 10 8 6 4 2

Arrow Books
20 Vauxhall Bridge Road
London SW1V 2SA

Arrow Books is part of the Penguin Random House group of companies
whose addresses can be found at global.penguinrandomhouse.com.

First published in Great Britain by Century in 2018
First published in paperback by Arrow Books in 2019

www.penguin.co.uk

A CIP catalogue record for this book is available from the British Library.

ISBN 9780099598961

Typeset in 12.07/15.75 pt Baskerville MT Pro
by Integra Software Services Pvt. Ltd, Pondicherry

Printed and bound in Great Britain by Clays Ltd, Elcograf S.p.A.

Penguin Random House is committed to a
sustainable future for our business, our readers
and our planet. This book is made from Forest
Stewardship Council® certified paper.

Praise for Katie Price's novels:

'A page turner ... it is brilliant' *Evening Standard*

'The perfect post-modern fairy tale' *Glamour*

'Angel is the perfect sexy summer read' *New Woman*

'A perfect book for the beach' *Sun*

'Glam, glitz, gorgeous people' *Woman*

'A real insight into the celebrity world' *OK!*

'Brilliantly bitchy' *New!*

'Celebrity fans, want the perfect night in? Flick back those
hair extensions, pull on the Juicy Couture trackie then join
Angel on her rocky ride to WAG central' *Scottish Daily*

'Crystal is charming. Gloriously infectious' *Evening Standard*

'Passion-filled ... an incredibly addictive read' *Heat*

'Peppered with cutting asides and a directness you can only
imagine coming from Katie Price, it's a fun, blisteringly
paced yet fluffy novel' *Cosmopolitan*

Chapter 1

December 2017

Jas collapsed into the back of an Uber, dropping the heavy bouquet and bulging Selfridges bag next to her. Her colleagues really were the best, spoiling her that afternoon with the flowers and lunch before she'd taken the rest of the day off to go shopping. Jas had treated herself to a Burberry eyeshadow palette, Jo Malone candle, Topshop ankle boots and her favourite Tom Ford perfume. It was her birthday, after all.

She let her eyes close momentarily and her navy-blue Prada heels slip off her feet as the Prius crawled through the bustling streets of Soho. It was the week before Christmas and, although it was only 6.30 p.m., groups of drunken revellers in Santa hats and Christmas jumpers were already laughing and singing. It was peak office

Christmas party time. Oxford Street was lit up by twinkling neon lights overhead.

Jas sighed. She might just have turned twenty-eight, but she felt more like fifty-eight! So far this week she had attended a launch for a major TV show on Monday and a drinks party for its crew on Tuesday. Wednesday was pre-birthday dinner and cocktails with her sisters, Megan and Lila; Thursday night she'd spent clubbing with her old mates from Manchester University, and today, her actual birthday, there'd been lunch with her closest colleagues before she went shopping. Jas was a TV producer in the entertainment division of Channel 6. This week she'd pitched what would be the biggest series of her career yet, a reality TV show called *Mr Right*, in which a houseful of female contestants would vie for the attention of one lucky man. It would be a dramatic, glamorous and expensive series and Jas was praying she would get the green light to go ahead with it. Her job was her passion and she needed a new project.

Jas wished she could have rejoined her team after work in the pub for a mulled wine, before going home to her flat in Hackney, East London. Usually she loved a night out, but at this point she could think of nothing better than a long, luxurious bath followed by a weekend under her duvet; phone off, make-up-free and bingeing on Netflix. Yet there was still one more event for her to attend: dinner with her husband Richard.

Most women would be thrilled at the prospect of going for a romantic, intimate birthday dinner with their husband. Then again, most husbands didn't stay out all night without their wives and eventually come home reeking of booze and cheap perfume. They'd been living apart for weeks now, Jas in their jointly owned flat and he in a temporary rental in Moorgate, a stone's throw from where he worked as a City trader. Nevertheless Richard had insisted that he take Jas to a small French restaurant in Islington where they had spent their last few anniversaries, saying this occasion was just as special.

She yawned and scraped her long, thick blonde hair into a messy bun, trying to muster up some energy but already mentally preparing for bed. Her phone beeped with a Whatsapp message. It was from Richard.

'Hey, babe, just checking you're on your way?'

Jas didn't reply, instead staring out of the window as the car approached Upper Street. Not for the first time that week, she started analysing where it all went wrong.

For years Jas had ignored their strained relationship, and Richard's increasingly arrogant and self-centred behaviour. Ignored the fact that they'd taken to sleeping in separate bedrooms months ago and barely touched or spoke to each other unless it was to say something negative. But when she'd seen his phone flashing with messages from another woman, read through their steamy exchanges, no doubt had been left in her mind that he was having an affair. She had thrown him out immediately. This dinner seemed to be his way of attempting to make things up with her, though she wasn't so sure one expensive meal could fix a broken marriage.

3

'Le Petit?' The Uber driver jolted Jas out of her train of thought. 'We're here, love.'

'Oh, thanks.' She slipped her heels back on. Let's just get this over with, she thought, fantasising about a hot chocolate and her pyjamas. Straight to the main course, no dessert, and you'll be home in a couple of hours.

Jas walked into the restaurant and was surprised not to see Richard at their usual table at the front by the window.

'Ms Whiteley?' asked a pretty maitre d', somehow knowing instantly who Jas was and what she was here for. 'Mr Butler is waiting for you at the back of the restaurant.'

'Ah.' Jas smiled and wound her way through the tables. Still no sign of Richard. The maitre d' pointed to a red velvet curtain, which Jas presumed led to a room even further back. *Weird.* She pulled the curtain aside.

'SURPRISE!'

Jas jumped back, screamed and dropped her bags and flowers to the floor. A huge area was filled with people she'd never seen before: grinning, popping champagne corks and bursting party poppers so confetti rained everywhere. 'What the ... ?' she started to say.

'Surprise!' Richard bounced over, planting a kiss on Jas's gobsmacked face and handing her a glass of champagne. 'Happy birthday, Jazzy. Sorry for scaring you but, you have to admit, you weren't expecting this!'

'No shit,' she hissed at him. 'You've just taken another twenty-eight years off my life. I was so shocked!' But before he could reply, throngs of strangers were kissing her on the cheek, congratulating her on how beautiful she looked, wishing her happy birthday and laughing that 'of course, this was all Richard's idea'.

Jas smiled at the crowd, not wishing to be rude, but shot a reproachful look at Richard, who simply winked at her then leant in to whisper: 'You do like it, don't you?' He looked so hopeful.

'Well ...' Her voice trailed off. She was feeling a tad guilty and wondering what was so bad about a party being thrown in her honour. She'd sleep when she was dead, right?

'It's just ... I mean ... who *are* all these people?'

'Colleagues. Mates. Friends from work.' It was typical of Richard to throw Jas a birthday party and invite *his* friends. He disappeared to circulate.

Then, thankfully, Jas saw her sisters, Meg and Lila, weaving through the crowd towards her. 'Thank God. People I actually like. And recognise! I was starting to feel like I'd walked into a parallel universe.' The three of them embraced in a warm group-hug.

Jas was the middle sibling. They'd grown up in a close family. Her parents had lived in and around Manchester their entire lives. Lila, the youngest at twenty-five, had recently moved to London too. The last Jas could remember, Lila was living in a warehouse in Seven Sisters and working in a pub in Camden, though she could never keep up with her sister's escapades.

As the eldest, Meg was 'the sensible one'. She ran a boutique in Manchester city centre and was happily married, though loved coming down to London to see her sisters. They'd each inherited their dad's green eyes and their mum's blonde hair. Jas's was long and, although naturally curly, she hit it with GHD straighteners most mornings, while Meg let her curls hang free to her shoulders. Lila's hair was cut just below her chin in a sleek bob.

Meg grabbed Jas's hand. 'I am *so* sorry about this. I knew you'd been out all week and just wanted to chill tonight. I'm still recovering from our night on Wednesday so you must be knackered.'

Then Lila interrupted, 'But Richard Facebook-messaged us both saying we *had* to come as it would mean so much to you. And we just figured, if you hated it then at least we'd be here to make you feel better.'

'And,' Meg continued, 'he says he has some other big surprise coming up and we couldn't miss that. So, I drove down and I'm going to crash with you and drive back up north tomorrow.' It was a given that Jas's sofa bed would always be offered to her sisters.

Jas gulped down some champagne. 'I don't *hate* it. It's just so typical of Richard. I've been telling him all week that I need space but he insisted we must talk and, he's right, we do need to get together at some point … ' She sighed. 'A quiet dinner is one thing but throwing me a big party when we're not even together? It's weird.'

Meg and Lila looked awkwardly at each other. They knew the ins and outs of Jas's marriage and how much she'd put up with from Richard over the years. Jas finding out he was sleeping with another woman was nothing new. He'd cheated on her several times but always managed to win her back. This last time looked like it was the final straw, though.

'Maybe he really is trying to turn over a new leaf?' offered Lila, but Jas raised an eyebrow. Her little sister still somewhat idolised her brother-in-law, thinking he was achingly cool with his big-shot City job and access to the most exclusive nightlife. She often stuck up for him, which could be annoying.

Jas gulped down her champagne. 'Listen to me, all grumpy. It's my goddamn' birthday. And it's a party! Let's go get more drinks. And there's cake, right? There better be cake otherwise I'm *outta* here!'

The three sisters giggled and Lila brandished a bottle. 'Drinks first, cake second, and find-me-a-hot-guy third. Richard works in the *City*. There must be a handsome, rich, eligible bachelor here somewhere!'

Be careful what you wish for, thought Jas. When she and Richard fell in love he was the charming, handsome bachelor fancied by everyone at their university. Six years older than Jas, he had taken an extended gap year (paid for by his parents' bulging bank account) spent drinking his way through Australia. Since his father had then insisted he 'get back to the real world', he was finishing a Masters degree in Economics at Manchester while Jas was in her second year of a Media Studies BA when they met. It wasn't long before he was offered a lucrative job as a trader in the City, complete with a brand-new flat for them to live in until they found their own place. Jas was head over heels in love with him. How could she not be? Richard was charismatic and gorgeous, with ash-blond hair, bright blue eyes and a dazzling smile. Sure, he was a little spoilt, Jas thought at the time, but no one was perfect. When he whisked her off for a surprise weekend to Paris the following year, and proposed in a restaurant overlooking the Eiffel Tower, she accepted instantly.

Now, four years after that weekend and three years since their lavish wedding, she could barely recognise the man she'd met when they were both students. Working in the cut-throat City of London with its big bonuses, sixteen-hour days on the trading floor, late nights spent in swanky clubs 'letting off steam', as he called it, and lavish expense accounts, had turned Richard from sweet and funny to power-hungry and status-obsessed. As Jas looked around the restaurant she wondered how many of these party revellers he was trying to impress. Then she heard the tinkle of a silver spoon tapped against a glass. She looked over to see Richard standing on a chair.

'Everyone, can I have your attention, please?' he called. 'First of all, thank you for coming. I know we gave Jas the fright of her life but that's what birthdays are all about, right?' Some of his co-workers started cheering at this. Meg, Lila and Jas looked at each other.

'Now, I've brought you all here not just to celebrate my beautiful wife's birthday, but because I want to make an announcement ... here ... in front of all our friends and loved ones. As you may or may not know, Jasmine and I have had a rocky few months. Marriages are hard. Especially when you have jobs as demanding, time-consuming and competitive as ours.'

Jas narrowed her eyes. She had no idea where Richard was going with this but she was already cringing. Her sisters aside, she recognised a couple of faces from previous Christmas parties held by the firm Richard worked for. Describing them as *loved ones* was a stretch.

'But I want everyone to know – and Jazzy, in particular, I want *you* to know – just how much I love you.' A few women in the crowd ahhhh-ed at this. 'And I've missed you.' He stepped off the chair and came towards Jas, taking her hand. 'I've really missed you, babe. And ...' At this, the crowd gasped as Richard knelt down on one knee.

'What are you doing?' whispered Jas in dismay. He held out a small blue Tiffany box and offered it to her.

'We've both made mistakes, Jasmine. Neither of us are perfect. But I want to keep trying. So ...' He opened the box to reveal a shiny set of keys. More gasps from the crowd.

'I've bought us a house! Well, I've made an offer on a house and it's been accepted! These aren't the real keys, of course. But they're a symbol of our future.' He sprang up. 'This is all for you, Jas, so we can be together again!' He kissed her as the crowd toasted them and cheered.

'Jas, this house is perfect,' he said, lowering his voice while the guests mostly returned to their own conversations, a few of them still patting Richard on the back and offering him congratulations.

'It's in Surrey ... huge, with a massive garden. It's totally rundown, of course, and needs a full overhaul. But that's a project for you! I know you've always wanted to do up a house. I'll keep the flat here, of course, and stay up during the week while you're decorating. Then I'll come down for weekends. It's perfect!'

Jas was speechless, turning to her sisters who, like her, wore shocked expressions. It took a few moments for her to find her voice. 'You've *bought a house*?'

'Had an offer accepted, yes. Don't worry, babe, my bonus covered most of the deposit.' He winked at her.

'For me to *do up*? While you *stay here*?' She spluttered out the words. 'Let me get this straight: you live here Monday to Friday, alone, in our flat, while I live, alone, in *Surrey*, decorating? What about my job? My life, my friends, my family? You do realise Surrey is in the south of England and my family are in the north?'

'I don't get it. Jazzy, I thought you'd be happy.'

'Happy? Richard, we're not together. We're separated!' Jas shouted the last word so loudly that the crowd quietened, listening in.

'Darling, don't make a scene.' Richard laughed, awkwardly, only infuriating Jas further. Just who did he think he was?

'This is nothing to do with what I want. You know this isn't what I want!' She looked around the restaurant. 'Jesus, Richard, I don't even like French food. In fact, I hate it! *You're* the one who insists on coming here every year and not once have you asked me where I'd like to go. And now you just want me out of the way in *Surrey*' – she spat out the word – 'tucked away like a good little wife so you can live the single life in London. This is over, Richard. OVER. I've told you so many times. I don't want to be married any more.'

'But I thought ...'

'What? That you'd throw me a party, put an offer on a house without even consulting me, plan out my life the

10

way *you* want it – and I'm just going to forget that you've been cheating on me ever since you got your fucking awful job?'

Richard turned red with rage. Jas knew she'd just crossed a major line. It was one thing rejecting him, quite another doing so in front of the people he desperately wanted to impress. Obviously, he'd thought he could buy his way out of this one but Jas didn't forgive so easily. She'd entertained the idea of giving their relationship another go, but who was she kidding? She'd been thinking about the inevitable ever since they separated and now she knew it was exactly the right thing to do.

'I was going to tell you this next week when I had the go-ahead from my lawyer,' she continued. 'I wouldn't have chosen to do so in front of a roomful of people but since you love big scenes so much – I want a divorce.'

Richard's eyes were fixed on her and glistening with fury. The whole room fell deadly silent. Lila and Meg stifled grins.

'I'm going home,' announced Jas. 'Now.' She dropped the Tiffany box of keys on the floor as Richard stared at her aghast. 'Keep your damn' house.' She raised her glass of champagne and knocked it back in one. 'Happy birthday to me.'

Chapter 2

June 2018

Kingley's nightclub was packed with revellers. As the most famous and successful bar in Liverpool, Saturday nights here were always the busiest of the week, but nothing guaranteed full capacity more than match day when England had been playing in the World Cup – and won. The long oak bar had ten black-clad mixologists behind it, furiously whipping up cocktails. The booth area was full of men in suits and women in tiny dresses and huge hair, dancing on tables and sofas to Rihanna blasting from the DJ stand. Outside, queues formed around the block with shivering patrons waiting to get in. They'd be there a long time. Without your name on the coveted guest list, there was a strict 'one in, one out rule' past 11 p.m.

Naturally, Jas had no trouble getting her name and Monica's on the list for Kingley's. A quick call to the PR and marketing manager for the club was all it took. Jas's charm and confidence – essential traits in her job as a producer – meant she could talk her way into anything, but a simple mention of the fact that she was looking for contestants for *Mr Right*, a hot new reality TV show on Channel 6, not only got her and her assistant producer in, but the manager gave them their own private booth and drinks on the house all night. Sitting in a corner getting pissed for free was not what the women were here for, though.

Jas jostled her way through the crowds, holding her gin and tonic in the air to prevent it from being knocked over her brand-new Reiss white dress. She nudged Monica's back and pointed in the direction of the ladies' room. 'That's where we'll find our stars,' she yelled over the music.

'Yes! Great shout, Jas,' replied Monica.

They snaked their way through the crowds, men turning their heads as the two women walked past.

Jas's hair was swept up into an elegant bun, her cheekbones shimmering with highlighter and her full lips painted in Mac's Lady Danger lipstick. She'd bought her dress especially for tonight and it fitted perfectly, short but with a high neck. When it came to Saturday nights at Kingley's, women in Liverpool did not do things by half. Hair and lips were glossy. Tans, eyebrows (and certain body parts) were fake, and plenty of skin was on show between designer dresses and sky-high heels. They were all dressed to impress and Jas had no trouble fitting in. She adored fashion and dressing up was one of her favourite parts of a night out.

They eventually reached the women's cloakroom and let out sighs of relief. There were two aisles of cubicles, sinks outside them, then a huge area with pink sofas, stools and mirrors outlined with light bulbs. The whole place was full of girls: reapplying make-up, chattering, taking selfies and spraying generous amounts of hairspray.

'Bloody hell!' exclaimed Jas, adjusting her strapless bra from outside her dress. 'I knew it would be busy but this is ridiculous. It took us ten minutes just to get here.'

'Seen anyone yet?' whispered Monica, smoothing her long slinky black dress and shaking her blow-dried brunette hair.

Jas nodded to her assistant producer. 'We'll have no trouble finding a few candidates in this place. We'll head upstairs to VIP later. The best-looking girls will flock to where the footballers are all drinking. But I think right here is where we'll hit the jackpot. Look around.'

Mr Right was a British version of the popular American show *The Bachelor*; Jas had had the idea months ago of bringing it to the UK. She'd worked tirelessly on the pitch and, to her delight, it had been signed off just after Christmas. She and Monica had been working solely on it ever since.

The premise was that one lucky man was to spend eight weeks in a luxurious villa living with fifteen women, all vying for his attention. 'Mr Right' would get to know each of the girls through a series of romantic dates, either individually or in groups. Week by week, contestants who didn't make the grade would be asked to leave. Everything would be filmed and the winner – the object of Mr Right's affection – would be chosen by him live on air and then they would, in theory, become boyfriend and girlfriend. They'd also jet off for a two-week holiday in a five-star resort in the Maldives and their relationship would be covered by a glossy and lucrative magazine deal – fashion shoot and full interview included. Channel 6 were predicting it would be their most popular show yet.

Jas had acquired a background in reality TV hits since joining the channel two years ago. She'd sought new talent for various other shows as well as producing a small but successful one-off special where celebrities helped brides-to-be get in shape for their wedding. But *Mr Right* was on another level – and, even though the whole idea was Jas's genius brainwave, she was not the big bosses' first choice of producer for it. Some of the bosses worried that she wasn't experienced enough. But the head of entertainment at Channel 6, Harry Burrell, saw something in Jas: hunger, passion and raw talent. He was a tough boss who liked to remind his team that everyone was 'expendable', but Jas had fought hard for her chance to prove herself – pitches, presentations and lengthy emails about just why she was the perfect woman for the job and more than capable of leading the show, helped by an experienced director and an assistant. Now, everyone was taking a chance on the young producer with big ambitions. If the show wasn't a success, she'd be waiting a very long time to get a chance like this again.

She'd already found Mr Right himself, a six-foot-tall gorgeous Australian single father called Dylan.

A semi-famous rugby player in England, he also had investments in a chain of restaurants. Jas had first seen him on Instagram and done some background digging, found his agent and approached him about the show. In person Dylan was the perfect gentleman: sweet but sexy with an appealing touch of cheekiness. He was sure to win over the nation. The hard part now was to find fifteen women to compete for his attention, and on the contestants Jas's brief was clear: there must be a mix of ethnicities, backgrounds, personalities, characters, ages and jobs, but all the women should have one thing in common. They must be stunningly beautiful. The most popular contestants were sure to become celebrities in their own right.

'I spotted Melody Mane in one of the booths,' continued Monica. 'You know, that beauty blogger? She has a hundred thousand Instagram followers. She's single after breaking up with that boy band guy.'

'We'll get to her,' replied Jas. 'But we need to make sure we have a few complete unknowns as well. Normal girls viewers can relate to as well as aspire to be.' She headed straight for the mirrors where a trio of women with thick Liverpool accents were shrieking with laughter at something one of them had said.

'Hi, ladies, sorry to bother you but my friend and I work for Channel 6 and are actually on the hunt for potential candidates for a new TV series we're working on.'

The girls screeched in excitement. 'We're going to be on telly?' At that, various other clubbers glanced over and not-so-subtly listened in.

'We'd like you to *apply* to be on telly,' continued Jas, filling them in on the premise of the show. 'Anyone single and over eighteen has the right to apply, but we've come here to vet girls we think are particularly special. They will go straight to the top of the pile of applicants.'

'Like us?' asked one of the group, eyes wide.

'Like you,' replied Monica with a smile. 'You've all clearly got the looks and confidence.'

'How do we know you're for real?' asked someone from the crowd that had quickly formed around Jas and Monica.

Jas took a pile of business cards from her green leather clutch bag. 'Here are my details and all the info for the show is on that website there.' She handed out her cards, which were grabbed instantly by a swarm of hands embellished with acrylic nails.

'Send a short video of yourself to that address or come to the Echo Arena tomorrow afternoon between two and five. We're holding a casting.'

By now dozens of girls were crowding the pair, desperate to know more. The chance to be on TV was a draw and the questions came thick and fast.

'Well, the villa will be in Ibiza and we start filming there in the last week of July, start of August, when it's nice and hot,' explained Jas. 'We'll finish at the end of September, so that's two months. Then we'll want to do follow-up interviews as the show won't actually broadcast until January 2019.' She hoped it would be commissioned for a second series and that after the first ended she'd be flooded with new applicants.

'How romantic!' came a voice from the small crowd. 'What about the guy?'

'Can't say anything about him, I'm afraid. It's confidential for now but, trust me, he's hot.'

As Jas chatted away, she noticed a beautiful mixed-race girl with thick, dark hair to just below her shoulders, full lips and dark eyes. She was striking but, unlike the other women, listened in silently to what was being said and kept her distance. There was something mysterious and intriguing about her. Jas knew talent when she saw it. But just as she caught the mystery girl's eyes, she scuttled out of the cloakroom and back into the crowd.

Chapter 3

'No, no, no ... they're all too bloody nice! Where are the bitches? We need drama, Jasmine. Drama and catfights and tears. *That's* what gets ratings up!'

Jas sipped her skinny latte and nodded. 'We've got a good mix so far, Harry, trust me. I think we're more than halfway there. We've done castings in Liverpool, Birmingham and Essex, and are still going through the video applications. We've been on it non-stop for weeks with the researchers.'

Harry Burrell tutted. 'Yeah, okay, but no more normos. I want some real talent in there.'

'We've got Melody Mane. And that Hoxton Radio presenter, Alex Adams. She's a model, too. Gorgeous. Loads of fans on social media and she's really mouthy and opinionated. She's from a tough background. Her single mum raised her on a council estate in South London. I don't think she'll take kindly to any competition. You'll get a lot out of her. We need a mix of high and low profiles, though.'

'Fine, fine. Keep going, keep updating me. It's crucial we get this element right, Jasmine. No one cares about Dylan. The girls are what's going to attract the viewers and headlines. We need people to root for and against.'

Jas nodded, busy scrolling through Instagram on her iPhone.

'Oh, and have you met Legal yet? They're up on the twelfth floor. You better do that sooner rather than later. As we get closer to making the final selection you'll need to get contracts drawn up.'

'Yeah, it's David Griffin, right? He drew up the contract for Dylan, I met him weeks ago.'

Harry tutted again. 'No, no, no. David retired last week. They've got some new chap over from news covering entertainment now. He's the contact for all things *Mr Right* for the foreseeable.'

Jas started scribbling on her notepad. 'Name?'

'No bloody idea. Now piss off.'

Jas smirked. Harry was notorious for being the grumpiest, hardest, most ratings-hungry executive in the company, which made him perfect for a high-powered role in TV. Jas wasn't scared of him, though. She knew the way to win around bosses like Harry: work your arse off, get results and, most importantly, show no fear.

'Right you are, Hazza,' she said, standing up from the black leather sofa in his office and heading to the door.

'Bloody insubordinate,' Harry muttered, though he smiled as soon as Jas was safely out of sight.

*

One evening a couple of weeks later, Jas arrived home just after 10 p.m. She and Monica had already found a brilliant final selection of willing contestants to present to Harry, but had still spent the afternoon going through more applications, just in case there were any fantastic girls they'd managed to miss, and trawling Instagram and Twitter to check there weren't any more semi-high-profile names they should approach. They'd finally called it a day at nine but Jas was satisfied the long hours were worth it as she'd found the perfect final contestant to make the show complete: a twenty-three-year-old fitness instructor from London called Charlotte – five foot three, with dark skin, glossy dark hair, huge brown eyes and a great figure. She was sweet and, Jas could tell, entirely genuine. Her video application, explaining how she'd been unlucky in love and just wanted to find The One, would be bound to win the viewers over. Jas was sure she was 'National Treasure' material, unlike some of the other more entitled-seeming girls, who were right for the show but for all the wrong reasons. 'Bitch players' she and Monica called them; the ones who were clearly fame-hungry and would do anything just to be on TV.

Arriving back home, Jas kicked off her black L. K. Bennett loafers. She had a weakness for luxury labels but was also a savvy shopper and adept at hunting out a sale. She considered her treasured finds investment pieces and, while she had the odd designer accessory or pair of shoes, the rest of her wardrobe was Topshop, H&M and ASOS all the way.

She poured herself a generous glass of chilled Sauvignon Blanc and threw herself onto the sofa. Richard had officially moved out for good last December after the disastrous surprise birthday party, and Jas had bought him out of the flat. She loved the freedom, but the downside was the financial burden of a gigantic mortgage on the Hackney property. In recent months her shopping fetish had come to an abrupt halt and she would no doubt have to start selling some of her wardrobe on eBay and borrow money from her parents to help with solicitor's fees for the divorce.

Still, she loved living alone, even if the flat still reminded her so much of Richard, despite her best efforts to redecorate within her modest budget. She'd found this place not long after they'd moved to London and were staying in the place provided by Richard's new employers. He had wanted to stay there for as long as possible but Jas felt it was important they had their own home. When she'd found this flat, he couldn't have been any less interested but she fell in love with it instantly and took pride in decorating it. There was a spacious, open-plan kitchen and living area, with marble worktops and chrome fittings throughout the kitchen and a black dining table with four chairs. An elegant grey sofa and rug stood in the living area, and there were framed black-and-white photographs on the walls. When Richard left, Jas replaced the pictures of them taken in happier times with photos of her own friends and family. And she introduced some colour and warmth into the previously monochrome interior in the form of potted plants, green and pink cushions, and a copper floor lamp.

Even after the party, Richard had begged Jas to come back to him, but she'd told him it was too late and that she was already in talks with divorce lawyers, so she'd been surprised when he had agreed to let her buy him out of the flat so easily and quickly. He'd even given her a generous deal. And, for a while, he stopped the incessant calls and emails. Fleetingly, Jas had wondered if she was making the right decision after all in letting him go. Was this a big mistake? Did she really want to be a divorcee before she'd reached the age of thirty? Maybe Richard could change after all, and go back to being the guy she fell in love with ...

Sadly, that wasn't the case. As soon as the ink was dry on the property settlement, Richard turned completely irrational, drunkenly declaring love one day, shouting spiteful words down the phone the next, or else refusing her calls entirely when she tried to contact him about the divorce. She'd had the papers couriered to both his office and flat and he was still denying receiving them, rendering it impossible for her to proceed.

'Clearly, he never expected you to go through with buying him out,' Meg had said last month. 'He probably thought that if he was nice enough to you, made it easy for you, you'd forgive him and take him back.'

'I did think about it,' Jas admitted.

'Exactly. So, when you didn't, he would have been furious and that's why he's behaving like a child now. The sooner you're rid of him the better, honey.'

As she took a gulp of wine, Jas thought back to that conversation and decided to phone her sister. They spoke several times a week. Meg answered on the first ring. 'Hiya, hun. How's the hunt for the next Charlotte Cronby going?'

'Charlotte Crosby, you mean!' Jas laughed. 'And I didn't know you watched *Geordie Shore*.'

'I don't. Keep seeing her on the *Mail Online* though. These celebs are all the same to me anyway.'

The girls chatted about *Mr Right*, Meg's boutique in Manchester and her husband Oscar, who worked as an estate agent.

'He made spag bol for tea and we're about to catch up on *The Walking Dead*. Bliss! Aren't you supposed to be at some fancy club tonight in the name of research?'

'Nah, not 'til the weekend. Clubs won't be busy on a Wednesday. Anyway, I think we've got our final fifteen. I might be able to just let my hair down rather than prowl for women! Are you still going to see Mum and Dad this weekend with Lila?'

'I'm supposed to be but she's gone AWOL again. Haven't heard from her since last week. Have you? Honestly, that girl. You know she got fired again?'

'Bloody hell, not again.' Jas sighed. It had to be the fifth time in six months that her little sister had left a job, either of her own accord or at her boss's insistence.

'What's the matter with her?'

'Lacks direction,' sniffed Meg. 'You know this. And you're the one down there in London supposed to be keeping an eye on her.'

Jas frowned. It would be easier to herd a bus full of schoolkids on a trip than it would be to keep up with Lila's escapades.

'I know as much as you do, Meg. She hasn't picked up her phone all week but I know she's alive because she's been posting on Facebook though I've no idea where she is, who she's with or what she's doing. I'll try her now.'

'All right, honey. Keep me posted. Love you.'

'Love you.'

Jas took another sip of wine and listened as Lila's phone rang out. Flipping on the TV to her favourite guilty pleasure, *Keeping Up with the Kardashians*, she threw her phone down on the other end of the sofa.

She couldn't help feeling slightly annoyed with Meg. Why should Jas be the one to 'keep an eye' on Lila? Meg was the eldest, the one with the quiet life and steady husband up in Manchester. *She* should be the one keeping tabs on their rogue little sister. Didn't Meg realise Jas had her own problems? The small matter of a divorce for one thing, a prime-time show to produce for another.

As Khloé Kardashian argued with Kris Jenner about the latest party they were planning, Jas started to analyse her life. By her twenty-ninth birthday she'd be a divorcee. That's if Richard ever agreed to the divorce.

And, as if dating in London wasn't hard enough already, now she was going to be seen as damaged goods. Though, she had to admit, she still received plenty of attention everywhere she went. Jas was five foot seven with long, shapely legs, a small waist, glowing skin, dark eyes with naturally long lashes and a wardrobe to die for. Not to mention a high-flying job in TV, her own property in London, a close family and an active, glamorous social life. But unsurprisingly, the divorce was making her feel tense and unsettled. Jas sighed deeply. She always tried to look on the positive side of life but lately it was proving to be more and more difficult. She'd started to question herself. Was she so upbeat because people expected her to be? Jas had to be the fun-loving sister for sensible Meg and the reliable big sister for Lila, as well as ambitious, tenacious and successful at work. But right now she was finding it exhausting keeping up on all these fronts. Her disastrous marriage to Richard had made her doubt herself. After all, could she trust her own judgement if she'd married someone like him?

When it came to relationships, Jas hadn't been single for longer than a year since she was twenty. When she'd decided to dump Richard for good she was excited by the thought of being free again, but now she just felt alone. And – though she'd never admit this to anyone – scared that she always would be.

Chapter 4

The next morning Jas yawned her way out of bed, determined to shake off last night's gloomy mood. It was a bright, beautiful day. After a treacherous winter that had seen record low temperatures and heavy snow, and then a pitiful spring, it was now a beautiful summer with a record heatwave. And it was Thursday, almost the weekend! Tomorrow she and Monica were hitting a few clubs. Seriously, what did Jas have to complain about?

She arrived at Channel 6's vast building in London Bridge dressed in loafers and a white maxi dress. Her blonde hair, straightened that morning, hung loose. She stopped to take a selfie in the sunshine, carefully positioning the camera so it showed just her outfit and not her face. Jas liked showing off her clothes but wanted to remain somewhat behind the scenes.

She worked on the sixth floor in the 'entertainment hub'. The office was entirely open-plan and she sat in a corner at a bank of desks with other producers and researchers, facing an incredible view of the River Thames.

'Just in time,' said Monica, placing a steaming skinny latte on Jas's desk a minute after she'd sat down and flipped her iMac on. 'Burrell wants to see you in his office. Now.'

Jas looked at her watch and groaned. 'It's not even ten and already I'm getting a bollocking? What now?'

Monica simply shrugged.

Jas walked across the floor. The blinds were up in Harry's office so she could see him deep in conversation with someone with their back to Jas. That someone had short, cropped hair and broad shoulders. Jas was staring so intently she almost walked right into the door.

'Ah, Whiteley. Come in.' Harry beckoned Jas inside and nodded to the man in front of his desk. 'This is Luke Hawkins from the twelfth floor.'

The man stood up and extended his hand, giving Jas a warm smile. He was gorgeous. Dark green eyes – or were they hazel? – cropped strawberry-blond hair, a touch of stubble around a strong jawline plus six feet of solid muscle. It was like Chris Pratt had come to life and was standing in front of her!

'Hi, good to meet you,' said Luke, shaking Jas's hand. *Oooh – and a northern boy*, she thought appreciatively, though she couldn't instantly make out where exactly he was from.

'Hi,' she replied, hoping that she was showing off a dazzling smile and not a goofy grin. Then she remembered. 'Twelfth ... the legal department?'

''Fraid so.' Luke smiled at her.

'Right, you've met now. Sit, Jasmine. We're down to the final girls, yes?'

'Almost. There's someone else I found last night – Charlotte Truss. We need her in. She's a sweetheart. Big smile, great look. She's perfect within the mix. I'll get her to come in for an interview as soon as possible. Then we've got a few more interviews next week, but we're getting close.'

'Provided they all check out, legally, and sign the relevant documentation,' put in Luke. 'I'll need to do basic background checks, just to make sure there are no alarming criminal records or red flags we need to be aware of. We'll ask them to sign consent forms, of course. There will be a lot for them to read with all the terms and conditions of taking part, so we should aim to get the documentation out as soon as possible so they have a couple of weeks to read and return.'

'Not a problem,' replied Jas coolly, already picturing her line-up of beautiful women looking disarmingly glamorous against the gorgeous, dramatic backdrop of the Ibizan hills. Her mind veered off to the opening scene where Dylan would meet his lucky ladies. She wondered if she should have them all lined up for when he arrived on the scene, or whether he should meet them one by one. *Perhaps there could be a party on the first night and he gets to meet them all then, dressed up in their finery?* Harry jolted Jas away from her thoughts.

'I've got another meeting in ten minutes so, Jasmine, have the final names, pictures and biographies ready to present to me at one p.m.,' he said, bluntly. 'Then you two can iron out all the legalities. How's the Ibiza place looking?'

'Booked, deposit paid and ready to start filming when we get there,' replied Jas. 'We've had official approval to film out and about on the island and Monica is sorting work visas for the crew. It's all under control, Harry.'

'Excellent. Now, bugger off both of you.'

'Nice chap, isn't he?' laughed Luke when they were safely out of the lion's den.

'Ah, he's not so bad.' Jas smiled. 'So, you've just started here then?'

'I've worked at the channel for a couple of years but I've been over in news. When David left they asked me to help out the entertainment section of the legal department for a bit. Makes a nice change from the Prime Minister's office threatening to sue us every other week because of some allegedly scandalous story we've reported.'

Jas smiled, instantly warming to this man. 'I'm afraid you might not find things any easier down here. Only last week some nutter threatened to sue me if I didn't put her in *Mr Right*. There are some crazy people out there and most of them are desperate to be on telly!'

Luke laughed softly. 'That's what makes it interesting though, right?'

At that moment Monica appeared, wide-eyed at the sight of Jas talking to this handsome new face. 'Jas? All okay with the boss?'

'Yep, all good, he just wanted an update on where we were.'

Monica cleared her throat and side-glanced at Luke as if to say, 'Who on earth is *that*?'

'And to meet our new lawyer,' Jas continued. 'Monica Bright, this is Luke Hawkins. He's taken over from David on twelfth and is going to make sure we don't get sued or jailed.'

'Nice to meet you.' Luke smiled, stretching out his hand to Jas's assistant.

Monica shook it, taking her time and fluttering her eyelashes. '*Very* nice to meet you, Luke.'

Jas could barely stop herself from laughing.

Luke clearly clocked on to the flirting but was either too polite or too embarrassed to do anything but look down with a sheepish smile. He turned to Jas. 'Anyway, I've got a conference call but let me know when Harry has approved your names so far and I'll do all the boring legal bits. I've got a fair bit to get through before birthday drinks for someone from news later at the pub across the road.'

'Oh, Sue Leonard?' Monica jumped in.

'That's the one.'

'Lovely Sue,' enthused Monica. Sue was a senior editor at Channel 6 but Jas, Monica and their team barely knew her. 'A few of us from entertainment might pop over. Especially now we know you're going to be there. What better way to get to know our new lawyer?'

'Great,' replied Luke. 'In that case I look forward to seeing you both later.' He gave Jas a quick nod and headed for the lifts.

Jas turned to her friend, laughing. 'What are you like? *Especially now we know you're going to be there.*' She said the last sentence in a baby voice.

'My God, if I was single, I'd have my tongue down his throat in seconds.'

'Lovely image,' dead-panned Jas. She walked back to her desk, Monica in hot pursuit. 'And by the way, we barely know Sue.'

'Everyone knows Sue. She's part of the furniture of Channel 6. And she did invite us. There's money behind the bar for the first couple of hours too, I hear.'

'She invited everyone. Harry's not actually expecting us to go.'

Monica raised her eyebrows. 'We're going. And you're going to make an impression on that hot lawyer.'

Jas shrugged. What else was she going to do tonight? 'Sure, why not? Try not to pounce on Luke straight away though, eh?'

'No promises.' Monica winked at her and sashayed over to her desk. Jas turned to her computer, mentally reviewing Luke's last words to her. *I look forward to seeing you later*. Was he flirting with her? Then again, wasn't that *seeing you both* later? She brushed aside the thought as she concentrated on her work, but secretly was pleased she was wearing her favourite dress.

The rest of the day was full on. Jas fielded calls and emails from prospective contestants, had her weekly content-planning meeting for the department in which everyone was expected to come up with fresh ideas, went through the list of candidates yet again with Harry, had a conference call with the owners of the Villa Valencia in Ibiza and arranged for Meg to courier down some glamorous dresses from her boutique. Jas figured she could get some of the girls to wear them on the show, plus steal a few outfits for herself of course. The perks of having a sister in fashion retail!

At 6 p.m. on the dot, Monica demanded they head over to the pub, having already applied a sultry smoky eye in preparation. Jas had retouched her own fresh make-up look with an extra coating of mascara and a slick of a red Tom Ford lipstick, making her green eyes pop.

Fuller's was packed and Monica and Jas, the only representatives from the entertainment department, seemed to bring a dose of glamour to a room full of black and beige outfits. Floor six was a medley of bright colours and designer jeans, but the news team were always required to wear plain suits.

After some brief small talk with Sue and quick hellos to the people they knew, Monica nodded towards the bar where trays of white and red wine, beer and orange juice stood ready. 'Come on, let's grab a freebie before they run out.'

'Ah, you beat me to it,' Jas heard a voice say behind her as she and Monica took the last remaining glasses of red wine from the tray. She turned to see Luke smiling at her and motioning towards the bar.

'Oops, sorry. Is red wine your drink, too? Here, take this one and I'll have white.'

But Luke held up his hands in refusal. 'You got that Pinot Noir fair and square. I'll grab a beer.'

Jas smiled back. 'More like the cheapest house red they've got.' She moved aside to let him reach for a beer and, as she did, was jostled against his chest by the crowd, getting a feel of his firm muscular build and a waft of a delicious musky aftershave. Monica was talking to someone else but saw the collision and winked at Jas who instantly looked away, hoping Luke didn't see.

'Sorry,' she said hastily. 'I didn't spill my drink on you, did I?'

'All good.' He smiled at her. 'But, why don't we move down the bar where there's a bit more space?' He stood back to let Jas go first and they huddled together in a quieter spot where they were able to lean against a wall.

'How's your day been?' he asked.

'Oh, you know, busy as usual. It's getting more exciting, though, the closer we get to Ibiza. I just want to make sure everything is perfect.' Even while she was speaking, Jas was mentally going over her to-do list for tomorrow. *Scene-play meeting, 10 a.m., budget meeting, 11 a.m....* .

'Well, you seem to be doing a terrific job so far. Burrell was raving about you this morning before you came into his office.'

'Really? Makes a nice change from him barking orders at me!'

'Nah, I think he's got a soft spot for you. And why shouldn't he? This was all your idea. He reckons it's going to be huge.'

'Well, it's a big team effort. I couldn't do it without Monica. She's amazing at budgets, problem-solving and logistics, whereas I've got more of a background in showbiz and reality TV. We make a great team.'

'She seems a lot of fun,' laughed Luke. 'And speak of the devil.'

Monica sidled up to the couple. 'I got stuck talking to Barry from accounts. Hello, Luke! What are you two gossiping about?'

'I was just saying what a fantastic job you're both doing on the show,' he said. 'There are whispers going round about how efficient you both are and that everyone is expecting this to be one of the channel's most popular shows. Burrell told me before Jas came in this morning that you're both doing a fantastic job.'

Jas was shocked to hear that their cranky boss would be so complimentary about them, especially to a man he'd just met, but Luke seemed so genuine. Normally compliments embarrassed Jas but she allowed herself to feel proud for once.

Monica wasn't quite so subtle. 'Well, we've worked our arses off, haven't we, Jas? Lots of late nights. And I suppose you two will be working very closely together, what with all the legal bits and bobs to sort through. Will your wife mind you staying late at work so often, Luke?'

Jas shot her friend a look and Luke scratched his head. 'Er, no, I'm not married.'

'Your girlfriend, then?' Monica was on a roll. At this blatant probing Jas felt she had to jump in.

'Mon, I don't think Luke wants to be interrogated about his personal life before he's finished his first beer of the evening.' She was mortified but still curious as to what his response would be.

35

'Um, nope. No girlfriend. Or boyfriend if that's what you were going to ask next. Anything else you want to get out of the way now? Star sign? History of mental illness?'

'Yes, and your blood type,' deadpanned Monica.

'Okay. Capricorn, no to the mental illness – that I know of anyway – and, actually, I have no idea what my blood type is so I'll have to get back to you on that.'

'Please, don't encourage her,' laughed Jas.

'I'm just getting to know the newest recruit to the *Mr Right* team,' replied Monica in her own defence. 'And where's that accent from, Luke?'

'Oh, to be fair, I was wondering that too,' said Jas.

'I was born in Cheshire. What about you? Let me guess ... Leeds?'

'Not quite. Just outside Manchester.'

'Look at you two, so much in common already,' teased Monica. At that, she was hugged by someone else she knew and distracted by the lively conversation that broke out, leaving Jas and Luke alone again.

'Sorry about her.'

'Don't be, she's great. So, is your family still up north?'

'Yep. Mum and Dad live in the house I grew up in. My elder sister Meg and her husband live about ten minutes away, and my little sister Lila lives down here.'

'Middle child?'

'Mm-hmm. Three girls. You gotta feel sorry for my dad, living with four women!'

'Ha! Me too. The middle of three, I mean. An elder brother and younger sister.'

'Do they still live in Cheshire?'

Luke shook his head and motioned to the bartender. 'Another drink?'

Jas looked around. Monica was over on the other side of the pub now, deep in conversation with Harry. 'Yes, please.'

Luke handed Jas a large glass of wine before taking a sip of his own beer. 'I lived up north until I was fourteen then my dad got a job in Hove near Brighton so we all moved down south.'

'And you've kept your accent? Very impressive!'

'Oh, yeah, that's not going anywhere! I go back up north quite a bit, to see friends and play rugby. Hove is a wonderful place to live though, have you been?'

'Yeah, my sister had her thirtieth birthday in Brighton a couple of years ago. Great clubs.'

'Hove is beautiful. Maybe I'll show you some time.' It was the flirtiest comment Luke had made since they'd met and he looked mildly embarrassed to have said it, scratching his head and quickly changing the subject. 'You know, for work. In case you wanted to film anything there.'

Jas smiled and moved the subject on to life in the north compared to the south. An hour later, drinks finished, she called it a night. She had an early spin class the next morning and was more than happy to leave Monica propping up the bar with Harry and some of the news team.

On the Tube home, Jas reflected on her evening. Luke was handsome, there was no doubt about it. She loved living in London but always maintained that northern boys had the best manners. She was so lost in her thoughts she almost missed her stop home. Walking back to her flat, she suddenly thought of Richard. It was hard not to, given that they had so much history together here, walking these streets, sharing the flat … The weight of the impending divorce dawned on her anew and she told herself not to think about Luke any more that night. Firmly, she reminded herself that romance was – had to be – the last thing on her mind right now.

Chapter 5

'Now, full breath out and slowly roll up. Make sure your head is the last thing to come up aaaaand – you're done! Well done, everybody, fantastic workout today. Give yourself a round of applause!'

Twenty women, sweaty and red-faced, clapped their hands wearily as they trudged out of the studio. The instructor, Charlotte Truss, who'd barely broken a sweat, started picking up and putting away the bars, steps and mats. One of her regular attendees, a sweet older woman, helped.

'Don't worry, Linda, I can handle this. Go and have coffee with the rest of the group.'

After the class, most of the women – housewives in Barnet – would have a leisurely coffee at the café at Fitness First. But Charlotte was always on the go. After she'd finished here, she'd be off to teach another Body Goals class at a gym in Crouch End. And later she was visiting her best friend Maya and her son – Charlotte's five-year-old Godson Rafi.

'They'll wait for me,' replied Linda. 'I want to hear all about that boy you were seeing! I've been married for forty years, Charley, I have to live my life vicariously through you! What was his name? Jamie? With the Ferrari? He sounded very exciting.'

Charlotte piled step blocks on top of each other. 'Yeah, well, exciting is one way of putting it. Flakey is another. He texted me every day for two months, but now I haven't heard from him for a week. I rang him and he said he was at his grandma's because she was sick.' She sighed. 'He promised to call me back but didn't. Then I looked on his Facebook page and there were pictures of him at a club surrounded by girls.'

'Oh, love. Not again. We do need to find you a nice boy!'

'I don't get it, Lind. He seemed genuinely sweet. We went on loads of dates before we ... you know. He never pressured me or anything, he was a complete gentleman. And he really opened up to me. Or I thought he did anyway. Now, completely out of the blue, he's disappeared! I've been texting him every day, a few times a day, but nothing.'

Linda came to the Body Goals class twice a week without fail and always pressed Charlotte for gossip about her private life, which Charlotte was happy to divulge, except it was usually heartbreak and let-downs rather than romance. To say Charlotte had a bad track record with men was an understatement. It was like she was programmed to fall only for bad men. With her curvy, petite and gym-honed body, glossy shoulder-length dark hair and caramel-coloured skin, men flocked to her. But she was also sweet-natured, only saw the best in people and was a true romantic at heart, which seemed to make her a magnet for players. It was the same pattern every time. At first, they were begging to see her, but as soon as they'd been dating for a bit the guy would lose interest and be on to the next conquest. Maya always scolded her for picking the wrong men but even the shy, not-that-great-looking guys screwed her over. True love was all she'd ever wanted. She was still only twenty-three but she longed to have children of her own and to find a decent man to settle down with. Her parents had been happily married for thirty years and Charlotte wanted what they had.

She must be doing something wrong, no matter how hard she tried to 'play it cool', as Maya would always advise. In lieu of a boyfriend Charlotte busied herself with her job, partly to keep herself occupied and partly so she could save up and one day buy her own place. At least the job was varied, interesting, social and kept her in great shape. Charlotte loved to exercise and, furthermore, loved helping other people feel good about themselves. Was it too much to ask for a nice man who had the same interests and shared her dreams?

'It's these young boys,' tutted Linda. 'You need an older man, love. Someone more mature. I keep telling you that my Quentin would be perfect for you.'

Charlotte tried not to smirk as she dismantled her microphone headset. Linda had been trying to set Charlotte up with her son Quentin for months. The poor woman had no idea that Quentin, with his perfect abs and impeccable dress sense, was as gay as the day was long. Charlotte saw him in the gym all the time and it wasn't her he was eyeing up, but the male instructors.

'Thanks, Lind, I'll bear it in mind.'

By the end of the week, Jamie still hadn't been in touch and Charlotte was devastated, repeatedly going over and over in her mind what on earth could have gone wrong. Was it something she said? Something she did? She'd really thought he was different. When would she learn?

She tried her best to distract herself with work, teaching her regular classes and covering for another instructor at Fitness First who was away. Charlotte taught Body Goals, Legs, Bums and Tums, Aerobicise and Abs Attack. Her warm, friendly nature made her a hit with members and she loved her job. The salary wasn't great, but she lived with her parents in Mill Hill and only paid a small amount in rent, which enabled her to save up for her own place. Her car cost a small fortune to run but was essential as she taught classes all around North London and needed to zip about quickly.

On Friday afternoon, after taking Rafi to feed the ducks and then for pizza, Charlotte drove him back to Maya's at 5 p.m. She checked her phone again for any word from Jamie. There was none. She put her phone on silent mode and stuffed it into her bag, in an attempt to forget about it and not check it obsessively.

'Was he okay?' Maya asked, hugging her son tightly after she'd flung open the door. Charlotte threw her khaki Misguided bomber jacket over the sofa. When she wasn't in gym gear her look was skinny jeans and ankle boots.

'A dream, as always. Do you want to finish dinner while I give him a bath?'

'Ah, I love you! Would you mind? I've got some pasta on the go for Rob and some nice chicken salad for us. Wait a minute, it's Friday night. Haven't you somewhere to be?' Charlotte wished she had. All her other mates were cosying up with their boyfriends. She shrugged and silently sloped upstairs to get Rafi ready for bed. Maya still hadn't come up after bathtime so Charlotte brushed his teeth and got him in pyjamas. Then, Maya appeared at her son's bedroom door dressed in a short black dress and blue high heels.

'Maya, what the hell?'

'Come on, Rafi, say night-night to Charley. She's going to get changed into the dress Mummy left out for her while I read you a story and put you to bed.' Rafi rifled through his books, carefully selecting *The Hungry Caterpillar*, and Maya turned to Charlotte.

'Rob's home now and I've told him we need a girls' night out. There's an open bottle of prosecco downstairs, grab yourself a glass and get ready. I'm sure your insanely gorgeous body could squeeze into one of my Topshop dresses. Now go. I'll get this little tiger to sleep.'

Charlotte didn't know what to say. She wasn't exactly in the mood but she was so touched by her friend's gesture that she scurried to get ready. Why shouldn't she have a night out?

They hit four cocktail bars in Camden before dancing into the early hours at Lock 17, a bar playing everything from Motown to Madonna. It was exactly the sort of fun-filled Friday night that Charlotte needed. She was having so much fun, and Maya was the one taking pictures on her phone all night, that it was only when she reached into her bag to order an Uber that Charlotte realised she'd left her phone at her friend's. Maya called a cab and, home at 2 a.m., Charlotte passed out on her friend's sofa, blissfully unaware that, while Jamie still hadn't been in touch, there were three missed calls from another number.

Chapter 6

Charlotte woke at 8 a.m. to the sound of Rafi singing along to *Frozen*. Her head was banging. Thank God she didn't have to teach a class until 4 p.m.! Saturdays were her one chilled day of the week.

'This is my favourite bit, Charley!'

Charlotte winced. She loved her Godson but this was one of the few times she was glad she wasn't a parent. Maya staggered into the room holding two cups of tea and handed one to Charlotte. 'Every morning,' she muttered, motioning to the TV.

Charlotte felt around for her phone. She'd fallen asleep before she'd had a chance to check it. She scrolled through her notifications: a WhatsApp message from her mum asking her to pick up milk on her way home, a few new matches on Tinder and an email sent at 9:04 p.m. last night.

Hi Charlotte,

I'm the producer for *Mr Right* and am getting in touch about your recent application to be a contestant on the new series of the show. We loved what we saw and I wondered if you could come to the Channel 6 office on Monday to meet me, my assistant producer and the head of programming. We're in the final stages of selection now and hope to decide on all the contestants by the end of next week. Please call me back to let me know when you can come in. I'm taking calls this weekend so the sooner the better.

I've tried to ring you a few times today. If you get this can you confirm I have the correct number for you?

Thanks and best wishes,

Jasmine Whiteley

After reading and rereading the email, Charlotte sat up straight. 'Bloody hell!'

'What's up?' Maya asked, trying to prise Rafi away from the biscuit tin and towards a banana.

'Remember when we went up to Liverpool for your birthday a few weeks ago? To Kingley's?'

'Uh-huh.'

Charlotte took a deep breath, crossed her legs and turned to her friend. 'I never told you this, but in the toilets I overheard these women talking. They were saying that they were up in Liverpool looking for girls to appear on a new reality TV show where all these women compete for the attention of a guy. Anyway, I did some research when we got back to London ...'

Maya was listening intently as Charlotte filled her in on the premise of the show.

'Soooo, I uploaded an application form online. I've just seen an email the producer sent me last night and she wants me to come to her office asap to talk it through!'

Maya put her hands to her face. 'What! Wow, Charlotte, that is so exciting! Why didn't you tell me, silly?'

'I was embarrassed. I thought it might seem desperate. And I didn't think for a second anything would actually come of it.' The words were spilling out now.

Maya tutted. 'Well, something has come of it and I'm delighted you finally told me. Oooh, I can't believe you're going to be on TV. We have to get you the *best* outfits for Ibiza. Let's diarise a shopping trip, pronto. Or shall we just do it all online now? When do you go? How long for?'

Charlotte was touched that her friend was as excited as she was, and did feel silly for not having been open with her to begin with, but wasn't Maya getting a little ahead of herself? 'Hun, it's just a meeting,' she said. 'It's entirely possible that nothing will come of it.'

Maya shook her head. 'You always doubt yourself. She emailed you at 9 p.m. on a Friday night. She wouldn't do that unless she was serious. Plus, you're single, drop-dead gorgeous, lovely, approachable and kind. The whole country will love you, let alone this dude!'

'Don't be daft.' But then Charlotte paused. 'So, if she asks me, you think I should do it?'

'One hundred per cent, you should do it!' Maya lifted Rafi onto her lap. He'd broken away from being engrossed in *Frozen* to wondering what his mum was chattering about. 'You're always saying that you want to shake things up in your life and do something crazy. Plus, you're a hopeless romantic and you might actually meet someone great out there. I think you'd be crazy not to do it. We'll vote for you, won't we, Rafi? Won't we? Yay!'

'Yaaaaaay!' The little boy started cheering, with no clue what he was cheering for.

'Well, if I've got Raf's vote that's all I need,' laughed Charlotte. 'Shall I phone her back now?'

'She said straight away, didn't she? Go for it! I want to hear every word.'

Charlotte kissed Maya on the cheek feeling, for the second time that weekend, a wave of gratitude that she had such a supportive best friend. She dialled Jas's number, tapping her fingers against the phone as it rang. 'Wish me luck.'

The following Monday Charlotte was waiting in the vast reception area of Channel 6 in London Bridge, nervously tapping her fingers, a habit she had whenever she was tense.

A tall, blonde woman approached her, smiling widely. 'Charlotte Truss? Hi, I'm Jas. We spoke on the phone.' Looking at Jas, dressed in cropped black trousers, a striped t-shirt and pink kitten heels, hair thrown up into a messy bun, Charlotte suddenly felt way overdressed in her tight dress and knee-high boots. But Jas had told her on the phone to wear whatever made her feel comfortable, and if she was auditioning to be on TV, Charlotte's idea of comfort was as glamorous as possible! 'You look great,' said Jas warmly.

'Really? Oh, thanks. I spend so much time in sweaty gym gear, any chance I have to make an impression, I really go for it. Although now I'm feeling a bit overdressed.'

'Nonsense! It's TV, we love a bit of glamour! Come on up and let's have a proper chat.'

Charlotte liked Jas instantly, and found her extremely easy to talk to. She sat down on a sofa in an office overlooking the River Thames. There was a camera in front of Charlotte. Jas secured it to a tripod.

'Just relax, Charlotte. I'm going to ask some questions, and when you answer me, look straight into the camera. The key is to be yourself. Viewers will want to get to know the real you and we're looking for a mix of different personalities so everyone who is watching will have someone they can relate to. There's no right or wrong here, I just want you to be as open and honest as you can. Sound okay?'

Charlotte nodded, wondering for the tenth time that day what on earth she was doing there – and whether she was making a huge, very embarrassing mistake. But the more they talked, the more Jas made Charlotte feel at ease. Charlotte proceeded to describe her job and how much she loved keeping fit and helping other people achieve their fitness goals, saying that eventually she wanted to start her own personal training business. She talked about her small family and quiet life in suburban North London.

'And how did you hear about *Mr Right*?'

'It's a bit embarrassing, actually. I was up in Liverpool for my mate Maya's birthday. A few of us were up for the weekend and went to Kingley's. I, er, overheard you and your colleague talking about the show in the ladies' cloakroom.'

Jas hit her forehead. 'That's where I know you from! I knew I'd seen you somewhere before! Why didn't you come over?'

'I was too embarrassed! Anyway, I went on the show's website the next day and, after deliberating for hours, finally decided to upload my video application. I knew you'd get thousands of applicants. I never thought I'd stand a chance.'

'Don't take this the wrong way, but you don't strike me as the sort of girl who wants to be on prime-time TV. Most of the contestants we've got are clearly desperate for their five minutes in the spotlight.'

Charlotte looked at her feet, tapping her fingers against the sofa. 'I've never done anything with my life, really. I've always lived at home, always gone to the same places. This seemed exciting and impulsive so I thought, why not?

'You know, Charlotte, even if you don't win, a show like this is terrific exposure,' Jas said. 'You might be interviewed for a fitness magazine or bag some celebrity clients to train. You never know who'll be watching.'

Charlotte lit up inside at that prospect. After a pause, she looked straight into the camera. 'That's really exciting.

But, you know, the main reason I'm here is that I'm looking for love. My boyfriend history is so terrible, finding my very own Mr Right would be the biggest dream come true of all. Oh, God, that sounds so cheesy!'

Jas switched off the camera. 'No, Charlotte, it was perfect. You're perfect. Can you wait here a few minutes while I go fetch my boss? Have you got time to fill in some paperwork? I think we'd like to keep you here for a little while.'

Walking out of the Channel 6 offices a couple of hours later, Charlotte wasn't sure if she'd just signed her life away, or signed up for the best experience so far. Either way, the ink was dry and it was official. She was going to be a contestant on *Mr Right* and in a few weeks' time would be flying out to spend a couple of months in a villa in Ibiza! She'd never felt so excited or nervous. But what did she have to lose? The paperwork was all very clear and straightforward: she'd had to agree to lots of confidentiality clauses, promising she wouldn't tell anyone except close family that she was going on the show, not reveal to anyone what went on in the villa, and certainly not talk to the press at any point. From the end of July, she and fourteen other girls would be living together in a villa, flights and all expenses paid, plus the show would compensate her for the money she was losing out on by not working at the gym.

Jas told her that she had as good a chance as anyone of winning but that didn't mean anything to Charlotte. It was the experience she wanted, the chance to do something crazy, impulsive and exciting. She imagined there would be a lot of contestants just looking to get famous but that wasn't Charlotte's game at all. She wanted to live a little. And, yes, hopefully not be evicted from the island of Ibiza too early on by the bachelor in the dramatic rose ceremonies, where he'd hand out flowers to all the women he wanted to keep in the competition, saying goodbye one by one to those he wasn't interested in. To be sent home first would be mortifying. But there was no need to think about that now. Charlotte hopped on the Northern line back to her parents' house, feeling a flutter in her stomach. Jas was right: this was an amazing opportunity. Charlotte was so glad she'd talked herself into applying. Only good things could come of it.

Chapter 7

Jas paced outside the Channel 6 building, willing Richard to answer his phone. He really was making this divorce as difficult for her as possible, denying any wrongdoing and pointedly ignoring her. She felt a headache start as his phone rang out. Since January, she had sent Richard divorce papers three times, all of which he'd claimed not to have received. It had got to the point that, on the advice of her solicitor, she'd hired a process server to turn up at Richard's office earlier that day and hand him the papers in person, proving once and for all that he had them in his hands and legally obliging him to act.

On her eighth callback, Richard answered. 'What the fuck are you playing at, Jasmine?'

'Me? What are *you* playing at, Richard?' Jas tried to avoid eye contact with anyone rushing through the revolving doors and into work.

'Sending someone to my office ... my place of work?'

Jas sighed. She knew that being served divorce papers in front of his own colleagues would be humiliating for Richard. 'You didn't leave me any choice,' she replied. 'Why are you making this so hard for me?' There was only silence from the other end of the line. 'Richard, this doesn't have to be messy. We both just want to get on with our lives. You know we're never getting back together, so why drag it out?'

He snorted. 'Do you have any idea how embarrassing this will make it for me with my family? To be the first Butler ever to get divorced?'

'Look, you're angry. I can tell that. But I'm sure if you just give it some time you'll feel better about everything.'

God, he was patronising! 'What, forget all the times you cheated on me? Came home at five in the morning reeking of whisky? Or didn't come home at all?' Her voice was raised now, and passers-by were glancing her way.

Richard paused and Jas heard muffled voices in the background as he put his hand over the phone speaker. 'I have no idea what you're talking about,' he replied calmly. 'I have never been anything but a doting and respectful husband to you.'

He was good. Richard knew that in order to divorce him, Jas needed to prove adultery or unreasonable behaviour on his part. He wasn't letting her have it that easily. That muffled voice was probably some advisor in his office telling him to deny everything. Jas realised that no matter how much Richard was to blame, he'd have the best lawyers in the business on his side. He was from a very wealthy family and would pay through the nose if it meant keeping himself free from scandal. Jas, on the other hand, was burning through funds she didn't have.

'So, you're still not going to concede?'

'I don't want a divorce, Jasmine, and I don't think I deserve to be cast aside. If anyone is being unreasonable, I'm afraid it is you. I am choosing to defend this unreasonable petition.'

'I bet you are,' she muttered before hanging up.

Richard threw his mobile across the room with such force it smashed open against the wall, dropping in two pieces on the cream-coloured office carpeting. The two men sitting with him chuckled.

'She's got you by the balls, son, that's for sure,' laughed one, a stout man with a gold wedding band on his stubby ring finger. 'I've worked with you since you started here and, believe me, it won't be hard for her to dig up dirt on you.'

Richard crossed his arms angrily.

'He's not wrong, you know,' put in Richard's boss, an older, red-faced colleague wearing braces and thick-rimmed glasses.

'Samuel, you just told me to defend the divorce!' argued Richard. 'You heard me say that to her, I can't back out now.'

Samuel Jones pulled a bottle of vodka out of his desk drawer and handed it to Richard with a nod. 'I said you had every right to defend it. But speaking not only as your boss but as a man twice divorced, the longer you drag this out the more it's going to cost.'

'How much are we talking?' asked Richard.

'Thousands, even tens of thousands,' Samuel replied.

Richard earnt a six-figure salary, and came from a wealthy family, but didn't particularly want to part with that much money. However, on the trading floor weakness was not permitted – and neither was losing. He didn't want to lose face in front of the two men who'd mentored him so he kept quiet, pondering his next move. He didn't relish the thought of breaking the news to his parents, but maybe they'd understand? Or he could give in, get it all done with as little fuss as possible.

At that moment, two younger colleagues poked their head around the door of Samuel's office, sniggering.

'We heard you got served, mate,' jibed one of them. 'After dumping you in front of all of us at the party you threw for her. Ouch!'

'Might as well just hand her your balls while you're at it, as well as all your money!' laughed the other one as they walked off.

Richard took another gulp of vodka.

'Steady on, Rich, they're just teasing,' said Samuel.

The thought of giving in to Jas suddenly seemed far less appealing. 'I'm a bloody laughing stock! Everyone on the floor will know about this now. The whole building will know by lunchtime!'

The fatter man stood up, took the bottle from Richard, returned it to Samuel and held Richard's shoulders, looking at him closely. 'Pull yourself together,' he ordered. 'She's upset. You know what women are like. God, if I had a quid for every time Nancy threatened divorce I'd be a lot richer!'

'She's not threatening divorce, she's bloody well doing it! And what if she speaks to that blonde from accounts I shagged at the Christmas party? Or Beth who puts our expenses through? She sees everything – the strip clubs, the 4 a.m. bottles of brandy at Scott's restaurant. The bloody underwear I bought for a woman who was most certainly not my wife. Jas really could take me to the cleaners.'

'Give her time. Be nice, polite, let her have her moment and it will all blow over. Women rush these sorts of decisions without thinking. Don't worry about anyone here. They won't talk. We'll very quietly and gently explain that if they disclose anything confidential about any employee of the business, they will have to look for work elsewhere. Okay? Now, pull yourself together and get back to work. Game face and all that.'

But Richard couldn't work. His concentration was all over the place. For the rest of the day people walked past glancing awkwardly at him.

By 6 p.m. he was agitated. He still had another three hours in the office and was in serious need of stress relief. He scrolled through the contacts on his gold iPhone X, wondering which of the many women listed there he could hook up with that night.

Arrangements made, Richard washed his hands in the men's room and looked at himself in the mirror. His ash-blond hair was still in good condition, with no signs of balding thankfully. His piercing blue eyes weren't quite as sparkly as they used to be. There were bags underneath them that weren't there before, and pinkness around his nostrils where they were sore.

But with his strong jaw and tall, slim frame, Richard was still eyed up by women everywhere. He was devilishly handsome, rich and utterly charming when he wanted to be. He'd been playing out without wearing his wedding ring for years and now didn't even know where it was. Somewhere in the new bachelor pad, probably.

He weighed up his options. It wasn't that he didn't feel anything for Jasmine. He was certainly crazy about her when they first met. We've just grown apart, he thought. As with every other marriage, that was bound to happen one day. No one stays happy and in love for ever, it's just naïve to think people do. Still, he didn't actually want their marriage to end. *Who wants the shame or hassle of a divorce?* Those other women didn't mean anything to him, they were just playthings. He'd loved having power over them but none of them was as smart and sexy as Jas. He'd thought that if he just played nice, gave her the flat, then she'd come round. And how did she repay his generosity? Sending a process server to his office ... what sort of stunt was that? Richard clenched and unclenched his fists. If it was a battle Jas wanted then she could have one.

Chapter 8

It was late afternoon before Jas had a moment to herself again. As filming for *Mr Right* drew closer, things were getting busier and busier at work. Despite Monica's brilliant budgeting skills, the sheer scale of a production of this level on location was nerve-wracking, and the two of them had to make a detailed pitch to Harry justifying their request for more money. Jas was nervous about putting down the deposit for the contestants' villa, and the crew's less glamorous but still expensive accommodation, without seeing them in person, and she and Monica agreed she needed to fly out there to inspect the properties and general surroundings first. They called it a 'recce' and argued it was essential. Fortunately, Harry was supportive and signed off a budget extension quickly, but with it came a reminder of just how high people's expectations of them were. Jas ignored the pressure and simply got on with the job, booking the cheapest easyJet flight she could find for later that week: a 7.30 a.m.

departure, returning at 11 that night. It would be a busy day!

With her trip to Ibiza taken care of, Jas scrolled through her phone until she found the number for Mackover & Staunton.

'Ralph Mackover, please.'

She was on hold for just a few seconds of tinkling classical music before her solicitor answered.

'Ah, Jasmine, what's the latest?'

'Not good news, I'm afraid, Ralph. He's contesting the divorce. Denying any wrongdoing. What on earth happens now?'

'One of two things. It will go to a court hearing, with a jury, or else straight to a judge to decide. Jasmine, I need you to collect all the evidence you can to prove unreasonable behaviour on Richard's part during your marriage. Statements from friends, text messages, voice messages, receipts and bank statements from your joint account if they show anything unusual. Everything you have. It will take some time. Start now. Call me when you have something and we'll take action to put it in front of a judge.'

'Okay, thanks, Ralph. I'll be in touch soon.'

Jas slid her phone across her desk and rubbed her temples. Her headache was vicious. She was worried. Maybe it would be easier just to stay married to Richard after all, and live separate lives? He would make things a whole lot easier for her if she did.

'Jas?' The deep voice made her jump and she looked up to see Luke standing by her desk, smiling. His broad shoulders rippled under a blue checked shirt, unbuttoned at the top to show the merest hint of chest hair. Jas glanced around. Luke was completely unaware of the stares he was getting from every woman – hell, even some of the men – around the office. The Luke Effect, as it was now called, was in full swing. Jas found it silly. He might be handsome, but everyone on the sixth floor seemed to be on constant heat since Luke had started working for the entertainment department. Was she the only one capable of thinking about anything other than the new lawyer on the scene?

His smiled faded to a look of concern. 'You look stressed. Everything okay?'

'Yep, yep, all fine. How are the contracts coming along?'

'Great. There's one girl, Gabriella Bellamy-Hughes, who has asked about money. She wants to know if the contestants who stay the longest get any sort of financial bonus and if so how much.'

Jas snorted. 'None of them will be paid, no matter when they leave! It's not *Who Wants to be a Millionaire?* She's also the richest and most spoilt of the lot. She'll give great TV though. Don't worry, I'll call her and explain that this is non-negotiable. Legitimate expenses and loss of earnings only. She's just trying her luck. Anything else?'

'Just a few things for you to sign off on.' He placed a folder of papers on her desk. 'Are you sure you're okay? Tell me it's none of my business if you want, but I saw you shouting down the phone to someone this morning outside the building and it looked pretty heated. I wanted to check you were all right.'

Heated was an understatement, but she had no intention of sharing her personal problems with Luke. Instead, she smiled and shook her head.

'I'm just a bit tired.'

'Okay. How about a drink tonight? You look like you could use cheering up.'

'Thanks, Luke, but I'm having dinner with my little sister tonight.'

'Tomorrow, then?'

'Can I let you know? Things are a bit mental and—'

'Sure. Anything for our star producer.' With that, he gave her another winning smile and walked back to the lifts. Jas was aware of the gawping women who'd overheard him asking her out. She turned back to work. Her life was complicated enough.

'Are you *mad*? He is utterly gorgeous!' Lila almost spat out her wine, peering in for a closer look at Luke's Facebook profile picture. The minute Jas had told her about him Lila had insisted on a visual aid.

Jas sipped her Dry Martini. They were at a trendy pizza restaurant in Shoreditch: exposed brick walls, low-level lighting, naked bulbs hanging from the ceiling, dark wooden benches and steel stools propping up patrons. 'He's not *that* gorgeous. And, besides, I can't go on a date right now. Not with everything that's going on with Richard.'

'He is! And what's the harm in one drink? Go on, Jas, have some fun. Nothing serious need come of it. Let him take you out and show you his muscles. My God! Does he live in the gym?'

'He goes a fair bit, actually. And plays rugby some weekends with his mates. I kind of get the sense he doesn't go out that much. His job is incredibly demanding and he's at work later than me most nights. He told me once that he goes to the gym after work then home for dinner.'

'Ah, so he's boring.'

'Not boring. Nice. Genuine. A salt-of-the-earth type of guy.'

'I think you like him.'

Jas shook her head but smiled. It was so nice to see her little sister again, though Lila looked even skinnier than usual. She was wearing leather trousers, biker boots and a black vest-top, rings on every finger and the top of one ear pierced. Her perfect cheekbones were lightly bronzed. She was the definition of cool, in Jas's eyes, though Lila idolised her older sister. They'd always been close. Too close, Jas sometimes thought. They squabbled frequently but, like most sisters, they made up just as quickly.

Jas wanted her sister to make something of herself. She had such potential and was so bright, but seemed to be happy partying her way through life.

Their pizzas arrived and Jas ordered more drinks. 'Enough about me. What's going on with you? Are you still living in that warehouse on Seven Sisters Road?'

Lila nodded, wolfing down a sloppy slice of Fiorentina. 'Six flatmates, tiny box room, one bathroom.' It was Jas's idea of hell. Lila read her mind. 'I know it's not to your taste. We can't all afford a flat of our own.' Jas didn't remind Lila that what little money she had was being blown on solicitor's fees and a huge mortgage.

'Anyway, I'm working full-time in that pub in Finsbury Park and it's paying the bills, so you all can get off my back.'

'I'm not on your back. We worry about you, that's all. You were always so clever in school. You got that graphic design degree in college and did really well. Don't you want to do something with it? Apply for some proper jobs?'

'It's so much work! All my life has been up to now is work, from school to A-levels to college. I just want to have a laugh! I work in a fun pub with fun people. I get to drink for free and it's fine. Okay?'

Jas was unsure how to respond. She couldn't help but feel that Lila needed to grow up a bit. By the time Jas was Lila's current age, twenty-five, she was married with a mortgage and steady job. Then again, that marriage didn't exactly turn out perfectly. And Lila was old enough to make her own choices.

'You've got to enjoy life,' she finally said, 'but I don't want to see you waste your talents.'

'Yeah, yeah. Anyway, speaking of enjoying life, are you going to take that man up on his offer of a friendly drink or not?' Lila raised an eyebrow but Jas simply rolled her eyes and started on her second Dry Martini.

Jas, Monica and Harry looked down at the big oak table in Harry's office where fifteen pieces of white cardboard lay, each depicting a different beautiful woman. Dylan's beaming face lay on a card in the middle.

'Yes.' Harry nodded. 'I love them. All gorgeous, all great characters, terrific stories. When do they fly out?'

'Friday the twenty-seventh of July,' Jas replied. She was giving her best poker face, showing Harry that she was the epitome of cool, calm and collected, but her head was reeling with questions. She'd seen the villa herself, but was it really good enough? Would the crew have enough room? Had she forgotten a permit along the way?

'We'll fly out the week before to start setting up,' she continued. 'Some of the crew are already out there installing cameras in the villa. And we'll start filming the girls' at-homes on Monday for some background stories to edit in later. It'll be good to show them in the first episode when we're introducing everyone. Let the viewers really get to know them.'

'Great. Get on with it, then. Out!'

Monica and Jas shuffled out of Harry's office and high-fived on the way back to their desks. Jas was proud of them. Fifteen contracts signed, sealed, delivered, and they were two weeks away from heading out to Ibiza for most of the summer. Jas couldn't wait to get away from London and into the Balearic sun, even though there was a good chance she might have to fly back at some point to see a judge about the divorce Richard was still vehemently defending. Back at her desk, an instant message popped up on her Google Hangouts on her email. Luke.

'So, was he impressed?'

'Uh-huh,' Jas wrote back instantly, adding a smiling face emoji.

'Congratulations, star producer.'

Jas smiled. Since asking her out he'd played it totally cool, alleviating any awkwardness by joking around with her as normal when they bumped into each other in the canteen, or had a meeting about the show. They had become mates. Mates who flirted occasionally, but it was stupid banter rather than anything romantic. They'd chat over Google Hangouts, he'd send her links to YouTube clips of *Black Mirror*, the Netflix show they were both addicted to, and she'd send him silly GIFs of animals playing in the snow. With everything else going on, having someone at work just to be silly with was very welcome. Jas considered this. She could really do with seeing Luke, actually, taking her mind off Richard and celebrating the success of the show. Impulsively, she wrote: 'I never did take you up on that drink offer, did I?' It came out much flirtier than she'd intended.

He didn't reply, but a green tick told Jas that the message had been opened and read. She suddenly worried that she'd come across as too forward. She'd turned back to her emails when he buzzed a reply.

'6 p.m. tonight?'

She grinned. 'Fuller's bar. Across the road. First round's on me.'

Chapter 9

Drinks turned into dinner, which turned into cocktails. At Fuller's they ate peanuts, drank wine and Jas laughed more than she had done in over a year. She realised just how miserable she'd been with Richard, even before they separated last year. Constantly arguing, worrying about his worsening drug habit, infuriated with him for staying out all night. It hadn't been a marriage, it had been a nightmare. She couldn't remember the last time she'd felt so relaxed in a man's company and was grateful she had a friend like Luke.

Over a table in the pub, they were debating the best pop music. 'Blur over Oasis?' he spluttered, an expression of genuine horror on his face. 'You really think Blur were better than Oasis? Call yourself a northerner? Shameful.' He shook his head and finished his glass of wine.

Jas couldn't help but giggle. He rarely reacted to anything with this much zeal. 'They were both great bands,

Luke, but at the end of the day it all came down to Damon Albarn over Liam Gallagher.'

'Disgraceful,' he muttered. 'I'd offer to inspect your Spotify, but I'm worried about what I might find on there now.'

'Eek! I don't know if you'd want to go there either. Lots of Kylie, Britney, Girls Aloud. A few old-school nineties dance anthems, too.'

Luke rolled his eyes. 'Sounds utterly dreadful. The only nineties music you need to listen to was recorded by men in bands, with long hair and baggy clothes. I was going to ask if you wanted to get something to eat but now I'm wondering if we can even be friends!'

Jas threw one arm around Luke playfully and leant in to whisper in his ear. 'Come on, I'm starving. I'll let you pick the restaurant.'

Luke put his own strong arm around her neck and sighed. They walked out of the pub, arm in arm. It was just playful, friendly banter, thought Jas. There was nothing in it.

He led her to an Italian restaurant tucked away behind London Bridge station and they ordered plates of creamy mozzarella, sun-dried tomatoes and dough balls to start, followed by sea bass linguine for Jas and a steak for Luke, washed down with delicious wine. It didn't go unnoticed by Jas that Luke always held the door open for her and topped up her glass before his own.

'Tell me more about your sisters,' he asked before the mains arrived.

'Well, Meg turned thirty-two in February and Lila was twenty-five in May. Meg is ace. Super-chilled and easy-going and very sensible. She's been with Oscar, that's her husband, for about ten years. They're dead sweet together and she'll be pregnant by Christmas, I reckon. Lila couldn't be more different.' Jas paused. 'I worry about her a bit. She seems reckless and has no ambition other than to party. What about your siblings?'

'Strangely similar. Michael is thirty-six and in a long-term relationship. He works for the civil service and lives down in Clapham. I see him quite a bit. My sister Kimberley is twenty-four. My parents had us quite young and her much later but I think my mum wanted to keep going 'til she got a girl. Kim is a PA at a PR agency in Hove but gets paid peanuts and still lives at home. It's a good job, I suppose, but I worry that she doesn't take it that seriously.'

Jas smiled. 'It sounds like you have a very accomplished family.'

The mains arrived and they ate in a comfortable silence for a minute before Luke launched into new territory.

'So, what about you? Any boyfriend on the scene?' Luke's eyes stayed on his plate as he tucked into his steak. Jas could tell that he'd deliberately dropped this into the conversation as casually as he could. She thought it was endearing, but felt a knot in her stomach at the thought of talking about Richard and sat back in her chair, taking a gulp of wine. She needed to change the subject quickly. She really wasn't in the mood to get into all that now. And technically she didn't have a *boyfriend* on the scene, so it was just a white lie, right?

'Nope, no boyfriend. I don't know how I'd find the time for one at the moment anyway. Work is taking over my life.'

'Ah, but you're doing a great job.'

Jas wished she could feel so confident. Her mind flashed to the opulent Ibizan villa filled with those brilliant women all falling over Dylan. She really hoped everything would go well. She and Luke continued to talk about the show and Jas felt utterly at ease and thoroughly relieved that she'd swerved the 'single' question and it never came up again.

Much to her embarrassment, Luke insisted on paying for dinner. 'I'm all about equality,' she pleaded truthfully, a firm believer in paying one's own way in life.

'Yeah, well, I'm all about being a gentleman. My dad raised me never to let a woman pay on the first date.'

Even though they'd flirted throughout the evening, at the word 'date' their eyes met for a brief, awkward second before Luke cleared his throat. 'A friends' date, that is. Anyway, I earn way more money than you,' he added with a wink.

'That's definitely true.'

'Although, if you insist, I will let you buy the next round. One for the road?'

Jas shrugged. 'Why not? We're celebrating a very successful work day. Come on, I know a great place.'

They headed to a swanky cocktail bar a few roads away. It was Jas's favourite bar in London, warm and friendly with the best Dry Martinis she'd ever tasted. She ordered one for herself and a straight whisky for Luke. Within minutes they were back to bantering, quoting clips of their favourite comedies to each other and doing impressions of Harry and the other top suits at work.

Sitting up at the bar on stools, their knees brushed against each other. 'Your Burrell impersonation is rubbish,' teased Jas. 'You've got the accent all wrong. He's a cockney, not a scouser.'

'It's spot on. You're just jealous that I'm better than you. In every way, I'd imagine.'

Jas playfully batted his arm. 'Yeah, right, *you're* just jealous that a woman is funnier than you.'

'Impossible.' And, at that, his hand fell lightly on her thigh. To her surprise and delight, he kept it right there as they carried on bantering.

This was no friend-flirting, thought Jas. She might have been drunk, but there was no question Luke was insanely attractive and the mutual attraction was getting hotter by the second. Luke slid Jas across her stool towards him. Their eyes met again but, this time, neither of them looked away. With one hand on her waist, he reached the other to her chin and gently lifted it so their faces were almost touching. Jas's stomach was flipping, her arms covered in goosebumps. He leant in so his lips were just brushing hers, then they were kissing, gently at first but with increasing passion as both his hands wrapped around her waist and her arms snaked around his neck. When they finally broke away she felt dizzy with lust.

'I don't normally do this on the first date, but do you want to come back to mine?' Luke asked softly. Jas's first thought was to say yes and get straight into a taxi with him.

She liked him a lot and, if his kisses were anything to go by, doubted that spending the night with him would be a disappointment.

But something held her back. Even through her drunken haze, the sensible, logical part of Jas's brain was telling her that this was a mistake. She had too much riding on her job without getting distracted, not to mention the ongoing divorce battle she'd failed to even mention to him. No, Jas needed to go home alone and sleep this whole thing off. Nip whatever was happening in the bud. It was just one fun night.

She must have been weighing up her options internally for a while as Luke prompted her quietly with another kiss. 'So?' he asked, softly.

Jas shook her head. 'I've had a wonderful evening, Luke. But I think we should call it a night. Busy day tomorrow and all that.'

He joined her in standing up. 'Of course. Let me call you an Uber?'

'It's cool, there are plenty of black cabs outside.'

He held the door of the taxi open for her and kissed her on the cheek. Jas had a fleeting urge to pull him into the car with her, but thought better of it. She didn't want to do anything she would regret later.

Chapter 10

Jas awoke the next morning with a sore head and a dry throat. She rubbed her temples and knocked back the pint glass of water she'd strategically left on the bedside table. She set her alarm on 'snooze' for an extra few precious minutes before she had to get up. As she did, the events of the previous night slowly came back to her, piece by piece. The flirting, the touching of knees, wandering of hands ... And that kiss. Jas turned her face into the pillow, both completely mortified and wracked with guilt. Thank God she had thought logically enough to go home alone! But, still, what the hell had she done? She was a married woman! And she'd not exactly been forthcoming with that information to Luke over their long and intimate date.

The alarm rang again angrily and Jas hit it off and begrudgingly lurched out of bed. Stepping into the shower and letting the cool water run over her and wake her up, a memory of last night's passion flickered through her mind. She batted it away.

Freshly showered, Jas threw on a green midi skirt, white t-shirt and red heels. Black mascara opened up her heavy eyes, and after a dash of Chanel foundation, brush of bronzer and slick of lipgloss she looked normal again, even if she didn't quite feel it yet. She popped two paracetamol with a glass of orange juice and strong black coffee. On the Tube into work her hangover lifted and she busied herself with answering emails, reading the morning's headlines and checking the Instagram sites of all the contestants to see what they were up to. Throwing herself into work was the best way to forget about last night.

'What, you didn't sleep with him?' Monica asked, aghast, an hour later as she and Jas grabbed a coffee from the canteen. Jas's eyes darted around but there was thankfully no sign of Luke. Stirring sugar into her extra-shot skinny latte, she shook her head.

'No, Mon. It's *so* not the right time for me to be starting up a new relationship or even anything close to that. Especially not with someone I work with. It's a bad idea.'

'You know you haven't done anything wrong, right?'

'It feels like I have,' Jas replied glumly.

'You've been separated for months! From an arsehole, I might add. And you haven't even had a sniff of a date. Luke couldn't be nicer, everyone knows it.'

Jas was about to reply when her phone beeped. 'Oh my God, it's from him.'

Monica grabbed the phone and read the message aloud. '"Hope your head isn't too sore this morning. I had a great night." Oh, Jas, he's so sweet!'

Jas snatched her phone back. 'Don't make me feel any worse!'

'You should have told him last night about Richard, he would have understood.'

'I need less drama in my life, not more. The best thing is to end this before it gets even more out of hand. Nip it in the bud.'

'Okay, but I think you're crazy. Every woman in the building has their eyes on that man. He's genuinely nice and he's clearly crazy about you!'

But Jas had made up her mind. It was one night of fun and that was the end of it.

She went back and forth over what to write back to Luke but, in the end, didn't reply at all. Logging on to Google Hangouts she expected another cheeky message. But there was nothing. Jas shrugged and distracted herself with work. With Monica and their team of assistants and researchers, she was finalising flight details for everyone and arranging venues around Ibiza for Dylan to take his chosen date. There would be picnics on the beach, dinners in fancy restaurants, boat trips with champagne, snorkelling and romantic walks. Harry had extended the budget even further to accommodate helicopter rides and flights to other destinations for the extra-special dates. No expense was spared.

Another huge task that was taking up a lot of Jas's time, and had prompted a closer working relationship with Luke in the first place, was carrying out background checks on all the contestants they hoped would make the final grade. Luke had walked Jas and her director, Lyndsey, through the finer details of the process. Any past convictions or criminal records had to be declared to Harry. It turned out that not only was one girl already on bail for assaulting someone in a nightclub, but on closer inspection another contestant had lied about her age and was just fifteen years old. Jas was stunned – this girl looked at least nineteen – but there was a strict rule that contestants had to be over eighteen, so Jas and Monica scrambled to find the two best replacements among their reserves.

Almost all the contestants were emailing asking what to pack. Gabriella, who'd tried unsuccessfully to demand money, was now asking for her own bedroom, claiming she couldn't sleep with other people in the room. Jas replied politely but firmly to the email, explaining that there were five bedrooms in the villa and three girls to each, but they all had double beds and plenty of room. Jas had personally flown out to inspect the villa – the bedrooms were massive! Gabriella was clearly just chipping away to get all that she could for free. There was always someone who tried it on.

At 6 p.m., exhausted and craving a huge bowl of pasta and a crappy comfort film on Netflix, Jas called it a day. But stepping into the lift down to the lobby, she came face-to-face with Luke.

'Hi,' she said awkwardly.

'Hello.' He smiled back at her. There wasn't much more they could say in a packed lift. At the fifth floor more people bundled in, meaning Jas was standing even closer to Luke. Dammit, he smelt good.

Safely in the lobby they got to speaking.

'How's your day been?' asked Luke coolly.

'Fine. I, um, haven't heard from you.' Shit! Why did she sound so desperate? She had to play it a lot cooler than this.

He looked confused. 'I texted you this morning. Everything okay?'

'Fine, fine … just, you know, a busy day …' Jas's voice trailed off. Back when she was with Richard, he would have been outraged if she'd not answered his text. Luke was so chilled out. And why should she care? She was going to break it off anyway, right?

'Up to anything tonight?' he asked. 'Because I'm pretty shattered but would love to make you dinner if you fancied coming round to mine. We could stick a film on.'

'Well, I …' Jas began. She'd rehearsed what she wanted to say to Luke a dozen times but now he was here, smiling so sexily and being so charming, she was entirely lost for words.

He leant down and whispered in her ear, 'I've been thinking about you all day.' Then he pulled back. 'And I'm starving.'

Jas was still lost for words. 'Um, well …'

'Or, if you prefer, we could go to yours, order in some food,' Luke continued, scrolling through his phone casually as it bleeped. He was standing close and Jas breathed in his aftershave – Armani, was it? Dior? Delicious. The thought of going back to an empty flat on a Friday night was hardly appealing. Snuggling with Luke all night on the other hand …

'I'd like that,' was all she said, deciding that her great plan would have to wait.

*

77

An hour later Jas was lying back on her grey sofa, a large glass of Sauvignon Blanc in hand and heels kicked off to the floor. Luke sprawled out at the other end of the sofa and gently lifted her ankles onto his lap, massaging the balls of her feet. It felt amazing. Jas was about to make a joke about how good he was with his hands but simply allowed herself to relax. She struggled to remember the last time she'd felt this good. She and Luke smiled at each other for a few seconds in a blissfully comfortable silence. He was the first to speak.

'My mum's a yoga teacher and massage therapist,' he explained, nodding to Jas's feet. 'You pick up a few things.'

'Ah, so that explains it. You use this technique on all the women you're trying to seduce, I suppose?'

'It's working, isn't it?' Luke smiled, giving her a cheeky wink.

'Smart arse.' But she smiled back at him. 'Is that what she's always done?'

Luke shook his head. 'She was a schoolteacher for years but had a bit of a career change when my dad got the job in Brighton and we moved down south. He's an IT consultant. She looked in a few schools in Brighton for a job but started getting more and more into the holistic side of things, retrained as a yoga teacher and now that's it. She says she's never felt happier.'

'That's so brave, just changing course like that. I don't know if I'd have the guts to do it.'

'You're still young. We both are. Everything seems important when we're this age but I reckon once you're older, you've had three kids and a thirty-year marriage, you start to chill out about stuff. It's not all about work.'

'Says the guy who trained for six years to become a lawyer.'

The level of training Luke had done for his law career was staggering, but he was equally in awe of Jas's job and found everything she did and said fascinating. She found herself opening up again about her uncertainty as to what her next career move should be. Luke never pushed any subjects but Jas felt she could talk to him about most things. Apart from Richard, that is. That part she was certain she wanted to leave out.

Family was clearly of paramount importance to Luke and Jas really liked that. She found it refreshing, especially after Richard who was ungratefully rude about his parents. It was funny how only now she was remembering the bad stuff about him. When they were first together she couldn't find any fault in him. Talk about rose-tinted glasses. The more time she spent in Luke's company, the more she realised what a shit Richard was compared to him. Not so much at the start of their relationship when Jas was truly happy, but certainly since they'd moved to London and he'd changed entirely for the worse. He'd never once offered to cook for her. Massage her feet? No way. Asked her about her own day at work, or after her sisters? Forget it! Jas wanted to know more about Luke.

'So, do you think you'll stay in this job for a while then?' she asked later, topping up their wine. Her stomach was growling for food by now.

'I think so. Entertainment law is pretty interesting. I'd probably like to go and work for a legal firm, though, where there'd be more money than at Channel 6 so I can buy a house, but I'm happy where I am for now. I don't think it's a good idea to try to plan too rigidly. Saving up for a house is one thing but I see people trying to map out the next five, ten years of their life and it's pointless.'

'I don't plan anything, that's the problem! I've no idea what the next five years hold for me.'

Luke paused. 'Maybe that's a good thing. I think people put too much emphasis on what they *should* be doing, but life doesn't always work like that. Expect the unexpected, that's the one thing I've learnt.'

Jas considered her own career. She adored working in TV but when she'd started out, interning on the newsroom floor, she had never imagined that when she finally landed a senior role she'd spend hours arguing with wannabe reality TV stars over how much they'd be getting paid to essentially go on holiday for eight weeks. Then again, she was about to go to Ibiza for eight weeks herself, so she could hardly complain. Why did she always over-think things? Why couldn't she be more like Luke? Nothing at all seemed to bother him.

'How are you finding the entertainment team anyway?' she asked, changing the subject. 'Do you miss being up on news?'

'I'm really enjoying it so far. It's fun. And different. But, really, so long as I'm working with decent people and getting paid, it doesn't really bother me where I am.'

'Nothing ever bothers you, does it? I wish I could be so content all the time instead of worrying constantly about what my next step up the career ladder is, whether I'm doing a good job, whether I'm being paid enough, whether I'm saving enough, am I a good friend, a good sister, a good daughter ...'

'Of course things bother me, as they do everyone,' replied Luke. At that, he leant over and kissed Jas lightly on her forehead. 'Give yourself a break. You're ace and everything will work out the way it's supposed to.'

There was something so calming about him, it made Jas feel happy. She really didn't want to ruin their perfectly lovely evening. Thankfully, she was literally saved by the bell as her entryphone buzzed loudly.

Luke lifted Jas's legs off his lap and sprang up to answer the door. 'Food's here!'

Seconds later he was chatting to the delivery guys about the balmy weather. Jas willed him to come back in with the food, she was starving! Her phone rang and, seeing Lila's number pop up, Jas hit the red button to reject the call. She'd call her sister back. Luke returned bearing two bags full of noodles, spring rolls, chicken, prawns and vegetables.

'*Et voilà!*' he said with a flourish, then went about fetching plates and cutlery from the kitchen.

Lila rang back. Again, Jas rejected the call. 'Nice one! I'm so hungry I can barely speak,' she called out to Luke. The phone rang yet again.

'Whoever that is, you might want to answer. They seem insistent,' Luke said, returning with the plates.

Bloody Lila! Impeccable timing as always. Jas picked up. 'What?!'

'Jesus, what's up with you?' Lila sounded genuinely baffled. 'Did I call at a bad time?'

Jas sighed. She was about to tell her sister that, yes, obviously it was a bad time as she'd ignored the past two calls, but decided against making a big deal out of it. 'Nothing, babe. What's up, you okay?'

'I've got a hot date tomorrow night and I need to borrow some clothes. I'm coming over in the morning. What do you have that's new and irresistible?'

Jas glanced at Luke, now stuffing his face with eyes fixed on the TV as he flicked through the sports channels. He looked cute. 'Er, I don't know, Lila, just come and have a look. You'll find something you like as usual. I want my denim jacket back, by the way, don't think I've forgotten.'

'Yeah, whatever, I think it's at Mum and Dad's now.'

'You *think*? Lila, that's my favourite jacket. Bring it tomorrow when you come over or else don't come over at all, I mean it.'

'Urgh, fine! Whatever, you're so annoying.'

'Urgh, you're so annoying,' Jas mimicked.

'So, you'll let me go through your wardrobe?'

'What sort of look are you going for?'

'I thought maybe that Maje blouse of yours.'

'No way! You'll only ruin it and it cost me a hundred and fifty pounds.'

'For God's sake, Jas, you have everything! Why do you have to be so selfish? I'd let you borrow anything of mine.'

'I don't want to borrow festival wellies and a crop top, thanks.'

'Pleeeeeeeeease, Jas. It will go perfectly with my leather trousers. I need some heels too. He's a City boy, much older, very serious but super-rich. So, I've got to look older.'

'Charming!'

Lila tutted. 'You know what I mean. Grown-up. Classic. Anyway, I'll be there at some point in the morning.'

Jas knew in Lila-speak this meant 'some time before 4 p.m.'.

'Just call me when you're on your way. I've got things to do tomorrow. Right, is that the wildly important question you needed to ring me three times for? Can I go now?'

'I'm bored. What you doing? Can I come over?'

'Nope.'

'Whhhhhy?' whinged Lila.

Jas playfully nudged Luke with her foot. 'I've got company.' He looked up and gave her a sly smile.

'Oh my God, who? Is it that fit guy from work? It is, isn't it? Cough once if it is.'

'Goodbye, Lila.' And before her sister could whine again, she hung up.

'That was my little sister. I hung up before she could invite herself over.'

Luke grinned. 'I get it. You want me to meet your family already.'

'Don't flatter yourself! I told her very specifically *not* to come over!'

But Luke was enjoying winding her up. 'I see your game, Whiteley. All right, all right, I'll go to dinner at your parents' house. God, stop harassing me!'

They both laughed and Jas gently kicked her feet against Luke's shin and then they were play-fighting. 'I do yoga too, you know, and I'm very strong,' she laughed as Luke effortlessly held her down with one arm while helping himself to a forkful of noodles with the other.

'Yeah, you're so tough,' he teased as Jas tried to wriggle out, but to no avail. His strength was such a turn-on ...

'I don't want to hurt you,' she protested, wrapping her legs around Luke's strong arm and guiding him down so he was on top of her. Their lips brushed and just as he leant in for a kiss she rolled away so he fell face down onto the sofa.

'Ha, I win!' She jumped up, triumphantly.

'Right, that's it. You're dead, Whiteley.' And in one motion he pinned her down on the floor and held her hands above her head as she tried to wriggle free but had no chance. They both burst out laughing. Jas wrapped her legs around his, pulling him in closer. They kissed, nervously at first and breaking away to laugh, then locking lips for longer and more intense kisses. Luke's hands stroked Jas's back and she coiled her fingers through his short hair.

'What was it you wanted to tell me?' Luke asked as he eventually pulled away.

'Oh, I can't even remember now,' lied Jas.

'Right, well, this food is getting cold so enough nonsense,' Luke mocked, turning his attention away from Jas and back to his plate. She pursed her lips. Just what was she getting herself into?

Chapter 11

Netflix was switched on and, two and a half hours of *Avenger*-superhero-fighting later, the entire takeaway had been demolished as had a bottle and a half of white wine. As the end credits rolled, Luke lifted the bottle but Jas shook her head, deciding to switch to sparkling water. She wanted a clear head for tomorrow. Even though it was Saturday, she'd be working.

'Come on then, tell me. What's wrong with you? There must be something,' Jas teased as Luke had dutifully cleared all plates into her dishwasher.

'I mean, you know the best Thai takeaway in London and even told me you can cook. You have a great job, you're close to your mum ...' Jas didn't want to massage Luke's ego too much by also adding how handsome he was. 'What's the glitch?'

He sighed. 'Small penis, I'm afraid. It's been holding me back for years.'

She almost spluttered her water out at the joke – or what she assumed was a joke!

'The truth is, I haven't had a relationship for a long time and my last one was pretty heavy so I'm just looking to spend time in good company. No hassle, no stress.'

Jas nodded slowly. She knew she was getting into dangerous territory talking to Luke about exes, and she was having such an enjoyable evening that she'd by now resolutely ruled out bringing up the subject of her awful husband. But she pictured Luke with a gorgeous ex-girlfriend that he'd never gotten over and felt a flash of jealousy. There was no harm in digging a little deeper, she reasoned.

'So, what happened?'

'I was engaged to a girl I met doing the law conversion course.'

Engaged?

'We broke up some years ago. I've had a few flings here and there since but nothing serious. That's it.'

He closed the dishwasher and, taking Jas's hand, led her back into the living room and sat them down on the sofa. 'Let's not talk about me.'

There was no way Jas was leaving it at that. 'No, I want to. Really. I've been talking about myself non-stop tonight.'

'It's not the best story.'

'No judgement, I promise. Please?'

Luke paused then let out a small sigh. 'Her name was Jenny. We were young and in love so, when we both graduated, I proposed.'

Jas took a sip of water and said nothing, signalling him to go on.

'She got pregnant.'

Jas's mouth dropped open.

'Yep, I know,' he said. 'We were twenty-seven, which I know these days seems a bit young to start a family, but I was delighted. We were financially stable-ish, and in love, so why not? But instantly things started to change. Jenny became really distant and short-tempered, always picking fights with me. I was stressed and would argue back. We weren't in a good place and started to grow apart pretty quickly. Anyway, one evening, I came home from work and she was just there, sobbing, clutching her stomach. I thought there was something wrong with the baby – it was within the first ten weeks and, you know, anything can happen in those early stages. So, I went to call an ambulance but she begged me not to. I couldn't get anything from her, she was so distraught, then eventually she admitted that she'd just come back from the clinic.'

Jas frowned. 'The clinic?'

'She aborted the baby without telling me. She said she freaked out, that she was too young to be a mother and there was still so much she wanted to do with her life before having a family. If she'd just talked to me I would have understood, but to go to the clinic without saying a thing, to keep it from me … I don't understand how someone could do that. I know it was her body but it was my baby, too.'

Jas was stunned. How could anyone do such a thing? She felt furious at this girl and protective of Luke, but kept her thoughts to herself. 'Then what happened?'

'I broke it off there and then and moved out of the house we were renting in Brighton. I rented a mate's spare room, pretty quickly got a job in London and relocated.'

'Have you seen her since?'

'She phoned me constantly at first, saying how sorry she was and begging for us to get back together. I was too angry to speak to her. A while later we met for coffee. I told her that I could forgive her but never forget and that's why we could never be together. I wished her a happy life but said I couldn't see her any more and that was it. Last I heard she'd moved to Australia.'

'Wow. I can't believe you forgave her, just like that.'

'It wasn't just like that, Jas. It took months for me to be able to say that. I was furious for a long time and took it out on people who didn't deserve it. I went out every night and had one-night stands with girls I never called again. I soon realised that I wasn't that sort of guy, though, and I never would be. I'm a relationship man. I like having a girlfriend. So, I ditched clubs for the gym, got myself into shape, started playing sports with the lads and spent time with my family. I started to realise what was important in life.'

'Wow,' was all Jas could say again.

'Jenny and I were clearly not meant to be,' Luke said. 'I came to realise that things were hard for her too and the decision she made was a horrible one. I didn't want to hold on to all that anger and negativity so I chose to forgive her.'

'But how could you?'

'Everyone makes mistakes, Jas.'

88

She considered what an amazing guy Luke was. It took a real man to forgive something like that and talk so openly about it. Luke clearly had his priorities in order and was secure and stable. Compared to him, Jas felt like a complete mess.

'I haven't freaked you out by telling you that, have I?'

'No!' she replied hastily. 'I'm really touched you told me. You have a lot more maturity then most men.'

'I don't usually reveal so much on a second date. There's something about you that makes me feel very comfortable.'

With that Luke slid his arms around Jas, sending sparks through her. 'And very turned on,' he whispered, nuzzling into her neck.

Jas bit her lip. Something switched on in her and she realised that her feelings for him were stronger than she had first suspected. This was crazy, they'd only had two dates! The physical attraction was clear, but this was more than that. And now it suddenly felt very real. At this realisation her body tensed up, as if it was reminding her mind that things were moving too fast and she just wasn't ready. It wasn't that she didn't fancy Luke; it was more that she didn't want the uncertainty of someone new in her life right now. Not yet. She wanted a divorce and then a simple life, not emotions that ran away with her. Surely now more than ever she needed control and stability. Jas was still adamant that she didn't want to talk about Richard. That was her business. But how could she carry on with Luke while holding back such a big secret after he'd just been so open and honest with her? Jas didn't feel right about being here with him. No matter what lustful urges her body might be feeling, she knew what she had to do.

'Luke, I need to say something too.'

'Enough talking, Jas.' He kissed her with more passion this time and Jas melted against his body before pulling herself away again. God, he was so distracting! But this had to end. Now.

'Luke, please, listen to me.'

His expression turned to one of concern. 'Okay. What's up?'

Jas looked at him; those gorgeous green eyes of his were boring into her. She felt rotten, especially after what Luke had told her about how badly his ex-girlfriend had treated him. But it would be wrong to lead him on.

'You're an amazing guy, Luke. But I can't do this.'

'Can't do what?'

'This. Us. Whatever it is, I can't do it. It's too fast and I'm freaking out.' This was true. It was all getting too much for Jas. Both fancying Luke and feeling too scared to let it progress any further was bewildering. She was feeling too much pressure. And how much did she really know about this guy? Sure, he seemed to be almost perfect, but hadn't she thought Richard was almost perfect when she married him? Jas wasn't sure if she was ready to trust anyone with her emotions again so soon. The relationship with Richard had damaged her so much. The marriage itself was painful enough, but the break-up was even worse.

Luke seemed confused and understandably so. He had no idea what inner turmoil she was going through. 'If there's anything you want to talk about, Jas, you can tell me.'

No, no, stop being so nice!

'We've had an amazing connection all night, don't tell me you didn't feel it?'

'This just ... isn't the right time for me. I'm away filming all week around the country for the girls' at-homes. I'll be so busy I won't even have time to speak to my sisters, let alone ... And then I'm off to Ibiza. It's the worst possible time to start up anything with you. This has to end. Now. I'm sorry.' It sounded much colder than she'd meant it to, but what else could she say?

Luke looked disappointed but simply shrugged and looked around for his shoes. Then he reached forward and, thinking he was reaching in to kiss her or convince her she was making a mistake, Jas darted out of the way. To her mortification, he was simply reaching behind her for his wallet on the side table.

'I'm going to go,' he said coolly.

Jas felt awful. She made a move to hug him goodbye but he got up quickly. 'See you at work on Monday.'

In the space of a few minutes the atmosphere had done a complete 180-degree turn from steamy to awkward. Jas longed to kiss Luke, apologise and tell him the truth, but her logical side stopped her. They said a formal, polite goodbye and he was gone. Just like that. Jas had got what she'd wanted, she was well and truly single.

Chapter 12

Reclining in the back of a blacked-out SUV and sipping the complimentary bottle of water, Charlotte felt as if she was in a dream. Minutes earlier, she'd been greeted at Ibiza airport by a runner for *Mr Right,* who directed her to a waiting vehicle and instructed her that the second she got out at the villa, cameras would be on her. They were recording the new arrivals in stages throughout the day. Charlotte had no idea if she'd be the first one to arrive or the last. She didn't know who the other girls were, where they were from or even a single thing about the Mr Right they were all competing for. She was both excited and sick with nerves. She checked her outfit once more: black Capri pants and an orange tank top. It was a casual look but showed off her flat stomach and hint of cleavage perfectly. She wondered if the other girls were also arriving in what they'd worn on the plane. She looked through her handbag for mascara, highlighter and pink lipgloss. Checking her hand mirror, she carefully applied make-up as the car drove along winding roads into the Ibizan hills. Clearly, speed limits weren't taken too seriously here!

Charlotte gazed out of the window as they sped along. She saw the glistening blue sea below but surrounding them now were luscious green trees. The white tops of villas peeped out from the wooded areas but they were all fairly secluded. The car eventually slowed down. Peering out of the front window, Charlotte gasped as they approached gold-painted gates leading to a ginormous white villa.

'Villa Valencia,' announced the driver in a thick Spanish accent. Villa? It looked more like a palace! There was a fountain in front and pots of beautifully bright flowers everywhere. Charlotte took a deep breath and stepped out of the car. Show time.

The front door was unlocked so she padded in, looking around for any sign of life. She'd been instructed to fight the instinct to look for the cameras, so Charlotte just took in the size and beauty of what would be her new home for the next two months. This place was gorgeous! And immaculate. Shiny stone floors, big plant pots and candles, a palatial living room with white sofas, leading to a huge kitchen of stainless steel and marble. She wondered into another living room, or cinema-room to put it more accurately, with a gigantic TV screen on one wall and cosy blue sofas, armchairs and beanbags facing it.

'Hello?' Charlotte called out.

'Out here,' a voice replied, and the sounds of laughter and women talking over each other came from another part of the seemingly endless villa, leading her outside.

93

'Wow!' Charlotte's jaw dropped when she found the terrace. Dark brown wicker chairs, sofas and tables were dotted around, all facing the most incredible view of green hillside and the blue, cloudless sky above. Steps led down to a swimming pool, hot tub, single sunbeds, four-poster Bali beds and a shady area with table, chairs and a fitted barbecue.

Three cameras were set up and the cameramen and women behind them waved. Charlotte remembered her pep talk from Jas and tried her best not to look into the cameras and pretend they weren't there. Easier said than done!

Five women, who were sitting on the balcony with glasses of champagne, all jumped up to greet Charlotte. A waiter in a tuxedo appeared from nowhere bearing another ice-cold glass, which she accepted gratefully.

'Hi, I'm Alex,' said the first woman, who had cascading black hair and glimmering green eyes. She had a coldness to her face but was beautiful and thoroughly friendly, explaining that she was a radio DJ for a local East London station and the first person to have arrived.

'And this is Melody.' She motioned to a woman who needed no introduction. Charlotte instantly recognised Melody Mane, a hugely successful beauty blogger who'd hit the tabloids last year because of a steamy romance with the lead singer of the boy band West Town. Melody had flawless black skin and her Afro hair was straightened and dyed red. She resembled a young Naomi Campbell. No wonder she had such a fan-following on Instagram, thought Charlotte.

'Hi, babes,' said Melody, planting a kiss on Charlotte's cheek. 'Wow, love your highlighter. Is it Bobbi Brown, right? You've got great cheekbones.'

Charlotte suddenly felt insecure around these glamorous women, but to her delight they all seemed genuinely nice. She was introduced to Carmel, a petite brunette with pixie-cut hair and huge brown eyes like a Disney princess; Natalie, an estate agent with glossy, tousled honey-coloured hair and a figure to die for, and Kat, a drop-dead stunning dancer from Liverpool. They chatted away about the house-of-dreams.

Within the hour, five more girls had arrived, including a social media manager, an executive assistant and a singer Charlotte recognised from the finals of a television singing competition on a rival channel last year. There really was a mix here.

Another glass of champagne down and Charlotte was starting to feel more comfortable, bonding instantly with Kat, the dancer, about exercise. Suddenly the clip-clop of heels stomped over the marble floors so loudly the entire group stopped talking and looked up.

'I'm HERE,' came the shrill voice of the stomper. A tall redhead appeared, wearing sky-high, snake-skin boots and a dramatic kaftan hanging more off her body than on it. Compared to the rest of the group, who were wearing denim shorts or casual dresses, she was heavily overdressed but certainly had the tall, slim figure to carry it off. Her bouncy red hair hung in loose waves down her back, pale face protected by gigantic sunglasses.

'Gabriella Bellamy-Hughes,' she announced, swiping a glass of champagne off the silver tray and resting one hand on her hip.

It was a bold entrance to say the least. Charlotte stretched out her hand and introduced herself, breaking the awkward silence. Gabriella pursed her lips in a tight smile, then went on to boast about her mansion in Hertfordshire and how she always stayed in villas when she was on holiday in Ibiza or St Tropez.

'Much bigger than this one though,' she announced, smiling. Charlotte caught the eye of the DJ, Alex, who rolled her eyes, making Charlotte giggle. Gabriella seemed a tad obnoxious, but what was it Charlotte's mother had said before she'd left for Stansted Airport? 'Be nice to everyone and don't judge anyone too quickly.' Charlotte figured that Gabriella was showing off because she was nervous. When the remaining girls arrived shortly afterwards, including Mackenzie, a publicist, Becca, a beautician, and Nysha who was a doctor, it became too busy and loud to notice any one person in particular. Just like everyone had said when she signed up for the show, Charlotte soon forgot all about the cameras.

'Ladies, ladies!' The crowd hushed as Jas appeared, blonde hair swept into a bun and wearing sunglasses, a red vest top and denim shorts, showing off a perfect, already tanned figure. This girl had the effortlessly cool look down to a T, thought Charlotte. She'd been following Jas's Instagram feed ever since they'd met and had developed something of a girl-crush on her enviable wardrobe and oh-so-perfect life. If only Charlotte could be as happy and successful as Jas was.

'Welcome, everyone,' she continued. 'I'm so glad you all made it here safely. I'm sure you're tired from the journey and excitement of being here so we've got a delicious buffet being prepared and plenty more prosecco. Tonight you can just chill. Tomorrow you'll have a relaxing day by the pool, get to know each other a bit, do some interviews with me and the crew, and then in the evening there will be the first proper drinks reception where you'll meet Mr Right. And I'm happy to reveal that his name is Dylan.'

A few gasps and excited giggles came from the contestants.

'Yes, yes, he's arriving tomorrow. Dylan has his own guest house to one side of the villa, with its own pool and garden. He'll watch the footage of each and every one of you making your entrance. Trust me, ladies, he is a going to be very popular in this house! Now, you all know how this works. Every week we hold a big ceremony in the evening where Dylan hands out roses to the women he wants to stay in the competition. The contestants who don't get a rose must leave immediately. We'll put you on the next flight home.'

More nervous whispers from the group. Of course, this was not news to them. The rules of the competition were clear on that aspect. But they'd also been warned that rose ceremonies could happen at any time, and it wasn't necessarily just one girl who would be sent packing. In fact, they'd all been warned to expect the unexpected, as the producers could throw in new rules and changes whenever they liked, if they thought it would spice things up. Charlotte had a feeling they would waste no time in doing so. And she was right.

'And, ladies, there's a slight twist I've introduced tomorrow. The first drinks reception isn't a formal ceremony, but Dylan will be handing out a rose. We're calling it the At First Sight rose and he's going to give it to whoever has impressed him the most within the first couple of hours of meeting you all. This girl will be immune from going home after the next ceremony.'

They really weren't wasting any time in making this a dramatic series.

Jas continued, 'Now, there are five master bedrooms with three double beds in each of them. We've allocated you rooms and taken your luggage up so you can go now and find which bed is yours, unpack, then meet back here to eat. Try to ignore the cameras. We'll be filming bits and bobs but soon enough you won't even notice them. Off you go!'

The gaggle of women rushed off to see who they were sharing with and chatter about what sort of man they hoped Dylan would be. The rooms were massive, each with their own bathroom three times the size of Charlotte's at home and complete with a rainforest shower and stand-alone tub. The rooms also had their own balcony with three cushioned sunbeds and a table, looking out either to the pool or to the hills, every view stunning. Charlotte found her pink suitcase next to a double bed and was delighted to discover she was sharing a room with Kat and Melody. The girls gossiped as they unpacked, freshening up their make-up before heading back down to dinner. It was now dark and the view of luscious green had been replaced with candles dotted around the lit-up swimming pool and twinkling fairy lights all over the terrace. It was the most beautiful place Charlotte had ever seen.

'No, I don't want my hair up. I told you, undone sexy. Undone sexy!'

'Does anyone have a pencil sharpener for my eyeliner?'

'Who unplugged my straighteners?'

Charlotte tried to drown out the dozen different voices coming from around the villa. Most of the contestants were running around in their underwear with rollers in their hair or fake tan drying on their arms, looking for their belongings in one of the five bedrooms with suitcases lying everywhere, clothes, shoes and make-up falling out of them. They'd spent all day sunbathing and tonight was the night they were meeting Dylan during a lavish drinks reception to be held on the terrace. The cameras would be on throughout and the women had already spent an hour getting ready. It was chaotic to say the least. The dress code was sexy and glamorous.

Charlotte had blow-dried her dark hair poker-straight so it hung just below her shoulders, going over it with GHD straighteners and spraying it with her favourite glossing hairspray. Melody kindly did her make-up and expertly applied brown and gold eyeshadow to give her a sultry smoky-eye look, often telling Charlotte what gorgeous skin she had. Afterwards, Charlotte stood ironing a floor-length mint green dress she'd bought from Miss

Selfridge during an online spree with Maya. She didn't feel the least bit bad about dipping into her savings. All the girls had been told to dress glam for these nights and were sure to look amazing, especially Gabriella who was carefully pulling a red dress out of a zippcd-up Valentino suit-bag. Charlotte hoped not all the girls had designer clothes.

'I thought my Reiss number would do the trick, I didn't know we'd be forking out for Valentino!' Melody nudged Charlotte and pointed to Gabriella, before turning back to chat to Nysha.

Gabriella headed straight towards them. Charlotte hoped she hadn't heard Melody poking fun at her expensive dress.

'Hey, what's your name again?' asked Gabriella, sharply.

'It's Charlotte. Hi. We haven't actually properly spoken, but—'

'Yeah, soz for being a total no-show by the pool today. I can't be outside in the heat for too long with my pale skin.'

'Oh, well, we were mostly sitting in the shade actually and—'

'I had to Skype my agent, I've got a big audition coming up for a Hollywood film.'

'Oh, you're an actress, cool. Have you been in anything I would have seen? One of the EastEnders actresses goes to my gym, I've given her training.'

'Wow, I hope you asked for her autograph,' said Gabriella dismissively. Charlotte frowned at the sarcastic comment. There was no need to be quite so rude.

'Anyway, you couldn't help me out, could you? And give this a quick steam for me? There's a proper steamer over there. You can't set an iron to a Valentino, of course, but I've already done my make-up and it will sweat out entirely if I get near the steam.'

Charlotte took in Gabriella's perfect make-up: a subtle gold shimmer to her porcelain skin and bright red lipstick covering her full, bee-stung pout.

'Well, I've had my make-up done too, Gabriella,' Charlotte replied softly, suddenly feeling even shorter than her five foot three against Gabriella who was closer to six foot.

'Oh, gosh! How rude of me. Ummm … you wouldn't be a darling and do it anyway, would you? We've only got another fifteen minutes and I'm running soooo far behind.'

'No, she won't,' came a third voice. Alex. 'Gabriella, stop being such a diva and steam your own damn dress.' Alex stood protectively in front of Charlotte, hands on hips, almost squaring up to Gabriella.

'I believe this was a private conversation,' she said, pouting.

'Yeah, well, you should get used to the fact nothing is private around here. I don't know what you're used to in your castle or wherever you live, but Charlotte isn't your private slave.'

Gabriella rolled her eyes. 'Take a chill pill. I was just messing with the girl.' And, with that, she flounced off, throwing Alex an evil look as she did so.

'Thanks, I never would have had the guts to stand up to her,' said Charlotte.

Alex smoothed down her own burgundy-coloured lace dress. 'Yeah, well, I know we're all meant to be competing or whatever but, where I'm from, girls look out for each other and we don't put up with bullies.'

Charlotte had spent a lot of time talking to Alex that afternoon. She was twenty-five and had grown up on a tough council estate. In consequence she was ballsy as well as beautiful. Hanging around with musicians and rappers from her estate got her into the music industry and she had a late-night DJ slot on Capital One Extra as well as her Hoxton Radio show. Charlotte was impressed by how fiercely intelligent and interesting Alex was but she would never want to get on the wrong side of her.

'I just can't stand these spoilt, privileged bitches who think they can treat everyone like dirt,' Alex continued. 'Anyway, hun, I've got your back.' And with that she winked at Charlotte and turned away.

Chapter 13

The cameras rolled as all fifteen girls gathered in the living-room area.

'That's it, ladies. Now all face the front,' called Jas from behind one of the cameras. She dashed back out into the main entrance where Dylan was waiting.

'How are you feeling? Nervous? Excited? Wondering what the hell you've let yourself in for?' she asked.

'Umm, how about all of the above?' Dylan replied in his soft Aussie accent. He'd lived in the UK for nearly a decade since falling in love with a British actress, but still retained his accent, a trait Jas liked about him.

'You'll be great. Now, go in there and show them what you've got! Remember what we said: big intro to all of them then you work the room and just see who you gravitate to. Try to get a few minutes with each girl. In an hour we'll get you back for a quick interview to see how it's going.'

'All right, here goes.' With that, Dylan marched confidently into the living area where thirty eyes were fixed on him.

Jas knew he would be an instant hit. He was 100 per cent gorgeous, with jet-black hair and a strong jawline, the effect softened by dimples and a goofy smile. A bit too pretty for Jas's personal taste, perhaps – she wasn't into men who had their teeth whitened and chest waxed – but Dylan was a lovely guy and the perfect bachelor for the programme.

Jas surveyed the action and got the thumbs-up from various cameramen and Lyndsey, so she knew things were running smoothly. It was the perfect moment for a break. She stepped outside and sat by the fountain at the entrance to the villa, letting the trickling sound of water relax her. She'd barely rested over the past few weeks.

Being rushed off her feet was a welcome distraction, though, taking her mind off Richard and the horrible way she'd treated Luke. She still felt sick with guilt and regret about how that had ended and, though she'd never admit it to anyone, she thought about him and their two nights together far more than she should. She felt rotten about the way things had ended and the one time they'd run into each other since, at the Tube station near work, was awkward as hell. He had looked handsome as ever and was walking with a pretty brunette girl, courteously holding an umbrella over her head. *Didn't take him long to get over me, then,* thought Jas bitterly.

She was struggling to process her feelings about Luke. Until she'd gotten things straight in her own mind, how could she possibly know what to say to him? No text, email or Hangout message seemed appropriate for talking seriously about things. She'd been so decisive when she broke it off. It was what she wanted, wasn't it? Why, then, did her mind so often wander back to being in his arms? Jas tried to find faults in Luke, to justify them not being together. Lila had jokingly said that one time he was boring – could she hang on to that? Nope, it just wasn't true. Luke was one of the most engaging men Jas had ever met. There was always the fact he was seeing that brunette girl. Obviously, he wasn't lying awake obsessing over Jas. She sighed, realising that she had made her bed and must lie in it.

And besides, she was settled in Ibiza now and staying in a villa with Monica and the rest of the film crew, close to the contestants. The crew's accommodation wasn't as luxurious as where the fifteen women were living with Dylan, but it had a swimming pool and gorgeous views of the Ibizan scenery and that was enough for Jas. She loved her colleagues and when they weren't filming or having meetings about the show they sat around the pool together, toes dipped in the water, drinking beer. Jas hadn't forgotten that she'd also got half a dozen gorgeous party dresses hanging in her holiday wardrobe, primed and ready to make their debut.

Her priority now had to be making *Mr Right* a success. Any feelings she thought she had for Luke needed to be ignored until they were pushed out of her mind entirely. That was the only thing for it.

There was also the small matter of her ongoing divorce battle. How Richard could have changed so much, be so totally different now from the man she'd fallen in love with six years ago, still shocked her. Truth be told, there had been so much pain, so many lies in the last couple of years, she'd never had a chance to mourn the man she'd lost. Wherever the old Richard was, he certainly wasn't coming back.

After weeks of gathering what evidence she could against him, she was still waiting for a date for the court hearing. The process certainly was dragging out and there was still a possibility that the statements from friends and her handful of text messages and emails to them, divulging that Richard had admitted cheating on her, still wasn't enough evidence to convince a judge. She'd tried to phone Richard to ask him to reconsider and avoid all this huge expense on both sides. Couldn't they just end this amicably and get on with their lives? But he pointedly refused to answer her. She had no idea what he was up to.

Jas's phone rang, breaking her train of thought. Meg's smiling face flashed up.

'I told you FaceTime was the best app,' Jas laughed as she answered. Nothing made her feel better than hearing her sister's voice. And since Meg had finally caught up with the twenty-first century and installed FaceTime, Jas had been regularly seeing her face, too.

'What's going on in Manchester then, missy? How's the big makeover coming along?'

Meg and Oscar were renovating their entire house, turning it into a real family home. Meg went into a monologue about paint swatches and the merits of track lights as opposed to spotlights. Then she casually dropped in, 'Oh, and you know Mum and Dad want Lila to move back home?'

Jas did not know this. It was so frustrating how they tried to coddle Lila all the time. 'Honestly, she's twenty-five. She is big enough to look after herself. She not only has her own place to live but she's currently got my whole flat to herself for eight weeks while I'm in Ibiza and she's house-sitting.'

'You know what they're like. They think she goes out too much, drinks too much.'

'Only 'cos she's the youngest,' said Jas, crossly. 'They didn't give two shits about us staying out all night when we were teenagers. We were a lot younger. God! I've barely heard from Mum and Dad since I've been out here. I'm the one with the personal life in tatters!'

'How's it going on that front anyway? You heard from Luke yet?'

Jas sighed. 'No. I think I need to accept that one is well and truly over. It's what I wanted. Want, I mean. It's what I want.'

'Aw, honey, you sound down. What happened to my fun-loving, bubbly sister, eh? You're in Ibiza, Jas. Ibiza, of all places! You're being *paid* to be there. Go out and let your hair down. Have some fun. You're young, gorgeous and single.'

'That last one definitely isn't true!'

'Well, it will be soon. In a few months, this divorce will be long behind you. I know it's stressful, but you have to enjoy life where you can. I didn't let you raid the rails of my boutique with a 50% discount for nothing.'

After the call ended Jas considered Meg's words. It *was* out of character for her to be so stressed and preoccupied. The old Jas would have been out every night, work or no work! Meg was totally and utterly right.

Monica called out from the villa's doorway. 'Jas? It's time for Dylan to give the At First Sight rose.'

'Great,' Jas replied. 'Hey, Mon. How do you fancy going out tomorrow night?'

'Ooh, fun! We're filming throughout the day but there's nothing going on in the evening that the pre-installed cameras won't catch.'

'How about I book a restaurant in the Old Town for us and the crew? And I know a guy from the club scene in London. He's taken over the Hard Rock Café for the summer. I reckon I could wangle VIP tickets. How about it?'

Monica was practically giddy with anticipation. Jas knew she could count on her best work-friend for a good time. 'Hell, yeah! Let's do it. I've been waiting for the old Jas to come back.'

Jas smiled, suddenly feeling totally revitalised. She wasn't about to let anything or anyone get her down.

The At First Sight rose was Jas's idea. She knew it would up the drama. Even if Dylan liked several women, he only had one rose to give that night.

Jas took in the scene of gorgeous girls draped around this picture-perfect villa in their figure-hugging gowns. It looked as perfect as she'd imagined. She was already picturing how it would be edited and the dramatic music to go alongside the close-ups and sideways glances. Monica and Jas took each woman aside with a camera to video their first impressions of how the night was going. Jas took Charlotte to the fountain outside the house, guiding her from behind the camera.

'Okay, Charlotte, look directly to camera, not at me, please. Tell me what you think of Dylan.'

Charlotte cleared her throat. Her eyes glistened. She really was incredibly beautiful, thought Jas. Sweet as well. Jas liked her and hoped she stayed in this contest for a while.

'I honestly didn't know what to expect, none of us did. We knew he'd be gorgeous and obviously he is, but he's really nice, too.'

'Uh-huh, and what did you two talk about?'

'Fitness, mainly. He asked what I did for a living. He keeps in shape too, obviously, so we talked a bit about that. Then just general chit-chat about the island, whether we'd ever been to Ibiza before, that sort of thing.'

'Mmm. And what about the other girls? Who do you see as your biggest competition?' Charlotte might be sweet but this was still a reality show and Jas needed some dirt.

'They're all lovely!'

'Really? What if you had to say just one name you weren't quite so keen on?'

'Honestly, it's a little too early to tell. Everyone seems nice and a bit nervous so we'll have to see how it plays out, I guess.'

'Okay. Thanks, Charlotte. You can go back inside now. Can you send Gabriella out for her interview?'

Charlotte headed back inside. A couple of minutes later Gabriella emerged in her eye-catching red dress, her Julia Roberts-red locks cascading over one shoulder and lips pouting.

'Look directly into the camera, please, Gabriella, not at me. Tell me, what are your first impressions of the other contestants? Made any friends yet? Or enemies?' Jas asked her.

Gabriella smiled, knowing exactly how to ham it up for the camera.

'There was tension in the house the second I walked in. People looking me up and down, whispering. Some of the girls seem lovely, but that Alex ... I don't trust her at all. And Charlotte? Don't let the butter-wouldn't-melt persona fool you. She's out to win.'

'And what are your first impressions of Dylan?'

'Oh, wow, we already have such a connection. I don't mean to sound arrogant, but he really stared at me in there! I really think there is something between us.'

Chapter 14

The evening was in full swing. Gabriella, Mackenzie, the blonde publicist with fake boobs, and the talent show contestant Georgia were vying for the attention of Dylan and the cameras and barely left him alone, while some of the other, more restrained contestants like Alex and Charlotte were hanging back and playing it cool. Dylan made sure that he engaged with every woman there, though, striking up conversations and getting to know everyone as they mingled between each other.

Later, it was time for Dylan to make his choice of who'd be the first woman to receive a rose. Gabriella, Mackenzie and Georgia were perched on a sofa out on the terrace. Charlotte could see they had struck up a friendship. But, with a rose in his hand and a cameraman behind him, Dylan merely smiled at the group and walked past, towards the pool where Charlotte was sitting on a sunlounger, sipping mojitos with Kat, Melody and Carmel.

'Charlotte, could I borrow you for a moment, please?' Like a perfect gentleman he stretched out his arm for Charlotte to take as he led her down to the Bali bed on the other side of the gigantic pool. She couldn't believe it! Charlotte could feel the rest of the girls stare after her and noticed a few whispering to each other. Realising they couldn't hear what Dylan and Charlotte were saying anyway, most went back to their own conversations, but not before Jas had motioned for the cameras to record their reactions. She had noticed Alex pursing her lips tighter and tighter as she saw Dylan and Charlotte walk away hand in hand.

'Surprised?' Dylan asked as they sat on the edge of the Bali bed, close enough that their arms brushed together. Dylan turned his body slightly so that he was facing Charlotte, his arm leaning on the bed behind her. Charlotte might not have known a whole lot about men, but she was sure she could read this body language – and it was positive.

'To be honest, yes,' she laughed, still not entirely comfortable with a camera tracking their date so closely. She took a sip of champagne for Dutch courage. 'Don't get me wrong, though. I'm very flattered.' Charlotte thought about Alex's jewel-like eyes and Mackenzie's perfect figure, both surely catnip to any man?

'Well, the first thing I noticed about you was how unbelievably beautiful you are,' Dylan replied coolly. Charlotte pursed her lips to stop a huge smile from spreading across her face. Was this really happening?

'And then we started talking,' he continued. 'We had a lot in common and I guess I just wanted to know more.'

'Such as?'

'Such as, how old are you? What do you like doing best? What made you decide to go on a show like this? What are your dreams and ambitions?'

'Talk about diving straight in!'

'Sorry, I don't mean to sound so full on. I guess I'm nervous.'

Charlotte now turned her own body fully towards Dylan's so they were facing each other, both of them smiling nervously. 'I am too,' she said. 'Hopefully there will be plenty of time for us to get to know each other.'

'Absolutely. Can I ask you one more question?'

'Shoot.'

'Do you have any kids? I have a four-year-old daughter, Ruby. I just want to be completely upfront with everyone in here that she's the biggest part of my life, so anyone who wasn't on board with that ... well, I wouldn't want to waste my time or theirs.'

This honesty and blatant devotion to his daughter was only a turn-on for Charlotte.

'Thank you for being so honest. No, I haven't got any kids but I'm hopelessly devoted to my Godson, Rafi. I've been best friends with his mum Maya since we were in school. She and her boyfriend Rob had him pretty young, at nineteen, but they're such amazing parents.'

'Wow, I love that. How old is Rafi?'

'Five. He's started school now, which is just too adorable for words!'

Dylan smiled and offered her the single red rose from his other hand. 'Well, you light up when you talk about him so he's clearly very special to you. If you'd accept it, I would really love to give you my first rose?'

'I'd love to have it.' She smiled back at him.

'I really look forward to getting to know more about you, Charlotte.'

Charlotte went to bed that night feeling exhausted but elated. She liked Dylan. He seemed friendly and funny but, then again, she always liked the guy. They just never seemed to like her. But being given the At First Sight rose was a big deal. It was the first rose to be offered and no one could take that away from Charlotte. She woke the next morning feeling confident. Maybe she would get her happy ever after for real?

The contestants ate breakfast on their huge terrace. There was a platter of sliced strawberries, melon, grapes and apple, bowls of yoghurt, nuts and different kinds of bread, granola and pastries. Normally the girls would be expected to take it in turns to prepare the fruit plates for everyone each morning but today, as a special treat, a chef had come to prepare eggs, any style. It seemed like a terrible waste as every girl was watching her figure. Almost all the pastries were left untouched, most of the fruit merely picked at. Charlotte sat next to Alex, who was chomping on an apple.

'Is that all you're having?'

Alex shrugged. 'I never eat much in the mornings and I'm allergic to nuts and melon anyway. I'll have a big lunch later.'

Gabriella sauntered past. 'Big lunch? With those hips? I wouldn't if I were you, babe.'

Alex stood up. 'What was that?' But Gabriella simply smiled sweetly and sat down at the other end of the table.

'Ignore her,' whispered Charlotte. 'She just wants a reaction.' Alex chomped furiously into the apple.

As the cameras rolled Dylan appeared, announcing that he would choose seven women to go on two group-dates with that day. Charlotte was delighted when he stated that she, Melody and the doctor, Nysha, would join him for a hike after breakfast. Gabriella was one of the four who got to have cocktails at sunset with him later on.

The hike was a lot of fun. Not only did Charlotte get to spend more time with Dylan, but she grew closer to Nysha and Melody. She really liked them both. Melody was incredibly funny and gorgeous with a curvaceous figure to die for, but totally down to earth. Thanks to Nysha's Indian heritage, she had long black glossy hair, big eyes and beautiful skin. She was just as boisterous as Melody, with a wicked sense of humour. Dylan was in his element, flirting with all the girls and trying to show off by listing facts about the island. Nysha was too quick for him, though, and often pointed out things that he got wrong and then the group would laugh about them.

Charlotte was convinced that Dylan held her gaze longer than anyone else's. When she slipped on a branch and fell over, he rushed to her side to see if she was okay and their eyes met for an electric second. However, when they returned to the house and Mackenzie was walking through the kitchen in her underwear, deeply tanned after sunbathing all day and her fake boobs barely contained by her bra, Dylan's appreciative glance didn't go unnoticed.

Charlotte reminded herself that there were fourteen other hot women here. A single man, especially one as good-looking and charming as this one, certainly wasn't going to commit to anyone this early. It felt so discouraging, knowing that everyone else would get alone time with Dylan at some point, but that was the game.

Over the next few days, more group-dates occurred and, when she wasn't involved, Charlotte hung out with and got to know the friendlier girls in the group. They'd chill by the pool, go to the beach or the busy town, and cameras would record much of their conversation. Most nights they would Skype friends and family back in England.

But beneath the dreamy atmosphere, tension was mounting. Gabriella and Alex, the two most outspoken and competitive of the group, were constantly bickering over anything from who ate the last yoghurt to who was hamming it up most for the cameras. There seemed to be cliques forming in the house. Gabriella, Mackenzie, Natalie and the singer, Georgia, had established a *Mean Girls*-style group and didn't talk to anyone else unless it was to say something passive-aggressive. Alex led the opposing crew, which consisted of herself and two others, Fiona and Jillian, who were nice enough but had strong opinions and a hard side to them. Charlotte wouldn't like to get on the wrong side of any of them. She, Kat, Melody, Nysha, Becca, Carmel and the final two, Delia and Hayley, tried to stay out of conflict entirely.

On the sixth night, Charlotte was busy putting on her blue pyjamas and scraping back her dark hair into a ponytail for a lazy movie night to be spent with Melody and a few others, when there was a knock on the bedroom door.

'Oh, hi, Jas, come on in.'

'Hiya, babe. I just wanted to check in on you to see how you're doing.' Jas plonked herself on one of the beds and flipped her phone so it was facing downwards. 'These first few days have been mental. Sorry I'm only getting one-to-one time with you now.'

Charlotte was grateful Jas was looking after her. She sat down next to her on the bed. 'I actually thought I'd be more homesick than this. I've never been away from home for more than a few days and we're almost through our first week already.'

Jas raised an eyebrow at this. 'Any of the girls giving you trouble? I hear Alex has been clashing with quite a few of the others.'

'I try to stay out of it.'

'We've seen footage from the fixed cameras in the living room. She's a fiery one, that's for sure.'

'She doesn't like posh girls. I think there's a big chip on her shoulder about that. Her and Mackenzie have been at loggerheads. And Gabriella ... though she's difficult anyway.' Charlotte felt bitchy for revealing as much.

Jas gave her a reassuring smile. 'Just keep going, you're doing great. Any problems, come to me, okay? Any time you want to chat, rant, cry, you name it.'

'Thanks, Jas, that's good to know.'

The following evening was the first proper and highly anticipated rose ceremony when Dylan would hand out flowers to the women he wanted to stay in the villa. As the recipient of the At First Sight rose, Charlotte was immune from leaving on this occasion, but still felt her stomach fluttering with nerves. The one unlucky contestant who did not get a rose would be on a plane back to England that very night. The atmosphere was tense. Charlotte figured that, with fifteen girls in a house, there was bound to be some clashing of personalities, and it was probably good TV. But no one wanted to be the first to leave.

They were dressed to impress, of course. Charlotte wore a red pencil skirt with a loose, beaded red camisole, her hair in an elegant plait. They all met for champagne on the terrace. On a silver tray sat a bunch of red roses.

From behind the cameras Monica asked the crowd for quiet as Dylan made his big entrance. Wearing a black suit and black shirt, his tanned skin freshly shaven, he looked extremely dapper. Every woman there was watching him, trying to make eye contact and smiling sweetly to try to get his attention.

Dylan cleared his throat. 'Ladies, thank you for coming this evening. You all look ravishing, I have to say.' A few giggles from the girls. He had them eating out of his hand. He then smiled directly at Charlotte. She took a sip of champagne and tried not to react. She didn't want to flatter his ego too much.

'I've had a great week getting to know you all on group-dates,' he continued. 'It's been a lot of fun and I'm truly excited to have the chance to get to know some of you a lot better on our individual dates starting tomorrow. I wish you could all stay so I could get to know you a little better but, as you know, someone will be going home tonight. But I have some news … It won't be just one of you. There are only twelve roses here. I am sending two women home tonight.'

The women glanced at each other; some gasped in surprise. Charlotte wondered if the producers had planned this all along, decided it just now, or whether two women had somehow offended Dylan and the decision had come from him. Who would be the first to go? Was her place in jeopardy after all? Was it something she said or did on the hike? Was that why he smiled; was he just toying with her?

'Charlotte, as we all know, you are immune tonight, so please make your way to this side of the room,' said Dylan.

Phew!

Dylan picked up the first rose and waited a few dramatic moments before announcing the first name.

'Mackenzie.'

Dylan didn't hear Alex mutter 'slut' as Mackenzie strutted up to him, but everyone else did.

'Will you accept this rose?' he asked.

'Of course!' she exclaimed, planting a kiss on his cheek and sashaying to the other side of the room to join Charlotte.

Gabriella, Nysha, Kat, Georgia and Melody all made it through. Then it was time for Dylan to reveal the name of the first contestant he was sending home.

'Fiona,' he said with a sigh. That was one of the girls from Alex's 'side'. She was a twenty-one-year-old student, mouthy and quite immature, Charlotte had thought.

'Fiona, I think you're a very sweet girl,' Dylan said, holding her hands. 'But I'm a father, I have a toddler and I need to be with a woman who is really on board with that. I think maybe you have some growing up still to do. I'm sorry.' Charlotte thought it was a considerate and heartfelt let-down.

The other girls' names were reeled off until just Alex and Jillian remained. Dylan finally handed the rose to Alex. 'There's a lot more I want to know about you,' he smiled flirtatiously at her. Charlotte wondered whether he was saying all this purely for the cameras or was actually something of a player.

Jillian, the glamour model from Surrey, looked devastated. She'd clearly hoped to stay till the bitter end, like they all did.

'I'm sorry, Jillian. You're very beautiful but I just don't think we connected. I wish you all the best.'

And that was it, thirteen girls remaining. Everyone said their goodbyes to Jillian and Fiona, who went upstairs to pack and go home. The rest trotted off for individual reaction-interviews for the cameras, but first Dylan had one more announcement to make.

'And Charlotte? Make sure you get up extra early tomorrow as we're going for a sunrise yoga class as our first alone-date. Goodnight, everyone!'

Chapter 15

Saturday night at Print Room was a glamorous affair. The bar was one of the hottest spots in London and a place on the weekend guest list was coveted. Richard scanned the room like a cheetah stalking its prey. He'd been called into work that morning to finalise a big deal and felt like celebrating afterwards with an indulgent lunch at Roka in Mayfair followed by some Dom Pérignon. He'd sloped off to a friend's flat that he'd taken to visiting every so often. He didn't like to use the word 'hooker' as it sounded so seedy. And besides, this girl – Frankie – was a total knockout and worth every penny. 'High-class escort' was a much more fitting description. They'd met at a big fundraising event where she'd been hired to be the date of a high-flying executive at a big City firm. Jas was there with Richard but he'd wasted no time in cornering Frankie and getting her number. They only hired the best girls for such functions. Frankie spoke four languages, had a Master's degree in philosophy and a flat paid for by a married and seemingly scandal-free politician. So what if she wanted to earn more cash on the side? Richard had since become a regular visitor. It wasn't that he couldn't get laid easily, he just got off on the power aspect of making a woman do whatever he wanted in return for cash. And now that was out of his system he was ready for another drink and some more fun, so he rejoined his colleagues at Print Room. By the early evening, those colleagues returned home to their wives and kids, but Richard was far from calling it a night. By his calculations, there were at least three women to every man in the bar. Before his eyes stretched a sea of high heels and tight dresses. His bosses were right: he'd really benefit from keeping up the pretence of being happily married. It made everyone more comfortable knowing they had a stable and committed chap on their hands. Single men never got promotions in his firm. He'd figure out what to do about his marriage later – right now he wanted some fun.

Freshly back from powdering his nose in the toilets, Richard propped himself up at the bar in the centre of the room, ordered a large Hendrick's and tonic and surveyed the landscape. He caught the eye of a busty blonde in the corner and a redhead smiled at him coyly. He did a double take when the most stunning brunette sauntered by, catching the attention of every man in the room. The girl had long, wavy, glossy hair and the biggest blue eyes. Richard had the feeling he'd met her somewhere before. She greeted another fit girl, shorter but with beautiful mixed-race skin and wearing the sexiest tight dress. *Hello, ladies!* Richard hailed the bartender.

'A bottle of Verve Clique, mate. In a bucket. Three glasses.'

Richard downed his gin and tonic and stood up to carry his offering over to their table, when suddenly he was stopped dead in his tracks. The girls had been joined by a man now, who had his arm around the brunette. Richard noticed a giant rock on her engagement finger. Bollocks! Richard recognised the guy instantly and remembered where he knew the girl from. Connor Scott. And that was his girlfriend. Or fiancé now from the look of things. Connor was an old friend of Jas's and Richard had met him a couple of times, though was so wasted at the time it was only a vague recollection. Damn! Why were the fittest girls always taken? Now he was left with a bottle of champagne and three glasses, looking like an absolute twat. Not wanting Connor to spot him, Richard sloped off to the dining section of the club. No point in letting a good bottle of bubbly go to waste, he reasoned. Better make himself comfortable at a table and wait for a woman to join him.

'Butler, is that you?' Richard turned to see the grinning face of Greg Simpson, a fellow trader who used to work on his floor before joining a rival firm. 'Maaaate!'

'Simpers! Good to see you too, mate.'

They two men hugged lightly, patting each other on the back as if in congratulation though neither of them knew for what.

'Here alone, Butler?'

'Oh, yeah, was just out with the boys after letting the ink dry on the Fitzrovia deal. Jones coughed up a bottle of

Dom P before being summoned home by his wife and so left me high and dry!'

'You landed the Fitzrovia deal?' Greg shook Richard's hand enthusiastically. 'Mate, that's impressive. You boys are cleaning up over there. The talk of the town.'

Richard smiled smugly. He knew how well his company was doing in the current climate, especially since his own recent promotion. He was the golden boy in a team of golden men. Life was good.

'Anyway, what are you doing here, Simpers?'

Greg nodded to his table in the dining room and Richard had to stop himself staring. For who was sitting there other than Lila Whiteley, pretty as a picture, idly touching up her lipstick in a hand mirror.

'I'm on a date. Our third, actually. She's fucking fit but I think she's losing interest. Still haven't managed to close the deal with her, either.' The two men laughed.

Richard couldn't help but stare. As Jas's baby sister he had never taken Lila too seriously. But tonight she looked undeniably hot. The ratty, moth-eaten vest she often wore had been replaced with a very sexy white blouse. Her white-blonde hair was shorter than the last time he'd seen her, cut to just below her chin and showing off her excellent bone structure.

'She's my sister-in-law.'

Greg looked aghast. 'Maaaate. Sorry, no offence, I didn't mean any disrespect. You're still married? I thought I'd heard you two divorced?'

Richard shook his head vehemently, then smiled slyly as a plan formed in his mind. 'Rumours, son, rumours. And no offence taken. Lila will be bang up for it, trust me. Listen, Jones left me with this bottle, barely drunk, and three glasses, would you believe? Why don't the three of us drink it? I'll talk you up to Lila. She'll listen to me.'

Greg grinned at him. 'Great idea, mate. Come on over and say hello.'

Fortunately for Richard, Greg was too preoccupied with the delightful prospect of finally bedding Lila that he didn't notice her look of contempt as he walked back to the table with their new guest.

'You two know each other, I presume?' But Richard had already sat down next to Lila and was pouring out three glasses of chilled champagne. 'Silly me,' continued Greg, 'I got up to go to the toilet, bumped into this guy and clean forgot I had to pee. Be right back.'

'See ya, mate!' Richard answered cheerily, knowing Lila would wait until he was out of earshot before she started to lay it on. And, as predicted ...

'What do you think you're doing?'

She looked even better when she was pissed off. 'All right, little one? Long time, no see. Champagne?'

'Why are you crashing my date?'

'Are you honestly going to tell me that Greg is doing it for you? I could sense your boredom from across the room. He's a nice guy but being in his company is about as exciting as watching paint dry. Where did you meet him anyway?'

Lila sniffed. 'On Tinder, if you must know. Where else do people meet these days?'

'Oh, you know. Bars, work, fundraisers ...'

'Huh?'

'Nothing. Here, have some champagne.'

'Do you have any idea what my sister would say if she knew I was sitting here quaffing champagne with you?'

'That she wished she was out having fun with us like she used to and that she should stop being such a buzz kill?'

'Hey! Jas goes out all the time.'

That was news to Richard. 'Really? Where?'

'Does it matter? And that's not the point. She's my sister and you've been a complete arse. Don't you know she tells us everything?'

Richard edged closer to Lila. He had lost count of the number of times Jas had moaned to him about how immature and irritating Lila was and that she needed to grow up. If he'd given it enough thought he might have felt sorry for Lila. Her parents blatantly spoilt her but no one actually took her seriously. Her desperation to be seen as an adult was so obvious to him.

'Lila, you're old enough and smart enough to know there are two sides to every messy break-up. Of course, Jasmine is going to paint me as the bad guy. You don't know the half of it, okay?'

It was that easy. Lila softened instantly. 'I suppose … But I know you've cheated on her, Richard. We all know that.'

Richard looked down at the floor and let out a dramatic sigh. This was getting to be quite fun. 'Lila, if you knew how much I cared about your sister … Everyone makes mistakes. I'm not perfect. There's a lot you don't know and

I bet Jasmine won't ever tell you. She's not squeaky clean either.'

'What do you mean?'

'Look, Greg's coming back to the table. I'll explain another time, if you'll let me. Let's just have a drink now and relax a bit. I'm dying to hear what you've been up to all these months. And we can't let this delicious bottle of champagne go to waste now, can we?'

'Okay, Richard. But only one drink and don't you dare breathe a word about this to Jas. She'd one hundred per cent go ape-shit if she found out I was fraternising with the enemy.'

Richard patted her arm. 'It will be our little secret.'

Chapter 16

Jas was getting ready for her first proper Ibiza night out. She'd found a manicurist that day and her nails were buffed, polished and painted a pale pink, which showed off her tanned hands and arms. She was starting to enjoy the way her hair looked when it dried naturally, having already gone even lighter in the sun and looking exceptionally full and healthy. It fell in soft curls over her chest. Monica insisted that Jas looked like Blake Lively when she wore her hair down. Tonight, Jas wore a silky, short, dusky pink kimono, low-cut with a sash belt. It was very sexy, so she kept her make-up look quite natural with highlighter, mascara, a touch of bronzer and a slick of nude lipgloss. She was just fastening the buckle on her chunky black sandals when her phone rang.

Richard.

'Is that really you?' she said, answering the call.

'Hey, Jazzy. Yeah, 'course it is. You haven't deleted my number already, have you, babe?'

So much for Jas's good mood. Instantly she was furious that he was acting so friendly, as if everything between them was normal. She'd been trying to ring him for days to talk about the divorce and he'd failed to answer or ring her back. *Be cool*, she told herself. *Just be cool.*

'Please don't call me Jazzy. You know I hate that.'

'I wanted to talk to you, Jazzy,' he said, totally ignoring her last point. 'Is this really what you want?'

'Are you seriously asking me that? You honestly think I'd take you back now?'

Richard sighed. 'I don't want a divorce, Jas. I really think that we can work through this.'

Jas closed her eyes. It was too late for all this!

'But, as I know that isn't what you want,' Richard continued, 'I've got a proposition for you.'

'Go on.' This should be good, thought Jas suspiciously.

'You know how frowned upon divorce is in my family. And at work. So I'm suggesting, for appearance's sake, even if you don't want me, we ditch the divorce anyway. You keep the flat, I'll stay in Moorgate. Lead your own life and I'll lead mine. We just, you know, borrow each other for the big stuff. Weddings, work functions, that sort of thing. And I'll pay the mortgage on your flat to sweeten the deal.'

He really was desperate. Jas actually felt a flicker of pity for him. The prospect of a divorce must be seriously worrying him. But no amount of money in the world would be enough to keep Jas in an unhappy, open marriage. She didn't see the point in having a row with Richard tonight, though, so decided to be civil.

'That is a generous offer,' she said. 'I can't accept it, though. I've told you, Richard, this divorce is going ahead. Either you can let it happen amicably or make me fight you, which will cost time and money and probably get ugly.'

'You're not even going to *consider* it?' Clearly Richard had expected Jas to jump at his offer. He'd better think again.

'No. I'm sorry.'

'Fucking ridiculous! Do you know what I'll do to you in court? Do you have any idea how long I could let this drag on for? I've got the money, sweetheart, don't you worry about that. What've you got? Some poxy savings? It's not like your parents are going to be any use from their hole in Manchester. Your dad is retired and your mum doesn't even have a job.' Jas didn't bother to point out that Richard's mother Celia had never worked a day in her life.

She let him rant on, knowing that he was acting out because he wasn't getting what he wanted, like a child. She refused to be drawn into a row, but his words stung and her eyes brimmed. Her parents might not have much money but they were loving, devoted, and would do anything for their daughters, unlike Celia and Harold Butler who had all the money in the world but never showed their son an ounce of affection. Jas remembered Richard confessing that his parents had never once told him they loved him. She had been speechless, wondering what that would do to someone's self-esteem. It seemed he was beyond help and Jas was only more convinced that she wanted to divorce him as quickly as she could. She'd sell the flat and everything she owned if that's what it took to pay the lawyers.

Jas momentarily thought back to their wedding four years ago. It had been sensational. A countryside church service was followed by a lavish reception in a marquee. It was largely organised by Celia, who had declared that it was to be the society event of the year when, in actual fact, she just wanted to show off to her snobby friends. Jas would have been happy with a knees-up in a pub, but 'doing things properly' clearly meant so much to Celia and the last thing Jas wanted was to get on the wrong side of the mother-in-law-to-be. Things became slightly awkward when Jas's own parents were handed a bill amounting to a small fortune for 'their half' of the over-the-top celebration they'd had practically no say in. Jas's family wasn't poor but they had nothing like the sort of money the Butlers had. Her parents were such kind, easy-going people – and could see how in love their daughter was – so, much to Jas's embarrassment, they agreed to pay up.

Richard was still ranting down the phone but Jas had had enough. 'Goodbye, Richard,' she said firmly, hanging up. She threw a few essentials into her evening bag, taking deep breaths to calm herself down. Richard really brought out the worst in her. She used to be so chilled and care-free. So much for her good mood.

Richard clenched his fists as the phone went dead. He really had expected Jas to have dropped this stupid divorce thing by now yet his final, last-ditch attempt to salvage their marriage had ended with her hanging up on him. He poured a generous amount of expensive tequila into a glass, threw in some ice and knocked back the whole thing, immediately pouring himself another. Letting the buzz wash over him, he slouched back into the expensive leather sofa.

How dare she? He'd offered to pay her entire mortgage! Just who did she think she was? The more Richard thought about Jasmine Whiteley, the angrier he felt. He finished his drink and poured yet another. Richard was stressed. He'd already lost a huge deal at work today, costing the company half a million quid. It was peanuts to them, really, but still. This was the first time Richard had ever messed up at work. Thoughts of Jas were preoccupying him and taking away his focus.

Richard sat back, tapping his fingers on the sofa, his mind whirring but coming up with no concrete plan to fix this situation.

He reached over to the table for his silver iMac and flipped it on, logging onto his Facebook account and lazily scrolled through. Amazingly, Lila popped up on his homepage. That was weird, he didn't realise she was still 'friends' with him. Jas and Meg had deleted him from their friend-list months ago. Whether from ignorance, scattiness or forgetfulness, it seemed Lila hadn't. Richard scrolled through her profile. It was full of pictures of her wearing very skimpy outfits and posing seductively with her equally fit mates.

'Frriiiiiiday, we're herrre!' was the caption under one picture of Lila in a miniscule dress that showed off her skinny frame. She was wearing dark purple lipstick. She was so beautiful, so youthful and sexy, she looked like she'd been Photoshopped. If Jas knew he was sitting there, perving over her younger sister, she'd be fuming. Was this going a step too far? It probably was. Richard started to close down his computer in order to direct his energy elsewhere when the flash of a green icon next to Lila's name appeared, notifying him that she was online now, too. Richard deliberated for a minute. To hell with it, he finally thought. He opened up a new chat in the Messenger section and started typing.

'I have a very important question,' he wrote to Lila.

There was no response. Minutes passed. Oh, well, he'd have to find his fun somewhere else that evening. He was just about to log off when …

'What's your important question?' came her reply.

Richard's sly smile returned. 'Just wondering when you got so beautiful. I remember when you were just a kid.'

'Not really sure you should be saying that to me … Thanx tho :-)'

'Sorry. Just been thinking about you since that night at Print Room. Is that bad of me to say?'

'Yes … Was nice to see u though. Been a while.'

'Oh, yeah, you have fun?'

':-) Ditched your loser mate, so boring, went to a party with my mates.'

'Wish I'd joined you. Maybe next time ;-)'

'Maybe. Can't tell Jas tho.'

Richard knew he was pushing the flirtation. No rush, he thought.

'Your secret is safe. Gotta run now but maybe dinner soon? Catch up properly?'

'Maybe,' Lila replied with a winking-face emoji.

'x'

And, with that, Richard logged off. Just what would Jasmine think about *that*?

Chapter 17

Jas winced as she knocked back a strong sickly shot of … well, she wasn't sure what it was. She made a face to Monica. 'That was foul!' Jas was back to herself again and determined not to let Richard spoil her night out. They'd sunk a bottle of prosecco in a funky bar with a neon dance floor and were now doing shots at the Hard Rock Café.

'Hey, you're the one who had the bright idea of coming here and getting us free shots,' Monica laughed. 'And we haven't paid for one drink since we've been here thanks to your mate. Does he own the place or something?'

'Connor? Nah, he runs a hotel in Miami and a club in London. You know 360, don't you?'

'Oh, yeah! I love it there!'

'I met him years ago when he ran Print Room but he's given that one up now. He's major. So successful. He's just helping run this place over the summer while the owners expand.'

'Well, he is fit *as*. And he's coming over!'

'Ha! Keep your hands to yourself, missy. He's engaged and his fiancée is as nice as they come. Connor!' Jas lurched into a slightly drunken but totally platonic bear hug. She'd known him for years through the nightlife scene in London. She'd also filmed a few episodes of previous reality shows she'd worked on at his club 360 at the trendy Degree Hotel in Notting Hill.

'All right, ladies?' He winked at them, motioning for the bartender to whip up another round of cocktails as Jas introduced him to her friend. Monica, undoubtedly tipsy by now, threw her arms around Connor. Ever the gentleman, he smiled politely.

'Sorry about her.' Jas rolled her eyes. 'How's Indigo anyway? Is she here tonight?'

'Flying out this weekend. She's trying on wedding dresses back home with the bridesmaids and, trust me, I didn't want to be there as much as she didn't want me there!'

'Quite right! Send her my love, won't you? We should try to all hang out while I'm over here. Seven more weeks!'

'Definitely. What about you, anyone special on the scene?'

Jas thought instantly of Luke. She'd done a pretty good job so far of putting him out of her mind, busying herself with the show and phoning Meg – Lila never picked up these days – or else talking to Monica any time she found her thoughts turning back to him. It might have been the several cocktails and mysterious shots blurring her perspective, but she suddenly felt sad. 'No. No one,' she replied.

'You're not still with that wanker from the City then?'

Jas bristled at the thought of Richard. Connor had met him once years ago and Richard had been embarrassingly obnoxious and rude, yet more than happy to sink all the free champagne Connor provided at their table in Print Room.

'Sorry, that was rude. Indi is always telling me I need to watch what I say and keep my thoughts to myself. Anyway, none of my business. How's filming going?' Jas filled Connor in on the different characters and filming locations for dates.

'Well, if you ever want to do anything in here, you're more than welcome,' he offered. 'It's not the most romantic of dates, it gets pretty rowdy most nights to be honest, but we can sort out a time when the couple can be alone and have drinks outside. The bar backs on to the beach. It looks gorgeous at the right time of day.'

'Really? Thanks, Connor, that would be fantastic!'

'No problem. Listen, I've got to get back to work but you girls stay as long as you want.'

'No can do, sadly,' Monica put in. 'Jas is up for yoga at sunrise in a few hours.'

Connor raised his eyebrows. 'Good luck with that!'

Jas whined in protest. 'God, I forgot about it. I don't have to take part, thankfully. Just oversee one of the dates. Better get going after this.'

'I'll call you a cab when you're ready,' offered Connor, ever-helpful and courteous. He waited until Monica was in the toilet before delivering a blow to Jas.

'Hey, Jas, one thing I thought you should know. Your sister texted me earlier.'

'Meg? What on earth did she want?'

'No, Lila.'

'Lila?! How did she get your number?'

'Your birthday at 360 last year? We all swapped numbers and I've sorted her out with guest lists a few times since, it's no biggie at all. She's a sweet girl. I actually also ran into her at Print Room a few weeks ago. I still pop in there from time to time. Anyway, this is a bit awkward but I thought you'd want to know. She was asking if I knew any drug dealers in London.'

Jas was shocked. She knew that Lila liked a drink, but drugs? Surely she knew better than that? Jas had had a few nasty experiences on drugs when she'd first moved to London. Once, in a bar with Richard and his work colleagues, she was certain her drink had been spiked. She'd blacked out and couldn't remember anything the next day, but Richard had said she was being silly and was probably far more wasted than she'd realised. She'd also tried cocaine with him a couple of times when he first started taking it, but both times it had made her paranoid, sick, and shaky for days afterwards. She'd never touched the stuff since. The more she saw Richard's habit escalating, the more she saw it changing him. Lila knew all this. How could she still be so stupid as to want to meddle in drugs?

'I told her I didn't,' Connor continued. 'That's not my bag at all. But if she's looking in London it won't be long before she finds what she's after. I just thought you'd want to know.'

'I do. Thanks, Connor, I really appreciate it.' Jas felt very protective towards her little sister. She hoped Lila wasn't getting herself into any fresh trouble.

Jas woke with a heavy head at 7 a.m. the next morning. She had twenty minutes to get ready and drive to the scenic hilltop where Dylan and Charlotte were having their romantic first alone-date.

Fortunately, it didn't take long for Jas to get ready. Ten minutes in the shower and a coating of suncream and she was done. She would have her big DKNY sunglasses on all day and never wore make-up in the sun, saving all her glam looks for the evening. She threw on a black romper from H&M, stripy nautical Kurt Geiger wedges, and let her hair dry naturally. A spray of deodorant and spritz of her Chanel Gabriella perfume and she was good to go.

She and one of the cameramen, Ken, filmed Dylan and Charlotte meeting for their date in the villa's white marble-tiled reception area. They were both grinning nervously.

Dylan drove Charlotte up through the hills in a 4x4 with a camera fitted inside, while Ken and Jas followed behind. The setting for the yoga class was stunning. In a secluded clearing shaded by trees, two purple mats were laid out with a view of the Balearic Sea below. The light was dusky pink when they arrived but got brighter as the private yoga class went on, making for some beautiful shots. The teacher was a skinny man wearing beads around his neck and with arms covered in tattoos. Charlotte flowed through his moves expertly while Dylan, with his height and bulky athlete's physique, was not quite so graceful. But it all added to the humour of the scene. Jas had to admit, they looked cute together.

After the class, Jas had arranged for an extravagant picnic breakfast for the couple – coffee, fresh mango and orange smoothies, and omelettes delivered by waiters. It was gorgeous. While Charlotte tucked into her food, Jas and Ken grabbed Dylan for a private interview.

'How do you think it's going with Charlotte?' Jas asked.

'Charlotte is adorable,' he said to the camera, flashing a megawatt smile that showed off perfectly straight and whitened teeth. 'She really impressed me with her yoga moves and has got an amazing body.'

'Mmm-hmm, that's great. What else do you like about her?'

'I feel there's nothing fake about Charlotte. But I also worry that she's holding back, and not really showing me her full character. There's something a bit nervous about her so I hope she will learn to just relax around me.'

'Excellent. Thanks, Dylan.'

After breakfast, he waited in the car while Charlotte completed her interview. If the contestants found it weird at first, being followed by cameras throughout their date then stopping to be interviewed about it, they did a good job of not showing it. Jas knew that they'd get used to the process before long.

'He's the sweetest guy,' Charlotte gushed. 'I'm having a fantastic time.'

'He's got an alone-date with Gabriella tonight. They're having dinner by the beach. How does that make you feel?'

Jas could see the disappointment in Charlotte's eyes and felt like a bitch for stirring things up, even though it was her job.

'Oh, I didn't know that.' Charlotte went quiet for a moment then gave a perky smile straight to camera, clearly not wanting to appear glum. 'I know Dylan is naturally charming and I'm sure all the girls in the house fancy him. I'll try not to read too much into one date. Even though I feel there's a connection there between us, I don't want to get my hopes up too much. We'll see.'

Gabriella's date with Dylan was much more flirtatious and touchy-feely. The setting was a white-clothed table on the beach, a roaring fire next to it in the sand. Jas laid on the wine, hoping for some chemistry for the cameras. Gabriella played it cool but seemed to have Dylan eating out of her hand. She regaled him with stories about her days backpacking around Thailand, Vietnam and Australia. As he was born and raised in Brisbane, the conversation flowed easily.

'Gabriella is definitely more confident than a lot of the girls in the house,' Dylan told the camera when Jas stole him for a quick interview. 'I guess because she's an actress she is very comfortable in her own skin, very easy to talk to. But I also want to be careful not to judge on first impressions too much. There are so many more women to get to know.'

Cameras followed Gabriella and Dylan as they walked back past the fountain, hands brushing. Jas noticed that the twelve other women were watching from a window upstairs, eyes glued to the scene, and had a full view of Dylan taking Gabriella's face in his hands and kissing her gently on the lips.

Jas nudged Ken's arm and pointed to them. She was very pleased: the first kiss so early on with one of the most controversial characters on the show was TV gold.

Chapter 18

Three weeks, two rose ceremonies – where the quieter members of the group, Delia and Hayley had both been eliminated – five group-dates and several more alone-dates between Dylan and the contestants later, more drama started to unfold.

There was a strict no social media and no outside news policy in the villa. The contestants were allowed calls back home to their families but everything else was very tightly controlled. The girls were free to roam around the island in their spare time, but the whole idea was that they were somewhat isolated. Jas wanted there to be a sense of glamour about the villa, of course, but also hoped the housemates would get on each other's nerves, thus creating exciting and dramatic TV, while their feelings for Dylan would intensify at the same time. If he was the only man they were in contact with for two months, apart from the men in the camera crew, Jas hoped that the women would develop feelings for him – or believe that they had.

All the tactics she'd used to make the girls more competitive were working. The fourth rose ceremony was tomorrow and at least one contestant would be eliminated. Tension was mounting in the house.

That morning the eleven remaining girls began their day. Some were already sunbathing by the pool, others drinking coffee in the living room. Charlotte was fresh back from a run around the hills and Georgia was slicing fruit and spooning yoghurt into bowls for breakfast. Kat was still in bed.

Carmel bounded into the living room, holding a black envelope and calling out to everyone to gather around. Charlotte, fresh in from her run and making a protein-packed smoothie in the kitchen, joined the group on the sofas, hoping she didn't look too red-faced and sweaty for the cameras.

'Look what just arrived,' Carmel sang, waving the envelope. She waited until everyone was there before opening the envelope and revealing a piece of gold card. She read aloud. 'It's from Dylan! He says: "To celebrate this year's World Cup I'm getting in the football spirit! The next group date is going be a five-a-side match. I'll be the referee, you'll be my players."'

The girls whispered to each other impatiently, wanting to know who the unlucky girl was who would be staying at the villa alone.

'Hurry up,' scolded Gabriella. 'Who's not going? And they better let us wear make-up! There's no way I'm running around a football pitch looking all sweaty without even a hint of mascara.' Charlotte then felt even more self-conscious, sitting in her drenched, unflattering running gear with not a scrap of make-up on.

'It's *football*, for God's sake,' spat Carmel, an un-characteristically sassy comment from her. Clearly, the tension was affecting most people in the house.

'She's worried she'll burn alive in the sun … like all witches.' This, from Alex, incited sniggers.

'Yeah, well, some of us actually care what we look like,' shot back Gabriella.

Georgia, sitting next to her, laughed out loud at that comment. With her golden skin, big blue eyes and long, tousled white-blonde hair, Georgia was classic bombshell-sexy, but wore heavy make-up constantly. In fact, Charlotte had never seen her without thick black eyeliner, blue eyeshadow and bubble-gum glossy lips. She'd lasted two weeks in the finals of the TV singing competition last year before a torrent of tabloid stories surfaced about her sending nude selfies to a married sportsman. She'd lost the public's approval overnight. Alex threw her a dirty look and Georgia simply stared her out.

'Got a problem?' she goaded.

'I have actually. My problem is the amount of collagen in your trout pout. Wasn't there an age limit to this show?'

Georgia's eyes flashed with rage. A few of the other women looked at the floor, others raising eyebrows to each other.

Charlotte sat upright. 'Ladies! Everyone chill. Go on, Carmel, read out the names.' She nodded and called out the ten names, missing Alex. Gabriella, Mackenzie and Georgia giggled.

'I hate football anyway.' Alex shrugged.

'Oh, wait, there's another card in here,' noticed Carmel. 'Oh, wow, Alex! You've got an alone-date with Dylan this evening! He's taking you out for a helicopter ride around the island followed by a candle-lit dinner!'

Alex smiled triumphantly and stood up, her long, glossy black hair rippling down her back, green cat-eyes sparkling. 'Have fun rolling around in the mud, girls. I'll be chilling by the pool all day, waiting for my hot date tonight.' With that, she sauntered out, several pairs of eyes burning into her back as she did so.

Later that morning the women huddled outside the villa waiting for Dylan to come down and for the SUVs with blacked-out windows to collect them. Charlotte was wearing cute yellow shorts she'd bought pre-holiday and a pink vest top. Mackenzie, typically leaving little to the imagination, wore tiny pink shorts and her gigantic silicone breasts were squeezed into an impossibly small bikini top.

Jas appeared from downstairs, ending a phone call. 'Kat's got a stomach bug and is confined to bed. We've sent for a doctor. She thinks it was the shrimps from the buffet last night. It's a five-a-side so obviously we can't just have nine players. Alex is going to take her place. I've told her. She'll be down in five minutes then we're leaving, so if anyone needs the loo, go now.'

Gabriella and Georgia tutted and muttered to each other but the second Dylan sauntered downstairs they smiled sweetly. 'Morning, ladies, ready for the big game?' He winked and half the group burst out in fake laughter like he'd said the funniest thing in the world. Charlotte was starting to get tired of the way they were all fawning over him, but when she felt his hand on the small of her back, she had to catch her breath.

'Morning, Charlotte.' He smiled at her. He was fully kitted out in an Arsenal shirt and shorts. 'You're a lot more used to physical exercise than some of these girls so I expect you'll be smashing it. That is, if you know how to play football.' He winked again.

'Ahem, I'll have you know I've been watching with my dad since I was five,' she shot back. 'Never had you down for a Gooner, though. My dad is Spuss through and through. I'm not sure we're allowed to be friends.'

Dylan opened his mouth to banter back when Gabriella appeared in front of him, literally shoving Charlotte out of the way. 'Dylan, you're not going to be too hard on me, are you?' she pouted. Charlotte stood back, rendered self-conscious by Gabriella's unnerving confidence.

Jas chimed in then. 'Gabriella, why don't you get in this car? Dylan, you go in that one, and Charlotte, you can ride with me. Let's go, hurry up now.'

Bitchiness between the girls reached boiling point throughout the first half of the game. Mackenzie was sent off for tackling Charlotte to the ground. She strongly suspected Gabriella and her minions were ganging up on her. There were constant sniggers and whispers from the Mean Girls posse, all while glancing over at Charlotte. She started to feel like she was in school again, with the popular girls circling the quieter ones as if they were prey. It was a horrible feeling, but Charlotte tried her best to ignore them and concentrate on the game.

And this treatment was nothing compared to what was bubbling up between Georgia and Alex. By half-time they'd both been given yellow cards by Dylan for fouling each other.

Jas, meanwhile, was starting to doubt the wisdom of her decision to put them on different teams in the first place. They clearly despised each other.

'It's TV gold,' Monica kept saying, relishing all the drama on the pitch. Jas tried to elicit some friendliness during half-time, when Gabriella was getting evil looks for flirting outrageously with Dylan, complaining of a sore ankle and asking him to massage it. Alex walked onto the pitch and bent over to tighten her trainer laces, her pert bum lifted right to his eyeline.

'Slag,' muttered Gabriella under her breath, when Dylan was safely out of earshot and talking to some of the camera crew.

'Gabriella, why don't you go over and help Monica bring over the protein shakes from that crate over there?' Jas said hastily. 'Everyone could use a little time out.'

Gabriella did as she was instructed, kicking the grass childishly as she left. Jas was starting to feel less like a producer and more like a babysitter.

'Some people have been getting more of a time out than others,' Alex laughed, throwing Georgia a dirty look.

'What's that supposed to mean?' the girl shouted, but Alex ignored her.

Less than ten minutes into the second half, Georgia tackled Alex so violently that she fell to the ground, crying out and holding her leg close to her chest. 'You bitch!' she shouted, and stumbled back to her feet, pushing Georgia to the ground in retaliation. They started wrestling, rolling around on the pitch. It was a bloodbath: hair-pulling, clawing, scratching. Two cameramen and Dylan rushed over to break them up, but not before Alex had tried to throw a punch at Georgia, narrowly missing as Ken, the older, stockier cameraman, used his considerable strength to contain her while she kicked and screamed. Georgia broke away and cried into the shoulder of the younger cameraman, Gary. Dylan stood in the middle, trying to calm the situation. Jas rushed over, telling everyone to take deep breaths.

'Oh, that's right, cry into the shoulder of your boyfriend,' Alex shouted over at Georgia. The pitch went silent except for her sobs.

Jas and Monica looked at each other in panic. 'Now, now, let's calm down,' said Jas speedily. 'Everyone's missing home, feeling the strain. We all need some time out.'

Alex rolled her eyes, still staring at Georgia and the cameraman holding her. 'It's so obvious. We all know you've been sneaking off to Gary's room every night. *And* Becca saw you giving him a blow job in the TV room.'

Becca looked sheepishly at the floor. Gary sprang away from Georgia, who tried to speak through her tears.

'It's – it's – it's not like that! Fuck you, Alex!'

Jas had had about enough. 'Right! Cameras off! We're done for the day. Everyone back in the cars NOW. Georgia,

I will speak to you privately later. Gary, Monica, Ken, get over here. The rest of you, back to the villa.'

'But what about my date?' whined Alex.

Jas let out a deep breath. 'That still stands. One of the crew will film you and Dylan later.' The group shuffled away, whispering together in shock. Jas felt a headache coming on.

Back at the villa, Monica had arranged for wine, sandwiches and snacks to be laid out by caterers. It was supposed to be a post-match celebration but no one felt like having a party, even though they were all ravenous.

After silently eating, the women separated into groups and went to gossip on the sofas in the living room, terrace or by the pool. Alex sloped off for a nap before getting ready for her big date. Georgia was being questioned by Jas and Monica in the study, admitting that, yes, for the past two weeks she and Gary had been sleeping together in his room.

And then, suddenly, a deafening scream rang out from Alex's room.

Chapter 19

Jas jumped up. 'What's going on?' The screams continued, so she and Monica rushed up to Alex's room where most of the other girls had gathered. Seeing Alex, Jas let out a gasp. The entire right side of her face had turned red and swollen up, causing her eye to close into a slit. Her hands had also swollen and were covered in an angry rash. Charlotte and Becca were trying to soothe her by rubbing her back, while Melody was throwing the contents of a make-up bag on the floor, looking for any cream or ointment that might help.

'I keep my EpiPen in that bag I take everywhere and now it's not there!' wailed Alex.

'Monica, call Dr Nichols, please,' Jas said firmly. 'Alex, sit on the bed with me, sweetheart.'

'You only need the EpiPen if you're struggling to breathe,' put in Nysha as she examined Alex's face. 'Have we got a first-aid box anywhere? Maybe there will be some antihistamines in there.'

'I'll go!' offered Charlotte, dashing down to the kitchen where the first-aid box was kept.

Jas was relieved to remember there was already a medic on the scene. But Alex only sobbed harder.

Charlotte returned with the box and Nysha quickly found the antihistamines, administering them to Alex while the other girls tried to soothe her. Monica returned, informing them that Dr Nichols was on her way.

Alex stopped screaming but hot tears streamed down her face. '*She* did this to me! Georgia did this!' she sobbed into Jas's shoulder. 'I'm going to sue! I'm taking that bitch to court!'

Charlotte bent down over the bed as Jas stroked Alex's hair. 'She thinks Georgia put something in her face cream. Almond oil or something else she's allergic to. They've been arguing for days and, apparently, Alex said last night that she was going to tell everyone about her and Gary and Georgia warned her not to. I didn't know, by the way. About Georgia and Gary. I swear I didn't.'

Jas knew that Alex and Georgia shared a bedroom and had been arguing like cat and dog, but she was sure Alex was exaggerating. It was a bold claim. Then again, could Jas be sure? From the behaviour she'd seen on the pitch today, she wouldn't put anything past this lot. She'd wanted rows for ratings, but this was ridiculous. Never in her producing days had she had to deal with anything like this!

'Alex, sweetheart, Georgia may not be your biggest fan, but she'd never do anything that extreme. How could she?'

'I'm suing,' cried Alex again.

Jas tried to remain calm but inwardly was feeling panicked. Could Alex sue Channel 6? She'd not only got a face like the Elephant Man but had a badly bruised leg after being tackled by Georgia on the pitch. And Georgia was a whole other story altogether. She'd admitted just minutes earlier that, yes, she had been sleeping with Gary. Now his job and her place in the competition were at stake. And to top it all off, Kat's stomach bug was still keeping her bed-bound.

'She definitely would do it,' wailed Alex. 'She's a cow!'

Dr Nichols arrived and cleared the room so as to give Alex some peace and quiet. She was about to administer a steroid injection to reduce the swelling plus a strong sedative. Alex would then be out for the count. Dr Nichols promised to check in on Kat next.

As Jas shuffled out, Monica pulled her aside. 'What a nightmare! I've never known anything like it.'

Jas nodded. 'We're going to have to call Luke, you know. I'm pretty sure there were a few libel issues thrown up today.'

'Babe, I called him the second after I called the doctor. He's getting a flight out tonight.'

Jas felt her stomach flip. Tonight? Couldn't he just have Skyped in to the team? The thought of seeing him again made her feel even more tense. The show, her job – her entire career even – could be affected by this. The last thing she needed was any distraction.

As if reading her mind, Monica reassured her. 'Don't worry. Luke is brilliantly capable and can help us much more by being here in person. Everything is going to be okay.'

'Of course it is. You're right, Mon, thanks. I don't know about you but I need a drink. I think we should stay here a while and make sure Alex is okay and that there are no more dramas. There'll be wine in the fridge.'

'I'm with you. What should we do about Georgia?'

'Let's wait 'til Luke gets here. I think the less drama in this household for now, the better.' As producers, Jas and Monica also needed to act as big sisters and agony aunts to the contestants and it was important that, now more than ever, the girls felt they had a strong support network. Jas followed Monica downstairs to join some of the calmer, less troublesome contestants in the kitchen. Charlotte, Becca, Nysha and Carmel had opened a bottle of wine and were talking over the day's catastrophic events.

As for Dylan, he seemed to feel more comfortable confiding in the male members of the crew, and after the football match had gone out for a beer with a few of them, to avoid any further drama in the villa. Jas was chatting with Charlotte on the sofa, well into her second glass of Australian Sauvignon Blanc, when her phone rang.

'Hello?'

'Jasmine, it's Ralph Mackover. Sorry to call so late.'

'No, it's fine. Is everything okay?' The last person she was expecting to hear from today was her divorce lawyer.

'Yes, it is. We've been given a date for a hearing before a judge. The seventh of October. No jury is required. The judge will examine the evidence provided by you both and determine whether you're eligible for a divorce on the grounds of unreasonable behaviour on Mr Butler's part.'

Jas was stunned. After months of waiting, now it felt like everything was moving almost too quickly. She thanked Ralph and finished the call. As soon as she did, a text message flashed up. It was from Richard.

'See you in court.'

That was it. It wasn't threatening, Richard would never be so stupid as to send her a text she could use in evidence against him. Yet hearing from him again after so long made her feel decidedly uneasy. For some reason, those four little words seemed laced with hate. Jas brushed the thought away, telling herself she was reading too much into this. Why, then, did looking at his message once more send a chill down her spine?

Chapter 20

It was 8 p.m. on the trading floor and Richard was exhausted. A heavy night last night began in the pub opposite his office, continued at a nightclub in Soho and had finished at Frankie's place in Mayfair until she eventually threw him out for being so drunk. He'd caught a couple of hours' sleep at home before picking up some more coke and heading into the office. Drugs were no longer something he took to liven up a party, but a crutch he relied upon to get him through most days.

'Butler? A word.'

It was his boss, Samuel.

'Yes, boss?'

'What are you still doing here?'

'Working. We've got the big Penton deal coming up and we need to close it and—'

Samuel talked over him. 'You're our hardest worker, Richard. But there is such a thing as working too bloody hard and I can see it's getting to you. You're rundown. You look like shit and I don't mind telling you that your work is suffering because of it. You're off Penton and I want you to take two weeks' leave, starting now.'

Richard was stunned. 'What?'

'You're no good to me at the moment. You're making mistakes and I can't afford mistakes. Just take some time off and you'll be right as rain. You haven't taken more than five days since you started here. You're burnt out – and don't think I can't tell how much of that rubbish you've been snorting. It's getting to you.'

'But you can't take me off the Penton deal! I brought that to the table, for Christ's sake.'

'Don't get sharp with me!' Samuel's fat cheeks turned crimson. Seeing Richard stiffen in alarm at his tone, he softened his voice.

'It's not right for you to be here right now. There will be other deals. Your job is safe, Richard, but you can't carry on like this. People are talking. You come in reeking of booze, your expenses are through the roof and you've lost your temper several times on the floor. I know the pressure you boys are under but you can't let it get to you like this. It's bad for morale. Have your fun, fine, I understand you all need to let loose from time to time. But we deal in billions here. I can't have my employees being out of control like this.'

'I am in control!' Richard realised he sounded anything but, so cleared his throat and lowered his voice. 'Things are tough right now. Jasmine is taking me to court.'

'But I thought you were straightening all that out? Jesus! No wonder you're such a mess.'

'She's not taking me back. I thought she would have caved by now.' Richard paused then admitted, 'The hearing date just came through. Seventh of October. It's going ahead. I need to work, Samuel, it's the only thing keeping me going. I'll quit the booze and coke, I swear.'

'Good. Then you can rest properly and come back clean as a whistle in a fortnight.'

'But ...'

'It's either that or suspension. Don't make another stupid mistake.'

Richard went home, seething. This was all Jas's fault. If she hadn't thrown him out, made him go off the rails, none of this would have happened. Getting that talk from Samuel had scared Richard and usually nothing scared him. His job was everything to him: money, power, status. For the past couple of years he'd been such a golden boy in the eyes of his bosses, he'd thought he could get away with anything. Tonight was a painful, stark reminder that it simply wasn't the case. The trading floor was a harsh place to be and second chances weren't given out lightly. Yet Richard knew he had just been given one.

At home, he took a long, steamy shower and stared at himself in the mirror afterwards. He looked like shit: ashen skin, thinning hair and bulging eyes. It wasn't a good look. Richard was no fool. He could see that his lifestyle was catching up with him. With a blue towel wrapped around his waist, he cleaned up his bachelor pad. Used condoms strewn beside the bed from one-night stands, half-drunk bottles of wine ... it all went in the bin. He changed the sheets for fresh ones. He hoovered, wiped and scrubbed, afterwards lighting a sandalwood candle and reclining on his king-sized bed, next to huge windows overlooking a twinkling night-time London skyline. He felt better already. He decided he would take the two weeks off. It wasn't like he had a choice anyway. He'd go skiing in Switzerland, take in some fresh air and have long sleeps. He'd be right as rain by the time he went back to work and would land an even bigger deal than the Penton one, get a promotion and a pay rise by the end of the year.

He wasn't going to let Jasmine humiliate him.

Despite the drama of the day, the atmosphere in Villa Valencia that night was the calmest it had been for weeks. Alex was medicated and fast asleep; Kat was still feeling sick but had stopped vomiting, so Dr Nichols was convinced that the worst was over and she just needed rest. Now that four contestants had been eliminated, there was more space in the villa and Jas rearranged the sleeping plan. She gave Alex and Kat their own rooms and moved Nysha in to share with Charlotte and Melody. Then she bunked Becca, Carmel and Natalie together. The fifth room was for Gabriella, Mackenzie and Georgia – or 'the three witches' as Monica had started to call them.

'Why do they get their own rooms and I still have to share with two others?' whined Gabriella.

'Just give me a break, Gabriella, please,' Jas said wearily. It was approaching midnight and she was exhausted. She wanted to add that there was every chance Georgia would be booted off the show anyway, but then figured it would be wise not to say anything until she'd had the legal sign-off. 'Alex has had a massive shock and I don't think you'd want to be anywhere near a contagious Kat. It's late, I think everyone should just call it a night.'

Luke, meanwhile, sent a text to Monica saying he'd booked a hotel in Ibiza Town as he would be landing at around 1 a.m. He'd be at the production crew's HQ, Villa Rosa, at 9 a.m. sharp.

Jas opted for a hot shower before bed, in an attempt to wash away the worry of the day. She let the steaming water pour over her, dosing herself with Rituals shower gel and her favourite Kerastase shampoo. She poured a generous amount of aloe vera after-sun lotion over her body. She had always tanned easily and her skin was now a deep golden bronze. She finally crawled into bed just before 1 a.m., sinking into the plush pillows and letting out a loud sigh. What a day!

But though she was exhausted, Jas couldn't sleep. What with the women causing havoc, a date fixed for her divorce hearing and that strange chill she'd felt when she'd read Richard's text, she was too tense to shut down her thoughts and rest. She couldn't help feeling that Richard was up to something. And then there was Luke ... she desperately wanted to see him, but didn't imagine he'd be keen to talk to her other than professionally. The thought made her feel a bit sick. But from a professional point of view, she was thoroughly relieved that he would be here soon. The legal implications of the past twenty-four hours were a total minefield and she needed his expert advice.

Chapter 21

Just before 9 a.m. the next morning Jas popped round to Villa Valencia to check on Kat and Alex but the whole household was still sound asleep. Jas started the short walk down the hill back to Villa Rosa. The only sound she could hear was the chirping of birds and the faint crunch of gravel and grass under her flip-flops. For miles around her all she could see was luscious green trees and a blue, cloudless sky. It really was lovely here, and so peaceful. Worlds away from the Ibiza Jas knew. She'd been once before, for her hen do in fact. It was a wild weekend spent going to the Super Clubs Space, Pacha and Amnesia in Playa d'en Bossa and Ibiza Town. This was a much nicer way to see the stunning island, though.

To reach Villa Rosa, the wide path led off to a side path where a few dozen narrow steps climbed up to the front door. She was about to turn left onto the side path when a taxi drew up and stopped right next to her. Luke stepped out.

He looked good, dressed in long, beige-coloured shorts, a white shirt and Ray-Ban sunglasses. Should they hug? Shake hands? 'Hey,' was all Jas could come up with.

'Hi,' he replied coolly, avoiding eye contact and busying himself by counting euros for the driver. He motioned to the path ahead. 'This us?'

They walked in silence until they reached the steps, which were so narrow they had to climb them in single file. Jas strode ahead with Luke directly behind her. She suddenly felt very self-conscious. Why hadn't she put on any make-up?

Thankfully, Luke seemed to pick up on the tension and broke the uncomfortable silence. 'So, how's it been going?'

'Oh, you mean apart from the attempted poisoning, cat-fights, shagging and norovirus?' Jas said cheerily.

'And let me guess, that's just between you and Monica?'

They both laughed and Jas felt a wave of appreciation that Luke was there, already making light of the drama and alleviating the tension between them.

'Exactly. *Apart* from all that, it's going great. Dylan's already snogged Gabriella, Alex, Mackenzie and Nysha.'

'Good lad! And the girls? Anyone there I'd fancy?'

Jas turned around and lightly batted Luke's arm, getting a quick feel of his muscles as she did so.

'Oi! Not you too, please! I assume you're all caught up on everything from Monica? Please tell me it's not as bad as I think it is.'

They reached the villa gate and Jas led Luke through to their kitchen. She busied herself with making a pot of coffee as he drew out a yellow notepad and pen.

161

'It's not as bad as you think it is. There aren't any legal restrictions about what Gary and – what's the girl's name?'

'Georgia.'

'Right. There aren't actually any legal restrictions about what Gary and Georgia did, per se, but it's not exactly ethical. From both their points of view. I mean, she's here to try to win the heart of someone else, that's the game. And Gary is here to work, not fool around with one of the contestants.'

'Certainly not.'

'I will need to get her account of yesterday's catfight on the pitch. And confirm that she doesn't believe that Gary has taken advantage of her at any point, which could mean huge implications for the channel.'

Jas gave a tight laugh. 'Trust me, no one could possibly take advantage of this lot, least of all Georgia. I don't think anything could break her.'

Luke nodded. 'I spoke to Burrell briefly this morning, to fill him in. He thinks it would be best if Gary came back to the UK and worked on something else. He gets paid regardless but it's better for the situation here with Georgia.'

Jas rubbed her temples gently, which she always did when she felt stressed, and thought about what Burrell would make of all this.

'He's not pissed off with you, you know,' Luke said, as if reading her mind. 'He's glad I'm over here and knows that together we can straighten it all out.'

Now they did look at each other and the all-too-familiar spark she'd felt last time she and Luke were together, at her flat weeks ago, jolted through Jas again. She was about to thank him for being so calm and reassuring but he quickly looked away from her and back to his notes, scribbling something down.

The kettle started whistling and Jas made their coffee. 'And what about Georgia? Do you think she should be thrown off?'

Luke shrugged. 'It's up to you, ultimately. There may be more bother for us if we do that, though. If she was clever she could come back and claim compensation, unfair elimination, that sort of thing. It's a hassle we don't really need. But I would say that if Mr Right – what's his name again?'

'Dylan.'

'Right. If Dylan doesn't know about this already, he will soon. All the girls will be talking about it, don't you think? Maybe you could have a word with him for courtesy's sake. It's up to him if he wants to keep her in the competition or not. If he chooses to let her go, it's all above board.'

'And if he doesn't?'

'Then that's his choice, too. Nothing about Gary and Georgia will be mentioned on camera unless you want it to be. The viewers won't have a clue and by the time the programme actually airs you'll think this is all old news. I think the best thing is for Gary to leave, and for Georgia to stay. Then everything will blow over.'

Jas smiled appreciatively and nodded. She trusted Luke implicitly and if he said the show wouldn't be affected at all, that was the important thing. She wondered why he didn't just tell her all of this over Skype or the phone, though. Then again, Georgia and Gary weren't the only concern.

'You know Alex Adams has accused Georgia of spiking her face cream with crushed nuts or something.'

Luke shot Jas a look of mock horror, causing them both to laugh out loud. Jas had missed laughing with him.

'It's serious! She had a face like the Elephant Man's. She could sue, couldn't she?'

'One thing at a time. Are the girls up yet? Let's see what they're all saying this morning. I'd better speak to Gary first and tell him what Burrell said. I've got a few things for him to sign, to confirm he's happy to go back to the UK, and also get his side of the story as quickly as possible to make sure our backs are covered. Then Georgia, then Elephant Girl.' He downed his coffee and got up. 'No rest for the wicked.'

'I'll walk you over now.' They headed out of the door at the same time, clashing into each other. The brief second of body contact with Luke sent another jolt through Jas and she looked up at him wide-eyed, but he simply apologised coolly and walked out, not even glancing at her.

They walked in silence over to Villa Valencia, as Luke was texting on his phone most of the way there. Jas wondered if it was work he was dealing with … or a girlfriend? That petite brunette she'd seen him with at the Tube station? She was desperate to ask, desperate to break the tension by talking to him about how things had ended between them, but every time she tried to catch his eye she failed. He didn't take any notice of her whatsoever.

'Here we are,' she announced as she used her key to let them into the contestants' villa.

Luke whistled in appreciation as Jas led him down the hallway, though the open-plan kitchen and living room and onto the terrace, where six of the girls were now huddled around the patio table drinking coffee. They all looked up and stared when she walked in with Luke.

'Morning, girls, this is Luke Hawkins. He's our in-house lawyer at Channel 6. He flew in from London last night after everything that went on yesterday. I don't think you need reminding of what happened, but I need you to all know how serious this is.'

The girls nodded solemnly but then Melody and Becca whispered something to each other and giggled. Jas was annoyed. Didn't they realise that everything was on the line here?

Gabriella, true to form, gave an elaborate yawn, stretching her chest forward and tossing her mane of red hair backwards, inciting more sniggers. Luke cleared his throat and looked at the ground. Jas couldn't quite make out his expression underneath his sunglasses, but was sure she could see a hint of a blush on his face. He was clearly embarrassed at the outrageous flirting. Unlike Dylan, that is, who seemed to grow more confident by the day when he was around the girls, and lapped up all the attention they threw his way.

Jas introduced Luke to the group. 'Where are the others?' she asked.

'Natalie, Kat and Georgia are still asleep,' replied Nysha. 'Charlotte is keeping Alex company upstairs. Her face has gone right down, by the way. I checked in on her earlier. She's in a foul mood, though.'

'I bet,' muttered Jas, dreading having to face Alex's wrath. She hoped the girl wasn't still planning to sue. That really would put the show – and Jas's career – in serious jeopardy.

'Do you want me to go and wake Georgia up?' offered Mackenzie, looking Luke straight in the eye and taking the opportunity to strut past him in her bikini. He looked away, awkwardly.

Kat padded down, wearing a white dressing gown and a pair of huge sunglasses over her elfin face. It was the first time she'd left her room in over twenty-four hours.

All the girls except Gabriella, who plastered on a fake smile but didn't move a muscle, rushed to give Kat a hug or offer her something to eat.

Jas placed a protective arm around her. 'How are you feeling?'

'Much better, thanks. Just very weak. I don't think sitting in the blazing sun today is a good idea but I was getting total cabin fever up there.'

'Dr Nichols will be round to look at you again soon. This is Luke Hawkins, by the way, he's our lawyer from Channel 6 and is helping us straighten out what happened yesterday. I'm sure someone told you about it.'

'Yes, Charlotte came in to bring me some tea last night and filled me in. I can't believe I missed all that drama!'

Luke knelt down to Kat's level and refilled her glass of water from the ice-cold jug on the table. 'Do you think the stomach bug has gone? Do you think perhaps it was something you ate by accident? A dodgy dose of medicine, perhaps?'

Kat shrugged. 'I haven't taken any pills or anything and only ate what everyone else did.'

Gabriella ignored her and rose from her chair, sashaying towards Luke and stopping to rest her hand on his arm. 'I'm so glad you're here. We need another man around the house.' Jas suppressed a smile. Poor Luke. This lot would eat him alive.

'Are we actually having any more dates with Dylan?' Gabriella asked, turning to Jas. 'No offence to Kat or anything, but I do believe the show must go on? I've not seen any sign of the prince yet but I assume he's due to take at least one of us out on a date today?'

'Speak of the devil,' whispered Becca, as Dylan strode into the kitchen.

'Morning, ladies! Man, I am starving! It gets pretty lonely eating out there in my guest house. Can I join you or is that only allowed to happen when the cameras are rolling, eh, Jas? Oh, wow, another bloke. Who's this? You're not my competition, are you, mate? I'm in trouble if so!'

Dylan was like an excited Labrador. Jas only ever saw him happy and had never heard a negative word come out of his mouth. She welcomed it during such a tense time in the villa.

'Don't worry, Dylan, you're still top dog. This is Luke Hawkins, our lawyer.'

The men shook hands. 'Gee, mate, that's big of you, to fly all the way out here on such short notice. I guess a phone call just wouldn't cut it. How much are they paying you?'

'Any excuse to join in the fun, pal. You seen the weather back home? It's meant to be the height of summer and it's pissing down now! You'll have trouble getting rid of me.'

The two of them laughed and immediately Dylan and Luke were the centre of attention, with the girls talking over each other to get a word in with the boys. All except for Kat, who sat quietly but did receive a big hug from Dylan. He asked how she was feeling then chatted to the other girls and Jas noticed his eyes meet Gabriella's for a second longer than they rested on the others. He also raised one eyebrow at her mischievously. Jas made a mental note to keep a close eye on those two.

Meanwhile Georgia appeared and Jas introduced her to Luke. 'I think you two should have a chat, if that's okay, Georgia?'

It was the first time she'd seen the girl without make-up on. She looked so much younger and somehow more vulnerable.

'I'm not going to get thrown off, am I?' she asked.

'Come on,' Luke said, motioning to the breakfast bar. 'Let's take a seat.'

Georgia looked genuinely scared that her place in the competition, her second chance of fame, was jeopardised.

Jas sat down with the rest of the girls but couldn't help glancing over at Luke and Georgia from time to time. Within seconds Georgia was smiling again and edging her seat closer to Luke's. God, he does look handsome, Jas thought, staring at his soft eyes and strong jaw. Her mind wandered ...

After a few minutes of talking to Luke, Georgia seemed entirely back to her old self. She bounded over to thank Jas and even give her a hug and an apology for all the unnecessary drama she'd caused, then bounced off to Skype her mum.

Jas pulled Luke to one side. 'Well, whatever you said it cheered her up!'

'Yeah, she understands she's got a yellow card this time. She's, er, quite flirty, isn't she?'

Jas rolled her eyes. 'Just ignore her. She's probably on the prowl again now she knows Gary is out of the picture.'

'Hmm, anyway, she wants to talk to Dylan. Says she wants to apologise.'

'Fine by me so long as it's in front of the camera.'

Luke leant in closer and Jas breathed in his fresh-smelling aftershave. 'I do think you need to carry on as normal,' he said quietly.

Oh, no, was she obviously desperate? He'd clearly seen her checking him out. *So much for being subtle!*

'I'm being normal,' she replied defensively.

Luke frowned. 'The dates with Dylan, I mean. This whole series is costing the channel a fortune and the crew are being paid regardless. Are there dates planned for today?'

He wasn't talking about her at all. Jas needed to get a grip! She nodded. 'There's actually supposed to be a group-date later, a boat trip. And there's supposed to be another rose ceremony tonight but I think we'll have to postpone that one for a few days. I'll call Monica now.'

It was back to business for the next hour as Jas and Monica ran through the day's scheduled events on the phone, Monica from the other villa while simultaneously getting all the camera crew ready and making sure the boat trip was on track. They filmed Dylan outside saying which four women he was bringing on the boat trip with him and why. He chose Gabriella, Mackenzie, Nysha and Carmel, and would later announce the names in front of all the girls for dramatic effect.

'There are a few I've probably grown closer to but I don't want to rule anyone out yet,' he said on camera. 'I find Nysha so attractive. I haven't spent enough time with Carmel yet and Mackenzie is certainly a handful, but something tells me that behind all that front is quite a sweet girl.'

Jas suppressed a laugh at the notion of ballsy Mackenzie being sweet. It didn't matter to her, though, as long as she was getting good footage.

'I think it will be a fun group,' Dylan continued. 'I feel really sorry for Alex and Kat, though, having been so ill. I'm going to take Kat on a walk tomorrow, if that's okay?'

'Of course,' replied Jas.

'I don't think the sun and a boat swaying on the sea would be too great for her.'

'That's very courteous of you, Dylan. And there's still time for you to get to know everyone. We're postponing tonight's rose ceremony.'

'Oh, that's good. I owe Alex a date, and after all she's been through, it will be nice to cheer her up.'

'I noticed a bit of chemistry just now between you and Gabby. Do you think she might be The One?'

Dylan considered his answer for a few seconds. 'Like I say, I don't want to rule anyone out just yet.'

Chapter 22

Monica gathered everyone downstairs to film Dylan's boat-trip choices but Alex sat in silence with huge sunglasses on and the minute the group-date had left she hid herself back in her room. Her face was back to normal, though even through the shades it was obvious that her eyes were red and puffy from crying so much. She was in a foul mood and skulked off to take a shower.

'How's she doing?' Jas asked Charlotte and Melody, who had been asked to coax Alex out of her room.

'We've been trying to cheer her up,' said Charlotte. 'We suggested going down to Playa d'en Bossa and chilling on the beach. Or else going shopping in town.'

Jas loved Charlotte and Melody. If any of the other girls had just found out they were missing out on a date with Dylan they'd be fuming, but these two saw it as an opportunity to hit the beach for a gossip and tanning session.

Jas knocked softly on Alex's bedroom door. 'Alex? Luke is downstairs, he's our lawyer. He'd love to chat to you.'

'Yeah, I'd love to chat to him too,' Alex angrily replied. She flung open the bathroom door and set about getting ready like a grumpy teenager, slamming drawers shut and tutting at everything. Charlotte and Melody didn't know where to look.

'I was surprised to see Georgia down there,' Alex continued. 'Why isn't she on her way home already after what she did?'

Jas sat down on the bed. 'Look, I know you're upset, but Georgia promises she would never do anything so extreme as what you are accusing her of. Monica feels terrible. She was the one who hired caterers for the snacks yesterday after the game and she told them about your nut allergy, but sometimes things just slip through. I know it's terrible and we're looking into it.'

'I could have died!' exclaimed Alex. She had every right to be furious.

'You're right. It was unacceptable. I'm so sorry, Alex.'

'You will be when I sue. I meant what I said last night. I'm not changing my mind. I've suffered serious emotional distress and my leg is badly bruised from Georgia's vicious attack.'

Jas didn't know if now was the right time to remind Alex that Georgia was covered in marks and scratches from the fight, too.

Alex stormed out of the bedroom, slamming the door in Jas's face. She was now very worried. Was her job on the line? How many court cases was she going to have to deal with?

'Are you the lawyer?' Alex barked at Luke when she found him downstairs in the kitchen.

'That's right. Hi, I'm Luke Hawkins. You must be Alex Adams? My little sister is a big fan of your radio show, by the way. She was so excited I was coming to meet you. I hope you're feeling better now. I'd love to have a chat and get your version of events, Alex. We're all on your side, remember.' Jas felt reassured that Luke was here.

'You better listen to what I have to say,' Alex stormed. Luke shot a look over at Jas who mouthed back 'sorry' as he followed Alex outside to a secluded table on the far side of the terrace.

Over an hour later, they were still talking. Jas had been catching up on emails and, in a fast-paced WhatsApp chat with Meg, bringing her sister up to speed. Now, she couldn't help but stare at Luke and Alex, deep in conversation. She was so fixated she didn't notice Monica sidle up to her, making her jump.

'Mon! You scared me.'

'Sorry. You're watching them pretty intently. What do you reckon he's saying?'

'I have no idea.'

Monica looked at her friend inquisitively. 'What's going on with you two, anyway?'

Jas made a point of looking away and making coffee to distract herself. She'd slept so badly last night she needed all the caffeine she could get today. 'Nothing. I'm worried about Alex, that's all. She is threatening to sue us, you know.'

'Uh-huh. And that's it? Don't think I can't see that there is chemistry between you and Luke. What's happened since you broke it off with him in London anyway?'

Jas had tried to downplay her feelings for him and hadn't let on to Monica how much she'd been thinking about him. But now she knew there was no point in continuing to pretend.

'I don't know what to think, Mon. I know he's only been here a few hours but there's something so familiar-feeling and reassuring about having him around. Every now and then I find him catching my eye and I think, there's this chemistry between us but maybe I'm reading too much into it. I'm pretty sure he's seeing someone else anyway. And I was the one who didn't want any complications. I don't know why he affects me like this.'

'Why don't you just talk to him about it, hun? Tell him how you feel?'

Jas shook her head. 'Where would I begin? "Oh, hey, Luke, I haven't been able to stop thinking about you even though I was a complete cow for dumping you. And, by the way, the reason I did is because I'm actually still married. Break up with your girlfriend for me?"'

Monica tutted. 'You're being overdramatic. And I've been speaking to the team back home. No one thinks he has a girlfriend. He never talks about one anyway. Maybe it was just a one-off you saw?'

'Maybe I'm just horny and have sunstroke! I'm being ridiculous. Everything with Richard and things here, it's all getting to me, I'm not thinking straight. Luke is not *all that*.'

Monica was about to reply when Luke and Alex sauntered back in, laughing together. Jas did a double take. Alex's expression had transformed from a mean scowl to a butter-wouldn't-melt smile, her green eyes sparkling. Even her body language had softened. She laughed again at something Luke said and went up to give Monica, and then Jas, hugs. They were both speechless.

'I'm going to the beach with Charlotte and Melody. Thanks so much for everything, Jas, you're the best.' And, with that, she practically skipped out of the room.

Jas and Monica turned to Luke with expressions that said, 'Well?'

'What an interesting girl. Did you know she got a First from City College and wrote her dissertation on the class divide in inner-suburban London? She's incredibly bright. She's not going to sue, by the way. She doesn't mind if Georgia stays. I'm going to head back to my hotel to do some work. See you later.' And, with a nod, he left.

Monica turned to Jas and folded her arms. 'Looks like he's saved the day. What was that you were saying about Luke not being *all that?*'

Chapter 23

Richard's two-week suspension had passed. He'd cut out the drugs and hookers and, instead, joined his parents for a skiing trip in the Swiss Alps, a favourite excursion of the Butlers. On his first day back in the office he was greeted by cheers, claps, pats on the back and assurances that it was 'good to have you back, Butler', and 'things haven't been the same around here'. By lunchtime he'd closed a major deal and celebrated with a four-hour champagne dinner, a strip club visit and a party back at his flat. The clean break was nice while it lasted, but impossible to maintain back in the City.

Meanwhile his plan to befriend Lila and get to Jas through her was right on track. After some weeks of chats over Facebook Messenger, they'd now progressed to frequent messages over WhatsApp. Richard would ask how her day was going and had even persuaded her to send him a picture of her outfit before going out last Friday, to which he replied with a wink and a flame emoji.

Lila loved the attention. She also clearly revelled in having a secret from Jas. Richard knew it. But, as far as Lila was concerned, he was nothing more than a mate. And much to his surprise, on the two occasions he'd suggested Lila join him for a drink, she'd said no.

One Friday night his team were celebrating the fortieth birthday of one of the more senior and most celebrated traders in the company. The plan was to be done in the office by 8 p.m. and then head straight to Mayfair for an expensive three-course dinner (though no one would touch the food) before they headed to The Box where they had a table reserved. The Box was one of the most notorious, decadent and glamorous clubs in Soho – nude trapeze artists included. In the taxi from the office, Richard drew out his phone to text Lila.

'What you up to 2night?'

'Nothing. Friend just bailed.' A pause for a few moments then: 'What u doin?'

'Mews of Mayfair 4 dinner then The Box. Full guest list, celebrities. We have a table. Come join?'

No point in messing about, Richard thought. He might as well be direct. It wasn't until the second uneaten course had been swiped from the table at Mews of Mayfair that Lila finally replied.

'The Box? Really? You can get me in?'

Richard smiled.

'Haven't you learnt yet that there is nothing I can't do?'

'What time?'

'10.30. Text me your address, I'll send a car.'

'That's easy. I'm at your old address. Send the car to Jas's flat.'

Richard booked the car. What was another Addison Lee on the company account? No way Lila was used to this level of treatment. A simple bit of Facebook stalking on her profile had shown Richard the sort of cretins she had dated before. A pathetic bartender with a nose piercing and baggy clothes. An out-of-work 'ethical artist' who no doubt used his dole money for weed. Really? This was her type? It was almost an insult for a girl that hot to be seen with losers like them.

His party rocked up to The Box at 11 p.m. Fortunately Lila was running late and her car pulled up just as Richard arrived. Her hair was glossy and her full lips painted a deep purple. She wore strappy black heels and a silky cream jumpsuit with the front open, covering her breasts but showing plenty of skin. She looked so much like Jas it was spooky. And very hot.

Richard dashed over to close the car door behind her and kiss her on both cheeks. He could feel eyes fixed on them from all sides. Who was the lucky guy with this stunning girl?

'Wow, Lila, you look incredible.'

'Thanks. You sure it's okay for me to turn up?'

'I'm delighted you did. Here, let's get inside and I'll introduce you to everyone I work with.'

'We'll be a while. Have you seen how long the queue is? It must be a good night!'

Richard laughed. 'Don't worry about it.' With his hand on the small of her back, he guided her straight to the front of the queue and slipped two £50 notes to the bouncer, who dutifully opened the red velvet rope as the people behind groaned in protest.

The club was packed. In the centre stood a stage with women wearing feather boas draped over swings suspended from the red ceiling. Weaving through the throng of people, Richard led Lila to a booth where several bottles of champagne had already been opened. He handed her a full glass and they sat in the corner so they could just about talk over the pounding music.

'Thank God Greg isn't here!' she said.

'Oh, yeah, I forgot you two were on a date when I ran into you at Print Room that time. I told you he was forgettable. You never went out with him again?'

'Nah. He texted me, like, every day for two weeks. Desperado just isn't my type.'

Richard smiled. 'Thanks for coming out tonight, Lila. These lot are great but I work with them every day. It's nice to have you here for a change.'

'Thanks for inviting me. And for the car!'

'My pleasure. If there's anything you ever need, you know you can ask me, don't you?'

She paused before replying. 'Really? Well, there was something I was going to ask you.'

'Of course!'

'You don't have any gear on you, do you?'

Richard laughed. Was this all it was going to take?

'Sweetheart, that's never a problem. Why, you want some?'

'Maybe later. After a few drinks. It is Friday night!'

'I'll drink to that! God, it's so fun being out with you. I wasn't going to bring her up but Jasmine was so boring about drugs. Like they're the worst thing in the world or something.' He shook his head for effect. 'So, um, have you spoken to her recently?' he asked.

'Not for a while. I think she's really busy out in Ibiza. They're over halfway through filming the series, then she's back.'

'You don't think she'd mind us hanging out?' asked Richard, feigning innocence even though he was fully aware Jas would absolutely hate it.

'Yeah, she probably would, to be honest. But I've known you for years too. Just because you're divorcing my sister doesn't mean we can't be mates, right?'

Richard topped up her glass. 'Right, Lila. God, you're so mature for your age. I can't believe a guy hasn't snapped you up yet.' He looked her up and down, appreciatively. 'Although looking like that, I'd better not let you out of my sight in here otherwise you *will* get snapped up and then I'll be left alone with these idiots again!'

Lila giggled. 'This is actually Jas's outfit. That's not weird for you, is it, me being here in your wife's clothes?'

'Ex-wife,' Richard pointed out. 'In all respects but the legal one. And, no, 'course not. You look a million times hotter than her anyway ... but don't tell her I told you that!'

Another giggle from Lila. 'She wouldn't believe you. She's been told she's the prettiest out of us three since the day I was born! Apparently the middle sibling is always the best-looking. I read that somewhere.'

Richard leant in so his body was right up against Lila's. 'Not from where I'm sitting,' he said. 'You don't really believe that, do you?'

Lila shrugged. 'Yeah, I guess so. Don't get me wrong, I know I'm not a hag but I don't stop traffic the way Jas does.'

That wasn't even an exaggeration. Richard remembered meeting her for a date early on in their relationship on a street in Manchester. A cyclist almost toppled over while turning to look back at her. She had that effect on men, it was one of the reasons why Richard had married her. He had the woman every other guy wanted. Not that he was going to say that to Lila.

'Nah. Obviously I was madly in love with your sister, but I always thought you had the best looks in the family.'

'Well, anyway, her wardrobe is a million times better than mine and I've got her key so I figure her wardrobe is available for my use while she's away.'

Richard sat up straighter. 'You've got her key while she's away?'

'I'm house-sitting. She wanted a dogsbody there to water the plants and make sure nothing got nicked.'

'Ahhh, *that's* why I sent the car to my old address.'

'That's right. Got the place all to myself.'

Richard nodded slowly, an idea forming in his mind that was so deliciously perfect it was almost too good to be true. What if he were to get himself back to the flat tonight, with Lila? The thought of how furious Jas would be if she knew he was back in what was now 100 per cent *her* flat.

Oh, it was too good to pass up. He raised his glass. 'Here's to friends.'

Lila clinked her glass against his. 'Friends.'

Two hours and many drinks later, Richard, Lila and their group were dancing on the tables in the packed and sweaty club.

Richard stood deep in conversation with a couple of his work colleagues before joining Lila and checking she was okay.

'What's going on?' she asked, wide-eyed and wired.

'Oh, nothing. George was just saying it's getting a bit rowdy in here now and he was talking about an after-party.'

'Great idea, my feet are killing me in these heels! Where are we going?'

'Well, that's the thing. George has a townhouse in Regent's Park but he's worried about waking his wife and the twins up if we go there. I'd have everyone back to mine but it's a construction site at the moment while the bathroom is being retiled. Everyone else lives miles away. I said I'd pay for a hotel suite in Mayfair so we could carry the party on. It's only a few hundred.'

'How many people are you talking?'

'Four or five.'

'You can't pay a few hundred quid for a tiny after-party, Richard. Just come back to Jas's. She'll never know.'

Richard's plan was working perfectly but he supressed his smile and shook his head sternly. 'No way. Jasmine would hate that and I don't want to put you in that position.'

'What position? Hackney is so close. And you've all paid for my entire night, it's the least I could do.'

'I don't know, Lila. Maybe we should just call it a night ...'

But she clearly had no intention of ending the night this early. 'It's not even two! Come on, let's go. It'll be totally fine.'

'If you're sure?'

She placed both hands on his shoulders. 'You paid for that flat, too, remember. Come on, Granddad, let's see if I can't drink you under your own table!'

Richard's car arrived within minutes and the raucous group piled in. They stopped at a twenty-four-hour shop on the way to pick up an expensive bottle of brandy. At one point in the cab, squashed in the back together, Richard's hand fell on Lila's momentarily. Drunk and giddy, she rested her head on his shoulder, smiling.

Twenty minutes later the group stumbled into Jas's flat. Shoes were kicked off on the floor, bottles were opened, Spotify playlists hooked up to speakers and lines of coke distributed onto Jas's expensive oak coffee table in the living room.

'A wedding present from some friends,' Richard said to Lila, gesturing to the table. 'I said she could keep it but now I'm missing it.'

Lila giggled, wasted now. 'You should reclaim it! Reclaim the whole flat!'

Richard made his way around the living room. It was the first time he'd been back since he'd let Jas buy him out. The look of the room had changed. Disgusting pink and green cushions all over the Habitat sofa. Arty fashion pictures hung all over the walls. It looked cheap. The oak bookshelf had been replaced with white built-in shelves filled with books, Jo Malone candles and framed photos: Jas and her sisters huddled around a table on Christmas Day; Jas and her parents standing on top of Primrose Hill, goofy grins on their faces like tourists; Jas and her friends tarted up in high heels, pouting to the camera in a club while holding champagne flutes. Richard couldn't stop looking at Jas in that one. Like she was deliberately looking straight through him, toying with him, teasing him. *'Look how much fun I'm having without you.'* The solid silver photo-frame next to the sofa on a side table, which once had their wedding photo in it, now boasted a picture of Jas and her sisters. Richard inwardly seethed.

He bent down to whisper in Lila's ear. 'Come on, let's see what she's done to the rest of my flat.' Giggling again, Lila took Richard's hand and let him lead her down the hallway. He poked around the bedroom, transformed from when he had lived there. The once-white walls were now painted midnight blue and the furniture was different, too. Barely recognisable. After he'd let her buy him out for such a good price, Jas had removed any evidence that he was ever here. And they were still married! If it weren't for his lucrative job bringing them down to London, getting their life started here, she'd still be in some poxy BBC job up in Manchester. This was how she repaid him?

Lila was swaying now, leaning into Richard as he stood in the doorway to the bedroom. He looked down at her glassy, bloodshot eyes and they looked up at him. Lila stood on tiptoe and closed her eyes, evidently waiting for him to kiss her. But instead he lightly brushed the top of her head with his lips. 'Come on, I think we've all outstayed our welcome and we should let you get some sleep. It's late and I don't want to intrude. We'll get out of your hair.'

'Nooo, stay!'

But Lila was slurring her speech now, minutes from passing out.

'No, darling. You go to bed and I'll order a car to take everyone home.'

There was no rush. After all, waiting would make it all the more satisfying.

Chapter 24

Charlotte seemed to be the only one in the house not giddy over Luke's arrival. At Bora Bora beach, he was pretty much all Alex and Melody could focus on. She honestly didn't see what the fuss was about.

'Did you see those *arms*?' gushed Melody, dramatically fanning herself with her hand.

Alex joined in. 'I couldn't stop staring into his eyes! So dark, so mysterious.'

The three women were stretched out on white sunloungers on the famous strip of sand that slowly filled up with more people as the afternoon went by, some already starting on the beers, others napping after a heavy night in Europe's club capital. The sun was scorching and there wasn't a cloud in the sky, though Alex wore a huge straw hat to shadow her face in case the sun caused a reaction on her tender skin. Charlotte thought the accessory made Alex looked even more glamorous than usual, like a film star from the 1970s. The sea fell in curling waves on the shore and jazz-infused house music played from a café behind them. It was blissful.

The girls had all brought magazines to leaf through but these were left unopened. The rare chance to talk without prying cameras everywhere was too good to miss and today no subject was off-limits.

'I don't know what you two are on about,' said Charlotte. 'Luke is cute but Dylan is much cuter, don't you think?'

'Nah, I like big men!' exclaimed Melody.

'Dylan has muscles!' Charlotte objected. 'He was a rugby player. And he's from a really poor family, he built everything up himself. The first thing he did when he made serious money was buy his mum a new flat.' She wasn't sure why she was trying to persuade the competition to fancy Dylan. But she found it necessary to defend him, somehow. And, besides, she and Melody had fast become firm friends.

'Woo-hoo, someone is getting defensive!' put in Alex. Charlotte still didn't trust her completely.

'It's so true,' teased Melody. 'I think you're genuinely falling for this guy.'

Charlotte frowned. 'But aren't we all? I mean, he's basically the perfect guy.'

Melody shrugged. 'He's not my type. He's nice enough, but we've not really got much in common. I'm not in it to win it, babe, I just want to get far enough into the competition so the audience remembers me and I get some more work off the back of it.'

Charlotte was confused. Wasn't everyone here because they were 'in it to win it'? Melody read her mind.

'There are no cameras around so I'm going to speak frankly and freely. We're all here to get something out of this, right?'

'Yep,' Alex nodded.

'I'm not convinced that winning is the be-all-and-end-all for me, that's all I'm saying,' Melody continued. 'Don't get me wrong, I'd love that holiday to the Maldives.'

'Who wouldn't?' laughed Alex.

'But plenty of girls get famous from TV shows without winning them. Besides, I don't think Dylan is going to pick me. We get on fine but I can tell he fancies other girls way more.' With that she peered briefly over her sunglasses at Charlotte. 'Anyway, if I flirt with him enough maybe he'll keep me in for a couple more weeks. And in the meantime I'm keeping out of trouble, being my cheery, likeable self and saying funny things about everyone else in my interviews so they'll definitely keep them in the edit. It's all tactical.'

'Whereas I know trouble is exactly what you need to get the viewers to like you,' said Alex with a wink.

Charlotte was gobsmacked. She hadn't been so naïve as to assume that no one in the competition was there just to get famous – the lure of becoming a minor celeb was a given – but she found Dylan so fanciable she couldn't believe that Melody and Alex didn't seem to be falling for him as hard as she was. She didn't want to home in on this point too much though. And she admired Melody's honesty and sheer confidence. But everything seemed so . . . fake. 'Wait a minute. Alex, you're saying all the fights, squabbles, everything with Georgia . . . You just put all that on for the cameras?'

'Oh, don't get me wrong, I hate that tart with a passion,' said Alex. 'And I hate all those stuck-up Mean Girls. But, yeah, I played up the fighting for more air time, just like they've all done too. Come on. Charlotte, you're not honestly telling me you don't have a game plan? Everyone's here for their five minutes of fame. At least Melody and I already have careers that are going somewhere. We just need an extra push. God, can you imagine how much exposure the winner will get? I'm going for that, all guns blazing! What've we got to lose?'

Melody nodded as if this was the most natural conversation in the world. 'True. Except I can tell Dylan isn't that into me. We're halfway through and I've still not had an alone-date. You, Charlotte and Gabriella have had loads.'

'Only one,' Charlotte said, somewhat defensively. 'But what about last night, Alex? You didn't really do that to your own face, did you?'

Alex pursed her lips. '*Obviously* not. *That* was low. I'm sure it was Georgia. You all know we've been fighting off camera too. The hatred is totally genuine. And it's true that I threatened to grass her up about Gary, which is why she poisoned me. Now there's a girl that's in it to win it!'

'Totally,' said Melody. 'My mate does the make-up for all the finalists on that TV show she was in and she said she'd never seen anyone as fame-hungry as Georgia.'

'Maybe she's just insecure,' Charlotte suggested. 'Gary certainly isn't going to make her famous. Maybe they're for real?'

'Don't stick up for her, Charlotte. She's poison and a total man-eater,' replied Alex, sharply. 'You never have a bad word to say about anyone, do you?'

But there was someone in the house who made Charlotte decidedly uncomfortable. She wasn't normally one to bitch but Melody and Alex had just been so upfront, she didn't want to act like she didn't trust them. 'Well, Gabriella looks at me like I'm an insect she wants to squash. There's definitely something about her I don't trust.'

'One hundred per cent.'

'Totally.'

'Dylan seems to love her,' Charlotte continued. 'And she's clearly very beautiful. But she never talks to me or when she does it's to say something patronising.'

Alex turned to Charlotte. 'I told you from the first night not to trust these girls. There's a reason she, Mackenzie and Georgia are all pals. They're the most stuck-up, affected ones in the house. Gabriella makes out like butter wouldn't melt whenever Dylan is around. It's creepy. If you ask me, there's more to that girl than meets the eye. I'd stay well away from her if I were you.'

The girls spent a couple more hours chilling and chatting before heading back to the villa, via a row of shops. Melody wanted to check out the make-up ranges in the local pharmacy and Alex went to enquire as to how she could replace the EpiPen that had mysteriously disappeared. Charlotte trailed behind, deep in thought. She felt silly. Of course she knew the benefits of being on a high-profile reality TV show. She thought back to her conversation with Jas, who'd informed her at the outset of the potential benefits for Charlotte's career, whether she won or not. But that was quickly forgotten when she'd met Dylan. Was she the only one with genuine feelings for him? And how much was he playing up to the cameras? Was he interested in falling in love at all, or was he in it just to get rich and famous too?

It was late afternoon by the time they arrived back at Villa Valencia and most of the girls were drinking wine by the pool or relaxing in their room. Charlotte was desperate to find out what happened on the boat-trip group-date and found Nysha applying make-up in the bedroom they shared with Melody. Charlotte grilled her for all the info.

'Well, it was a positive flirt-fest,' said Nysha. 'Gabriella and Mackenzie – oh, my God – they were outrageous! We were all sunbathing on the top deck and, no joke, Mackenzie was full-on topless and asked Dylan to put suncream on her boobs.'

Charlotte banged her fist on the mattress. 'No!'

'Yup.'

'What did Dylan do?'

'I thought he'd jump at the chance, every other bloke would, but in fact he was the perfect gentleman, handed her the bottle and said she could probably reach that area herself. Lol! Then we were all having lunch and Gabriella literally draped herself around him in front of everyone. Carmel and I didn't know where to look. Dylan didn't seem to mind though.'

Charlotte's heart sank a little, picturing gorgeous Gabriella and a laughing Dylan.

'Anyway, he was really good at making sure all four of us were involved in everything and that no one was left out. We just sailed around all day, jumping in the sea, swimming through caves. It was utterly dreamy. Then, right at the end, he dropped the bombshell that he was taking Alex out to a gig at Hard Rock Café tomorrow night as he still owed her an alone-date from last night. Well, as soon as we got back to the villa Gabriella did a full-on tantrum, moaning that it should've been her and that Alex was getting in her way or something.'

'Wow.'

Nysha rolled her eyes. 'She's just a drama queen. But *then*, one of those black envelopes came through the door. You know, from Dylan. He announced two more alone-dates for this week. One daytime date with Kat. They're going for a hike somewhere. And a night-date on Friday. He's cooking dinner in his guest house for – guess who?'

Charlotte's eyes were wide.

'Gabriella. You can imagine what a show she made of *that*. And they're holding the fourth rose ceremony on Saturday. I'm pretty sure I'm on my way out. We had one kiss on our alone-date in week two and since then he's been quite distant with me.' She looked disappointed. 'I thought we connected.' Charlotte liked Nysha but couldn't help but feel a prick of jealousy at the mention of her kiss with Dylan.

'Anyway,' continued Nysha, 'there's one advantage to going home, I suppose. I'm not sure I can keep up with all this drama.'

Chapter 25

On Friday night Charlotte was making pasta for herself, Nysha, Alex, Melody and Kat, who was eating normally and looking like herself again after her nasty stomach bug, in preparation for a film night in the villa's cosy living room. Becca, Natalie and Carmel were getting stuck into their third bottle of wine out by the pool while Mackenzie stayed in her room. Georgia sat alone on the sofa, quietly giving herself a manicure. She and Alex had been keeping well away from each other and the mood in the house was lighter and calmer already.

Charlotte looked over at Georgia and, despite Alex's hatred for her, felt a little bit sorry for the girl. There the five of them were, having fun cooking together, and just a few feet away sat Georgia all alone. Since Gary had been sent back to the UK she'd been much more subdued. Charlotte didn't think that anyone should feel lonely and Georgia didn't seem to have any allies now, which didn't seem right to Charlotte. She started to make her way over to the sofa area to speak to her when the entrance of Gabriella stopped Charlotte dead in her tracks. It might just be a casual dinner in Dylan's guest house, but she was dressed for the Oscars. A dramatic floor-length white silk dress clung to her slim figure and her red hair was straightened, hanging long down her back. A diamond necklace decorated her décolletage, which was extremely low cut.

'You realise it's a barbecue by his pool, not caviar at The Ivy, right?' Alex smirked.

Gabriella smiled sweetly. 'Well, he's coming to pick me up like a proper gentleman and, in my experience, you can never make too much effort for a man. Besides, we might skip dinner and head straight for dessert. And I wouldn't want to miss *that*.' Gabriella looked Charlotte straight in the eye for the last comment. Alex was right: there was something unsettling about Gabriella. Her outfit choice was wildly inappropriate.

Moments later Dylan strode through the open door, dressed in surf shorts and a Hawaiian shirt with short sleeves, fully open to show off his bronzed, hairless chest. The stark contrast between his and Gabriella's attire made everyone but her giggle.

Dylan kissed Gabriella lightly on the cheek then joined the group in the kitchen to say hello before their date.

'Whoa, Gabby, you look amazing! I should've made more effort,' he apologised.

Gabriella simply shot him a megawatt smile. 'Nonsense, darling. I know I'm way overdressed but I think it's so important for a woman never to let herself go, especially on date night. I've brought my bikini too, just in case we decide to have a midnight dip.'

Charlotte cringed. Talk about forward!

'Cool. How's everyone else doing ... all good, ladies?' He moved closer to Charlotte. 'Something smells good.'

She blushed as their eyes met. 'It's just pasta. Well, with pesto. I made it myself.'

Dylan's eyes widened. 'You're kidding? Pesto is my absolute favourite. And my daughter's. You make it from scratch, really?'

'It's super-easy and much healthier. You just blend the pine nuts with some olive oil and basil.'

Gabriella stroked Dylan's arm, throwing Charlotte a dirty look before flashing her smile back at Dylan again. 'I'm starving, darling. Can we get going? I'm soooo intrigued to see what you'll whip up in the kitchen.'

And with that she smiled so seductively even Charlotte couldn't take her eyes off her. She had to admit she was in awe of Gabriella's confidence. Charlotte could never in a million years be so sexy. No wonder Dylan wanted her all to himself tonight.

'Sure, babe, let's do it. I'm starving. Oh, wait, before I forget ... Charlotte, I've got tickets to the Barcelona versus Real Madrid match tomorrow and wondered if you wanted to come with me?'

'Wow, Dylan! Thank you. But, wait, isn't that match in Barcelona? You don't mean the real, actual game, do you?'

'Yep. We'll fly out first thing and come back tomorrow night in time for the rose ceremony. We might as well spend the day there. It's only an hour and a half by air. If you want to, of course?'

Charlotte smiled from cheek to cheek and could feel Melody nudge her affectionately in the ribs. 'Yes. Yes, absolutely I want to!'

'Great. I'll pick you up at eight tomorrow morning, don't be late! Come on, Gabs, I'm starved.' And with that, Dylan grabbed Gabriella's hand and bounded out, but not before she had stared over her shoulder at Charlotte. It was just for a few seconds, but it was a look of pure unadulterated hatred.

With the girls safely occupied in the villa, the crew headed out for dinner in a tapas restaurant not far from their HQ that had become something of a regular spot for them. It was a sweet, family-run restaurant with Spanish guitar music playing softly from the speakers inside. The crew always sat outside, though, under the fairy lights winding through trees and plants. The waiters knew them by now. Lyndsey, the show's director, immediately ordered dozens of different plates of hot and cold tapas for the table. Jas, dressed casually in denim shorts and a long-sleeved red and white top, checked her phone constantly in case any trouble should occur back at Villa Valencia.

'Just relax,' Monica whispered to her as the jugs of sangria arrived. 'Everything will be fine. Come on, have a drink.'

Jas smiled. She didn't tell Monica that the troublesome houseful of women wasn't her only concern. It had been a

196

while since she'd heard from Richard and, for some reason, she felt anxious about that.

'You're right, Mon. I'm just over-thinking things as usual.' Jas raised her glass. 'Right, what are we drinking to?'

She was about to make a toast when Luke approached, holding his phone in his hand. 'Sorry I'm late, guys,' he announced. 'That phone call went on for much longer that I'd hoped.'

'Luke!' cried Lyndsey from the table. 'You made it!' A few of the cameramen got up to pat him on the back or shake his hand. Ken even gave him a hug. Luke was still staying in a hotel but would come by Villa Rosa every day to work from his laptop or answer Skype or conference calls back to the Channel 6 office. He'd quickly fitted right in. The entire crew seemed to have bonded with him and, especially as it was predominantly male, loved having another bloke on the scene to break up the monotony of catfights and bitchiness in Villa Valencia.

'He's made friends fast,' Monica whispered to Jas. 'Everyone sure does love him.'

But Jas was mortified. It hadn't even occurred to her that Luke would join them for dinner. Not only was she dressed entirely unsexily, she didn't have any make-up on and felt immediately self-conscious.

'You didn't tell me he was coming,' she hissed to Monica.

'Why *wouldn't* he come?' Monica hissed back, then got up to greet Luke with a kiss on each cheek.

'Here, Luke, take my seat and I'll squeeze in next to Lyndsey. We have a few budget issues to go over anyway.'

'Oh, come on, Monica, no work tonight,' cried Lyndsey from across the table, but Monica shot her a look. Jas went bright red as Luke sat down next to her. Could Monica have been any *less* subtle?

Typically, though, Luke alleviated any tension instantly and made some football-related joke to Ken, seated to his left, before turning to Jas on his other side. Luke was wearing stone-coloured chinos, a blue V-neck t-shirt, and as usual smelt divine.

'What are we drinking? Ah, sangria, my favourite.' He topped up Jas's glass before filling his own. 'I've been meaning to ask how you are. I know everything's been a bit hectic here. I just wanted to check you were holding up okay?'

How was it that no matter what Jas was feeling, Luke had the ability to relax and reassure her within a few sentences?

'Hectic is one way of putting it.' She smiled at him ruefully. The first round of plates arrived and were distributed around the table: squid, *patatas bravas*, ribs, chorizo and vegetables. They talked about work for a few minutes and, as always, conversation flowed easily. Jas thought it was like being back at the Italian restaurant in London Bridge all those weeks ago, where it seemed like even in a busy place packed with noise and people, she and Luke were the only ones there.

The main courses and more jugs of sangria arrived.

'You're doing a terrific job, Jas,' Luke said.

Jas was already feeling the effects of the booze and didn't even notice that by now she and Luke had instinctively moved so close to each other that their knees were touching. 'I admit, it's a lot of pressure. There's stuff going on back home, too …' She stopped talking, realising she'd said too much and that her looming divorce case was *not* a subject she wanted to explore out loud tonight.

'Like what?'

'Nothing. I think I'm just missing my family a bit. I'm used to speaking to them every day and seeing Lila quite often but I haven't heard from her in a while. That's all.'

'You shouldn't be so hard on yourself.' And with that Luke stroked Jas's knee and kissed her on the cheek. 'I've really missed you,' he whispered in her ear.

Jas's heart skipped a beat. Their eyes met. Neither of them turned away. It seemed to her it had been so long since they'd looked at each other properly like this, and in that moment Jas knew that she and Luke were each thinking exactly the same thing.

Suddenly, Lyndsey lurched to her feet, wobbling ever so slightly. 'Shots!' she exclaimed, and several waiters arrived carrying trays of shot glasses filled with tequila, which they handed out to everyone.

'Oh, God, I can already feel this beginning to get messy,' Jas laughed.

'Let's make it a night to remember,' announced Luke, looking directly at her before everyone at the table rose to clink their shot glasses and then down them. They all roared a toast and more shots were ordered. Thankfully, everyone was so tipsy and engaged in their own conversations they didn't notice Jas and Luke holding hands underneath the table and talking into each other's ear.

'I haven't been able to stop thinking about you, Whiteley,' he said.

'Me neither,' she confessed. 'I really thought you hated me after ... well, after how things were left last time. I felt so rotten, Luke. I really feel I should explain.'

But he brushed this away. 'Jas, I know we're not exactly on holiday but we are in a holiday location. How about we don't ruin it by getting into all that?'

Jas was so relieved. While she felt that she owed him an explanation, a deep and meaningful chat was the last thing she wanted tonight.

'So, what do you want to do?' she asked quietly.

'I want to get out of here immediately and go back to my hotel. Or your villa, whichever is closest.'

'My villa is ten minutes' walk away.' Jas smiled as she spoke. She had to admit that this strong, decisive side of Luke was turning her on so much – and making her inhibitions fall away. If only she'd worn better underwear, or at least some make-up!

Fortunately, Luke didn't seem to mind. He threw a generous bunch of euro notes on the table. 'We're done. Those shots went straight to my head! I'm going to walk Jas back to the villa.' All the production crew were by now well on their way to getting plastered and they waved Jas and Luke off cheerily, thankfully without asking any prying questions. As soon as they were out of sight Luke pulled Jas to him and kissed her more passionately than he'd ever done before. His hands clasped her waist so tightly her feet left the ground, while her arms wound around his neck.

'You sure you don't mind me dragging you away from your mates?' he said when they eventually pulled apart.

'I only wish we'd left sooner,' she replied, and they walked away with Luke's strong arm wrapped around her.

Back at the villa and safely in Jas's room, Luke shut the door and gently pressed Jas up against it, lifting her so that her legs wrapped around his waist. They kissed feverishly for a few minutes. She felt small against Luke's tall, muscular frame, which made her weak with lust. She nodded towards the bed. Whether it was the heat of Ibiza, the buzz of the alcohol or pure lust, every second spent with Luke felt so right, like they'd waited all their lives for this very moment.

They fell onto the bed and tore off each other's clothes. Luke was on top of Jas, hands exploring every inch of her. As his fingers slid inside her she gasped and came so quickly it made her giggle, while he was all the more turned on.

Groaning, he lifted Jas on top of him, leaning up to kiss and suck her nipples while she straddled him. Then he was inside her, moaning gently as she gasped again. The sex was every bit as good as Jas had imagined it would be. Feeling free and relaxed for the first time in months, she let her inhibitions go and was overcome with wild desire. Luke was just as turned on, hoisting her into different positions, kissing any part of her body he could reach as they made love, alternating between slow and sensual then downright dirty. Two more mind-blowing orgasms later, Jas fell back into the sheets. Luke pulled her close, wrapping his strong arms around her as they both fell into a deep slumber.

Chapter 26

Charlotte was too excited to sleep that night. The World Cup was long over so it was just a league match, but Camp Nou was the biggest stadium in Europe and a huge deal. She Skyped her dad to show off about the football match and he made her promise to tell him all about it afterwards. Then there was a quick phone call to Maya and Rafi, to send them her love. Then what felt like a hundred outfit changes with the help of Melody, who picked out a blue floral playsuit and gold sandals. Charlotte was so excited about her day trip she didn't give a second thought to Gabriella and Dylan's date.

She woke up at 7 a.m. the next day, bounded out of bed, showered quickly and dressed in the outfit she'd carefully laid out the night before, her cross-body bag already packed with lip balm, suncream, Euros and her bank card plus make-up essentials: SPF lip balm, mascara, blusher and a small bottle of perfume. She threw in a deep red lipstick for good measure, just in case they hit a bar or two before flying home.

Dylan was already waiting outside the villa with a taxi to take them to the airport. He was wearing chino shorts and the famous red and blue Barcelona FC shirt.

'Where've you been hiding that?' laughed Charlotte in the taxi. Ken the cameraman and Monica were in a taxi behind and would be shadowing Charlotte and Dylan's date.

'Hey, after Arsenal, Barça is my favourite team. I've always wanted to go to Camp Nou. This is like a dream come true for me!'

Dylan's genuine excitement was adorable. 'And how on earth did you swing these tickets?'

'Don't laugh, but I got up in the middle of the night when they went on sale and waited in the online queue before spending a small fortune on them. I knew it would be right in the middle of the show but figured it was the perfect date for someone special.'

At that, he and Charlotte smiled at each other.

'You flirt,' she said, playing it completely cool even though her stomach was flipping. 'And the flights, did you pay for them, too?'

'Nah, that was all Jasmine. She's amazing. She blagged the flights for free in return for a credit on the show. She's behind all the other incredible dates. I know she has a great team with Monica being here and others back in the UK office, but Mon told me that most of them are arranged through Jas's contacts.'

'I know. She's fantastic. She's doing so much for all of us, including hanging out and listening to our problems when she should be off having fun with Luke.'

'Luke the lawyer?'

'Haven't you noticed the chemistry between them? I didn't at first but seeing them yesterday, hanging around our villa with all of us, they seemed like the most perfect, loved-up couple. Definitely the hottest I've ever seen too. I'm certain something is going on there.'

'You think they're the hottest couple?' At that, Dylan leant across and planted a quick kiss on Charlotte's cheek, making her face flush beetroot red. Fortunately he was distracted then by the taxi pulling into the terminal. 'Oh, look, we're here!'

The seats allocated to them on the flight meant Ken and Dylan were sitting together at the back, and Monica and Charlotte right at the front. 'It's perfect.' Monica winked at Charlotte. 'It'll give him a chance to miss you for a couple of hours.' Charlotte tried to brush away the comment but just the thought of Dylan missing her made her smile.

After they landed there was time for a quick stroll around Barcelona and lunch before heading to Camp Nou. Monica suggested a tapas restaurant off La Rambla, a famous street in the heart of the city that was bustling with tourists, street performers, shops, restaurants and bars.

They ordered a selection of meats and cheeses, a glass of sangria each, and Dylan whipped out his iPhone, typing a message.

'Sorry, I know it's rude,' he said. 'I just want to check in on my mum. She's got Ruby while I'm away.'

'Ah, I was wondering why they let you have a phone and not any of us but I guess it makes total sense if you've got a daughter back home,' said Charlotte.

'Yeah, I speak to her twice a day on Facetime. I miss her so much. But she seems happy enough being looked after by her nana, who's spoiling her rotten no doubt. Mum lives back in Perth and doesn't get to see Ruby as much as she'd like, so she's happy to share her with my ex for a few weeks. Would you like to see some photos?'

'I'd love to.'

Charlotte looked on as Dylan scrolled through hundreds of images of his beautiful blue-eyed girl.

'She's gorgeous, Dylan. You must really miss her.'

'I do, terribly, but Mum's coming out here with her in a couple of weeks and staying for the last week of filming so I'll get loads of time with her then. It's important that whoever I end up with has a good relationship with Ruby.'

'I wish I could show you pictures of Rafi. My phone is full of them. He's the sweetest little boy and the closest thing I've got to having kids of my own. For now, anyway.'

'You want children?'

'Some day, definitely. With the right guy. I love the idea of being a mum and having a family ... a husband.' She stopped talking then, feeling embarrassed and wishing she hadn't sounded quite so full-on, but Dylan smiled.

'That's lovely, Charlotte. Family is important. I'd love for Ruby to have a little brother or sister before there's a massive age gap.'

'Is that why you wanted to come on this show?' Charlotte hoped desperately that he genuinely had been hoping to meet someone special rather than simply chasing the fame game.

'For sure. It's one thing meeting people out and about, but when you're offered the chance to spend eight weeks in Ibiza with fifteen gorgeous women, you're hardly going to turn down that opportunity.'

Charlotte immediately felt silly. Of course, she was just one of many vying for his attention.

He shook his head, looking a bit shamefaced. 'I sounded like a real prick just then. It's not just about hooking up for me, I hope you know that, Charlotte.' He placed his hand on top of hers.

'I guess I don't know what to think,' she admitted. 'There are so many beautiful women, as you say, and you've had alone-dates with so many of them.'

'Charlotte, that's the game.' He looked around but the cameras were off briefly while Ken and Monica were having their own meal.

'Can I be honest with you? The flirting, the banter ... Jasmine told me I needed to ham it right up. It's just for TV. She wants me to fall for someone in the villa, and for them to feel the same way, but in the meantime everyone has to get dates. Surely you know that?'

He was completely right. But was Dylan spinning Charlotte the same line that he was spinning to Gabriella last night? And Alex the night before? Charlotte so wanted to ask about those dates but knew it was none of her business.

'Dylan, you don't have to explain anything to me. It's a reality TV show, I know the rules.'

'Okay, but I want you to understand I'm really not that sort of guy. We can talk more later. Let's get the bill and make our way to the stadium. It's going to be a great game.'

Camp Nou was so big and grand it took Charlotte's breath away. She'd only ever seen matches played at Tottenham's stadium before this. There was really no comparison. Almost 100,000 seats and every one of them full of loud, cheering supporters, waving flags and chanting at the tops of their voices.

The atmosphere was electric. Even though the teams drew 1–1 it was a heart-pounding game. Dylan and Charlotte grabbed hold of each other every time Barcelona tried to score and jumped up to hug each other when they succeeded. She wasn't particularly rooting for either Barcelona or Real Madrid but, as they were in the home section of the Barcelona stadium and it was Dylan's second team, it felt only right to cheer for them.

Afterwards, they headed back to La Rambla where Dylan ordered a jug of sangria and two shots of sambuca in a quaint bar off a side street from the main strip.

'I'll be wasted, especially with all this adrenaline running through my veins!' Charlotte protested, laughing.

Dylan pulled her in for a friendly hug. 'Come on, we've got just over an hour before we need to get a taxi back to the airport and I want to make the most of being with you.'

She had no idea if this was for the cameras or not, but she was loving every second of being in his company.

Chapter 27

While Charlotte was busy having her feet swept off the ground in Barcelona, Jas was wading through emails and holding planning meetings back at Villa Rosa, her mind wandering off every so often to her night of passion with Luke. Though she had plenty of work to keep her occupied, she bit her lip every time she had a flash of him gripping her waist, thrusting inside her, kissing her neck or stroking her hair as she fell asleep. That morning, he had kissed her goodbye and slipped away before the rest of the house woke up.

The open-plan kitchen and living room at Villa Rosa had been turned into a makeshift office with equipment lying about everywhere and laptops, headphones, running-order scripts, notepads, phones, cables and empty coffee mugs strewn all over the table and breakfast bar. They referred to it as the 'office' and whoever wasn't out filming would be working in it. As Lyndsey came in with a sore head but full agenda, Jas brushed away all thoughts of Luke for the next few hours.

'Jas, have you seen the footage from last night's date with Gabby?' Lyndsey asked, taking her headphones off. 'I'm watching it now.'

Jas sprang up at once, having clean forgotten about the date with one of their most volatile characters. 'Shit, no, not yet! Will I be disappointed?'

Lyndsey smiled, peering at Jas over her thick-rimmed glasses. 'You will not. There's some chit-chat while he's cooking on the barbecue but *this* is where it gets really interesting. Halfway through the second bottle of prosecco.' She pressed play on the monitor and handed Jas the headphones so she could listen. The shot showed Dylan and Gabriella in his hot tub, giggling like schoolkids and sipping wine straight from the bottle. Gabriella swished back her long hair so it fell into the water and let the drips cascade in Dylan's direction. He laughed nervously before leaning in for a long kiss. It was certainly steamy.

Jas slammed her hand on the table in satisfaction. 'Just what we wanted.'

'Check out her interview this morning about it.'

Gabriella sat on the terrace with the Ibizan hills as a backdrop. 'Last night our relationship went to a whole new level,' she began. 'The connection between Dylan and me is *insane*. I know he's out with Charlotte today, and obviously there's still a long way to go in the competition, but I'm pretty confident that my place is safe. I can see myself marrying him, no question. He's *mine*.'

'Oh my God, she is perfect,' Jas said. Gabriella might not be someone Jas would want to spend much time with away from the show, but she and Alex, especially, were exactly the sort of characters needed for the soap-opera dramatics that would keep viewers hooked.

'Busy day?' The familiar voice startled Jas.

'Luke! Hey ... I was catching up on some footage. Stuff is getting wild.' They smiled at each other. Jas felt like a schoolgirl running into her first crush!

'Morning, Lynds. How's the head?'

Lyndsey simply raised her glass of water with a smile and popped two more paracetamol.

' Yeah, that Gabriella seems like a handful.' Luke smiled, gesturing to the monitor.

'Aren't they all? Anyway, what are you up to?'

'We've had a ton of complaints back home over the new Friday late-night chat show. Too many swear words and too much sexism, apparently.'

'Crikey. That sounds fun. Well, it's the fourth rose ceremony tonight, I hope you're, er, going to stay around? All the crew will be having drinks here afterwards ...' Jas was well aware she was asking Luke out and Lyndsey pricked up her ears when she realised it too, peering over her thick-rimmed glasses again and smirking at them.

Luke smiled back. 'Sure, you bet. Anyway, I've gotta make some calls back at the hotel. I just came to collect some papers I left here. I'll see you later.'

Jas waved him off. Everything seemed different since his arrival, and, of course, more so after last night. Jas felt the most at ease she could remember since arriving in Ibiza five weeks ago. Just having him here was reassuring, like nothing could go wrong. She didn't know what last night meant but she wasn't going to ruin it by over-analysing the situation. She was determined to enjoy the rest of her time here.

'It's nice having Luke around,' Monica observed as she and Jas walked over to Villa Valencia for the rose ceremony later that evening. 'I thought he was only flying out for a day, though?'

'He decided to stay a bit longer and work out here,' Jas said. 'He says it's the closest thing he's had to a holiday in over a year and he wants to make the most of it. Burrell is letting him expense every penny. I'm sure he feels more secure, having Luke on the scene.'

'Uh-huh,' said Monica slowly, raising an eyebrow.

Jas shot her an incredulous look. 'What?' She hadn't told anyone about last night, not even Monica. Thankfully everyone had got so drunk they'd barely noticed Jas and Luke slip off, and when Monica had asked her about it, Jas said that the sun and sangria had got to her and Luke simply walked her home safely. Unfortunately, it looked as though Monica was now fully sober and in the mood to pry again.

'I was just thinking Burrell isn't the only one who likes having him around, that's all,' she said knowingly.

'Oh, you mean the women in the house? Definitely. Have you seen how much flirtier and competitive they are, with another man here to impress? It's like they're all on heat! And Dylan's loving having more male company, too.

Every time I turn around they're talking about rugby or football.'

Monica rolled her eyes. 'I'm talking about you and you know it. What is going on with you and Luke anyway?'

'We're friends. Everything is good. Anyway, he's only been here a few days. I'm concentrating on getting footage tonight, that's all.'

'Is that why you look even more gorgeous than usual?'

Jas gave her an innocent look as if she didn't know what Monica was talking about. So what if she was wearing the revealing red playsuit that she knew showed off her tanned back and legs? And so what if she'd paired it with her trusty MAC Lady Danger lipstick for the full-on glam-effect? It was a rose ceremony after all. Nothing to do with Luke and certainly nothing to do with making up for her low-maintenance look the previous night. Nothing at all to do with that …

At Villa Valencia, the eleven remaining contestants were draped on sofas around the pool when Jas and Monica arrived. The furniture had been moved down to the pool area for the evening, and the whole space had been decorated with twinkly fairy lights by the crew. Dressed in glamorous gowns, with perfectly groomed hair and carefully applied make-up, the women sipped champagne and small-talked through the tense atmosphere, in between eyeing each other closely. Tonight was a double-elimination, and everyone was speculating about which two contestants would be sent home.

Jas popped outside with Dylan to film an interview.

'Dylan, have you chosen the two you're sending home? Was it a hard choice?'

'You know, Jas, every week we get further into the competition, there are definitely women I feel more of a connection with and some I just don't at all. I wish I had much more time with them all. But I have to make my decision and it has to be final.'

'What about your date with Charlotte? And last night with Gabby?'

'I really like both of them. They're gorgeous girls and amazing in totally different ways.'

Jas made a sign with her thumb and forefinger signalling that Dylan's reply was perfect. He was, too. The past few dates couldn't have gone better, with serious sparks flying. He'd kissed Gabriella in the hot tub last night, Alex in the club the night before, and was clearly interested in both Kat and Charlotte – Charlotte in particular from what Monica had told her about their day in Barcelona. Dylan had certainly listened when Jas had told him to spice things up for the camera.

'Cut there. Great, Dylan. We'll leave it a few minutes before you go into the villa. You feeling okay? You're doing a good job, by the way.'

'Thanks, Jas. I do feel bad sending two of the girls home, though.'

'Like you said, you have to make your decision and stick to it. It's all part of the game. Though of course I have no idea who you've chosen, so for all I know you can chop and change right up until we call "Action."'

Dylan laughed. 'Thanks. I'm pretty sure I know who will be going, though.'

Jas instructed all the women to discuss their dates with Dylan in front of the cameras, to help stir things up. Charlotte was the last to arrive. She said her hellos to the crew and joined the crowd of contestants, having changed into a short white lace dress. She'd wrapped her dark hair into an elegant ponytail and finished the look with dark eyeshadow and glossy lips.

Gabriella, Natalie and Mackenzie sat together, eyeing up Charlotte and sulking that she'd had the most extravagant alone-date so far. Georgia, dressed in a loose, barely there, pale blue dress, nonchalantly looked at her nails but it was obvious she knew she was going home after her fling with Gary had been revealed. Becca and Carmel sat with their arms folded defensively. The aura of jealousy was palpable and Jas loved it. These women didn't even need directing. Melody beckoned Charlotte over to the sofa.

'Come on, then, miss, don't keep us all in suspense! How was it? From the massive grin on your face, I can tell it was good!'

Charlotte blushed, but she really couldn't stop smiling. She didn't want to seem like a show-off, though, so downplayed her perfect day with Dylan.

'Oh, you know, it was fun. The match was amazing, Real Madrid had the upper hand until the last ten minutes and then Barcelona scored a penalty. Amazing!'

'No one cares about the match, silly! Tell us about Dylan.'

'Yes, tell us,' said Gabriella. 'I'm dying to know how he had the energy for such a full-on day after our date last night.'

Everyone turned to face her. Jas made sure Ken got a close-up of Charlotte's smile dropping. 'What happened on your date last night?' she asked, quietly.

'Did you and Dylan get it on?' screeched Melody, revelling in the gossip.

Gabriella had a smug look on her face. 'Please, I would never sleep with a man so quickly. He begged me to, of course. You can't blame him after hours of kissing.'

Gasps from the others. Charlotte looked crestfallen.

'Don't look at me with those droopy eyes, Charlotte, you can't possibly think you're the only one with a chance?' There was spite in Gabriella's voice.

The women turned to Charlotte for her reaction, but confrontation only made her shy away.

Thankfully, Dylan's entrance halted this conversation. He strolled in wearing the same beautifully cut black suit and black shirt he'd worn for every rose ceremony.

'Good evening, ladies.'

'Good evening, Dylan,' they chimed in unison. *Like butter wouldn't melt*, thought Jas, watching the spectacle unfold with glee.

'How are you?' gushed Alex and Mackenzie at the same time, flashing each other dirty looks before smiling sweetly back at Dylan.

'I'm good, thanks, how are all of you tonight? Shall we sit and have a drink together?' He took a seat on a sofa and the girls flocked to him, Gabriella and Natalie sitting either side of him straight away.

'Dylan, I'm so sorry, can I interrupt?'

'Hey, Georgia, what's up?'

'Could I talk to you in private for a minute?'

Dylan nodded. 'Of course. Let's walk over to the garden. Ladies, we'll be right back.'

The women looked at each other in surprise. One cameraman followed Georgia and Dylan as they walked hand in hand to the garden at the side of the villa where Georgia led Dylan to the loveseat nestled next to a rose bush. Another camera stayed to film shocked reactions from the other girls.

Jas crept into the garden, eager to see what Georgia had to say. Her revealing dress with its plunging neckline left little to the imagination. Dylan and Georgia sat hand in hand and she gave him her most winning smile.

'I know we haven't had much time alone together, Dylan, and I know you've probably heard some things about me.' A tear slid down her bronzed cheek. By now, everyone else had followed them outside and was trying to catch what was being said from behind the camera.

Dylan took Georgia's hands, looking comfortingly at her. *This girl is good*, thought Jas, loving the crowd of women behind her hissing 'Oooooh my God' and 'I *cannot* believe her'.

'I really feel that I deserve to be here,' Georgia went on. 'And that I'm a good person. Everyone makes mistakes. Everyone deserves a second chance. I've been feeling really lonely here. All the girls are ganging up on me and I don't seem to have any friends.' Tears started streaming down her face and Dylan took her in his arms, stroking her hair. 'Shhh, it's okay, Georgia. It's okay.'

'I know you're probably going to send me home, but please don't, Dylan. I really want a chance to make it up to you.' And as her tear-stained face looked up at his, she leant in for a kiss, wrapping her arms around his neck and pushing her breasts against his chest. Georgia knew everyone was watching and the collective gasp from the other women was audible.

Jas ushered them all away. 'Come on, ladies, get back to the pool and let Ken do his job, filming all of this.'

Charlotte looked as though she was about to cry.

'It's just a TV show, remember that,' Jas whispered in her ear.

'I feel so silly. I'm really falling for him.'

'I told him to flirt with everyone and get a few kisses in for the cameras, babe. Don't take it personally. Besides, you saw the way she threw herself at him.'

Charlotte joined Melody and Alex who were desperate to gossip about what they'd just seen. After a few minutes, Georgia and Dylan emerged from the garden and joined the crowd as if nothing had happened.

The evening went on being filmed like any other rose ceremony, with everyone vying for Dylan's attention and pointedly ignoring Georgia, not that she seemed to mind.

Jas was observing the action when Luke came up beside her. Dressed in shorts and a white shirt, a slight tan emerging, he was so handsome.

'You look sensational,' he commented, gesturing to her outfit and kissing her on both cheeks. The pair of them stared at each other. Jas giggled and he bit his lip, looking her up and down appreciatively. Jas didn't know what had gotten into her but she liked it.

Luke kissed the top of her head. 'So, is it always this dramatic?'

'Yup. Surely you know that by now? Do you think Burrell is going to like it?'

'I think you might be on your way to the TV BAFTAs, Whiteley.'

They smiled at each other.

'Still on for the party back at yours tonight?' Luke asked.

'Well, it is Saturday night.'

'Cool. It'll be, um, a nice send-off.'

'Send-off?'

'I wanted to tell you straight away. I spoke to Burrell an hour ago and he wants me in the office first thing Monday. I'm catching a morning flight back to London tomorrow. I'm sorry.'

What? Just when they'd finally got together, he was leaving? But work was work. Jas nodded. 'I'm surprised Burrell let you stay this long anyway, to be honest. Obviously, I'm disappointed though ...' That was an understatement. Every bone in her body was desperate for more time with Luke. Alone-time, preferably. 'Guess we'll have to make the most of our last night?'

He smiled at her and nodded his head.

An hour later it was time for Dylan to distribute his roses. The women lined up in two rows with Dylan standing in front of them. Jas motioned for a production assistant to carry in a high table covered with a white cloth. The red roses were piled on top of this.

Dylan left a dramatic pause and then took a deep breath for effect, just like Jas always told him to do.

'Today was different,' he began. 'It was the first time I'd been off Ibiza in a month, it was my first time in Barcelona and it was a really amazing day.'

Everyone's eyes turned to Charlotte who smiled at Dylan.

'It made me realise that I'm not just here for a bit of fun or to be on TV,' he continued, reaching for his first rose. 'I really want to meet someone special. Someone I can, hopefully, spend the rest of my life with. As the competition goes on, I need to think carefully about that.'

Another pause.

'So, without further ado, Charlotte, will you accept this rose?'

The camera zoomed in on Charlotte's beaming face as she walked up and hugged Dylan. 'Of course I will,' she replied.

Woman after woman accepted her rose until Becca, Natalie and Georgia were the last three standing. Only one rose was left on the table.

'Now for the hard part,' Dylan said. 'Ladies, I've enjoyed spending time with you all. And this evening has also made me reassess certain preconceptions I might have had about some of you. It gave me a lot to think about – not just my own behaviour, but that of everyone here. Georgia, I think there's more to you that I'd like to get to know. Will you accept my final rose of the evening?'

The blonde's face lit up and Becca and Natalie fixed stony stares on her.

'Yeah, I bet there's a lot more of her he'd like to get to know,' muttered Luke, who was grinning openly, loving watching all the drama unfold. Jas elbowed him gently in the ribs. She was surprised, though. Everyone had been convinced Georgia would be on her way out tonight. Georgia joined her fellow lucky contestants, with Alex, Gabriella, Carmel and Mackenzie all turning dagger eyes on her.

Becca and Natalie said their goodbyes to the other girls, hugged Dylan and went to pack. They'd be on the midnight flight and back in London and their old lives by sunrise the next day.

Chapter 28

Once filming was finished for the night, Jas left Dylan alone with the remaining nine contestants to carry the party on. The fridge was fully stocked and the women circled him like sharks. Everyone had taken note of Georgia's tactic and each of them took it in turns to 'have a quiet word', which meant getting Dylan alone for five minutes and making the rest of the group wild with jealousy about what they could be up to. Jas hoped there would be lots of snogs to spice things up.

She half-wished she could stay and see what happened next but the cameras installed around the villa were always on and it would make for great viewing tomorrow. Besides, she had her own party – and Luke – to get back to.

At Villa Rosa someone set the playlist from their phone up to the speakers by the pool. Beers were cracked open and handed around as the crew laughed and toasted another successful filming week. Jas was enjoying herself. She felt relaxed. The sun, scenery and pace of life in the glamorous Ibizan hills were far removed from the busy vibe in London, not to mention her complicated life there.

Monica picked up on her mood. 'You look the happiest I've seen you in months,' she said, clinking her bottle of Corona against Jas's.

'I feel much more peaceful,' Jas admitted. 'Like I can take on anything!'

'There's the spirit! You can't let that bastard Richard win.'

'I know. I actually feel so much better about the situation. Like, I've finally come to the conclusion that whatever mess there is between us, it will soon be sorted out one way or another. I definitely don't want it dragged out any further, but I've also realised that I just have to accept I can't control everything. And, in the meantime, guess what? I've got the job of my dreams. Look where we are! People fantasise about this.'

Monica hugged Jas closely to her. 'Babe, I can't tell you how happy I am to hear you say that. I was worried the old Jas was disappearing, but I knew deep down that nothing could break you. You're the strongest person I know.'

'Aw, thanks, Mon.'

'By the way, Luke hasn't been able to keep his eyes off you the whole time we've been speaking. And don't look now because he's making his way over.'

Jas beamed. 'How do I look?' she whispered.

'Ten out of ten as always. Incoming!' And, with that, Monica spun Jas around quickly so she was face-to-face with the familiar, handsome face of Luke.

'Sorry to break up the love-fest.' He smiled. 'Were you two having some best-friend moment that I've just ruined?'

Jas turned around but Monica had disappeared. 'Looks like you're not interrupting anything! Having a good time?'

'Oh, yeah. It's pretty hard not to have a good time here. It's paradise.'

'I know what you mean. I love the hustle and bustle of London and Manchester but it's only when you get away for a decent amount of time that you realise how full-on city life is.'

'Agreed. That's why I keep going back to Cheshire and Brighton. It's nice to get away, go somewhere quieter where people are actually polite to each other! Although Brighton is so hipster these days it's basically turning into London with pebbles.'

'At least you have a beach. That's one thing London and Manchester certainly don't have! I've barely spent any time at the beach here.'

'Why don't we fix that, then?'

'Fix what?'

'Let's drive down to the beach. I've got my rented car here and I've only had half a beer. I'm good to drive. I found a lovely little stretch of beach this morning I reckon will be very beautiful in the moonlight.'

Jas didn't need to be asked twice. She didn't want to miss an opportunity for alone-time with Luke on a moonlit beach before he flew back to London. It would be weeks until she'd see him again.

'You're on, Hawkins. But if you think for a second I'm going skinny-dipping, you've another think coming.'

Luke snaked an arm around her waist and pulled her close to him. 'What a nice thought,' he murmured.

Luke pulled up his rented 4x4 in a car park that looked out over the sea. Steps led down to the beach. It was indeed utterly beautiful in the fading light and much more secluded than Jas had imagined it would be. And colder. She was still wearing her revealing red playsuit and hadn't thought to take a jacket when she'd raced upstairs for her handbag. The second they were on the shore, she was shivering.

'Come here.' Luke pulled her in. His body was like a furnace. She snuggled against him. 'Do you want to go back up? I have a jumper in the car you can wear.'

'Not yet. It's so stunning here.'

'Worth shivering for?' Luke said, and before Jas could reply he was kissing her, softly at first then more passionately. Her arms were tucked into his chest for warmth but she reached them around his waist and pulled herself tighter into him. She wanted to feel him close against her. The kisses grew more intense and his hands stroked her hair, her back, and squeezed her bum. Her hands explored him, feeling every glorious, sexy muscle beneath his t-shirt.

'Still cold?' he asked when their lips finally parted.

'Worth it,' she murmured, drawing his head down for another delicious kiss. She stroked her hands over his chest appreciatively, then started rubbing his groin slowly.

Luke groaned. 'Jasmine Whiteley, you are trouble,' he said in between kissing her neck.

Jas was feeling so frisky she didn't want to wait a second longer to take things further with him again. What setting could be more romantic?

At that thought, her phone started ringing in her handbag. 'Oh, God, it's Lila. Impeccable timing as always. She's house-sitting for me. I'd better answer just in case it's serious.'

'Why don't you take the call and I'll go and get my jumper from the car? I'm pretty sure I saw a blanket in the boot too.' He kissed her on the lips again before heading off. Jas was grinning from ear to ear but the phone was still ringing loudly.

'This better be good, Lila. It's nearly ten o'clock.'

'Charming! I was only phoning 'cos you haven't contacted me all week. I could be dead for all you know.'

Jas rolled her eyes. 'I've been busy. It's called a job. What's going on anyway, little one? You behaving yourself? How's Meg? And I trust my flat is still in one piece?'

'Speaking of jobs, I've got a new one, you'll be pleased to know. A grown-up one. And, to answer your questions, the flat is just as perfect and obsessively clean as when you gave me the keys. The plants are all watered and nothing is dead yet. Meg's grand. Going on about mixer taps and wooden flooring for the loft extension. Where are you anyway? It sounds windy.'

'I'm on a beach, freezing my arse off. Don't ask. Let's go back to that job you mentioned.'

'Oh, yeah, I've got a nine to five now and a proper salary. I'm the new receptionist at Curtis Stoddard in the City. How great is that?'

'Lila, that's fantastic, I'm so proud of you! I think a serious job is exactly what you need.' Then Jas frowned. 'Wait. Curtis Stoddard? You know that's where Richard works, right? Eurgh. Well, maybe if you just keep your head down he won't even notice you're there'

'Notice I'm there? He was the one who got me the job.'

Jas might have been shivering on the outside but suddenly it felt as though her blood was running cold. Even the sight of Luke reappearing in the distance, clutching a blanket and jumper, didn't stir anything in her.

'What do you mean?'

'It's nothing to worry about. He texted me to tell me they were hiring, made sure my application went straight to the top of the pile and put in a good word for me. Look, I knew you'd get mad so that's why I phoned. You were going to find out anyway now we're working in the same building. It's nothing.'

'Stop saying it's nothing! What do you mean, he texted you? Why was he texting you?'

'He's my brother-in-law, Jas, you weren't the only one who knew him. We ran into each other at Print Room a few weeks ago. That's it.'

Jas dropped to the ground and sat cross-legged on the sand. She didn't understand what she was hearing. 'And what ... now you're best friends? You do remember what he did to me, Lila, don't you? You remember how broken I've been these past few years?'

'Of course I do, Jas. You're my number-one priority, you know that. But Richard's just been super supportive and—'

'Supportive of what? What the hell have *you* got going on?' Jas knew it was a nasty comment but she was furious. She felt as though Lila was betraying her by fraternising with the enemy.

Luke approached. As soon as he saw the pained expression on Jas's face his smile dropped. 'You okay?' he mouthed, but all she could do was shake her head.

'Oh, so you're the only one with goals, dreams, ambitions? I can't have any of that because it's all about you?'

'That's not what I meant, Lila. But how do you think it feels to hear that one of the people who is closest to me in the entire world has been in communication with the man who ruined my life?' At this Luke looked over at her but Jas was so irate she didn't notice.

Another deep sigh from Lila. 'You're currently being paid to live in Ibiza. I hardly think your life is ruined, Jas. And Richard practically gave you the flat. He feels really bad about things, you know. If only you'd give him a chance, you might see that there are two sides to every story.'

She sounded so emotionless and aloof. Hot tears filled Jas's eyes. Luke wrapped his jumper and his arm around her but Jas took no notice.

'How – how could you say such things, Lila? You know what he put me through. What he's still putting me through.'

'I think we should talk tomorrow. You're upset. It'll give you a chance to calm down.' And with that, Lila hung up. Tears streamed down Jas's face. How ironic that all this time she'd wanted Lila to grow up and get serious; to land a proper job. In the space of a phone call Jas had learnt that not only had her sister achieved all of that, she had broken Jas's heart in the process.

'What was that about?' asked Luke.

Jas wiped her face, shaking her head. 'It's nothing.'

'Don't give me that. Talk to me.'

'Just my sister. She's hanging out with my ex. They're texting.'

'Well, that doesn't sound so terrible.' Luke's attempt to make light of the situation only made things worse.

'You don't understand,' Jas replied, coldly.

'So tell me. Come on, it has to be serious if it's got you this upset.'

Jas stood up, letting Luke's jumper fall to the ground, and started marching back up the steps towards the car, her arms folded.

'Hey!' Luke caught up to her and took her hand but she angrily pulled it away and kept marching.

'Oh, this is mature,' he said sarcastically. 'Jas? JAS?'

'What?'

'What's wrong with you?'

'Nothing!'

'Then tell me what could possibly make you so upset about Lila being in touch with your ex?'

Jas stopped and turned round to confront Luke, her expression furious. 'Because he's not my ex, okay? He's my husband. There? Happy?'

She didn't wait to see his reaction. She wanted to get away. She stormed into the car park and yanked at the passenger door of the car, but it was locked. She slammed her fist against the window, causing no damage except to her ego. It hurt her hand, too. Jas didn't care.

'You have a husband? You're *married*?'

'Let's just get in the car,' she snapped back at Luke. She knew she was acting like a child throwing a tantrum. It was completely out of character but it felt satisfying to let out all the anger she'd supressed over the months. Years even.

'Whoa, we're not going anywhere until you tell me what's going on.'

Jas folded her arms tightly to her chest, suddenly feeling exposed and vulnerable. She couldn't bring herself to look at him but knew she had to face up to this now. There was no escaping that.

She bit her lip. 'Yes, I'm married. But we're separated, have been for months. I filed for divorce and he's refusing to give it to me.' It certainly wasn't the way Jas had wanted to come clean to Luke but, man, did it feel good finally to say it out loud.

'It's been hell. I'm sorry, Luke. I should have told you.'

Luke was shaking his head. 'How could you have kept this from me?'

Tears were streaming down Jas's face but this time Luke didn't offer her any consolation, just stared at her with an expression she couldn't decipher. 'I wanted to, but I didn't want to ruin what we had.'

'So you lied to me?'

'No! I mean, yes. But it wasn't like that.' Jas moved closer to him but he swerved aside, walking over to the driver's side of the car and unlocking the door.

'Get in,' he said.

Jas got in the car. Luke sped away. He turned the heating on and warmth spread over Jas, calming her down. The tears dried and she sniffed, talking deep breaths as Luke drove on. Jas didn't know what to say so waited for him to speak first. They sat in silence for what seemed like hours.

'Why are we following signs to the old town? I thought we were going back to your hotel?'

'I'm dropping you home. Then I'm going back to my hotel.'

That made sense. But he wasn't planning to leave things like this, surely?

'Okay, we can talk in my room.'

'I'm going back to my hotel,' he repeated.

'Oh, no, please don't leave like this, Luke. I wanted to tell you so many times, but there was never a right moment. I know that sounds ridiculous. That's why I ended it, because I didn't want things to get more complicated until my divorce was final. I swear, to all intents and purposes I am single and what I feel for you is real.'

'Okay, Jas, okay.' His voice softened. 'It's a lot to take in right now. I'm tired. It's late and I have an early flight. I think we should leave it tonight, let things cool down a bit and talk again in a couple of days.'

He pulled into the parking area at Villa Rosa.

'We're here.'

Jas wanted to argue with him but, really, what justification did she have? The least she could do was

230

respect Luke's wishes. Feeling miserable, she got out of the car.

'Call me when you land, okay?' she asked, hopefully. But he'd already sped out of the driveway.

Chapter 29

Jas barely slept that night. She'd always been a good sleeper but when her marriage had started falling apart anxiety made her unable to relax. Where once she was calm and easy-going, she started getting paranoid and tetchy and her formerly sound sleeping pattern turned into restless nights; too tired to think, too wired to sleep. This time, she tossed and turned for hours, obsessing over the evening's events. She felt terrible about the way she'd left things with Luke. He'd had every reason to drive away. And, in fact, in the circumstances he'd been a lot nicer to her than some men might have been. The childish tantrum she'd thrown certainly hadn't helped. She felt mortified the more she thought about it. Why hadn't she just told him about Richard in the first place, like everyone had told her to? Was she just hoping it would all work out fine? Since when was she so naïve? And what did last night mean to Luke anyway? So much had happened yet they'd never had a straightforward and honest conversation about their feelings for each other.

The situation with Luke was just one problem keeping Jas awake. The conversation with Lila had been more than upsetting; it had chilled Jas to the bone. Not only was Lila acting as if her so-called friendship with Richard was completely normal, there'd been something uncharacteristically cold in her voice. Richard had really gotten to her quickly.

Over the next few days, the main communication Luke and Jas had was via emails with other members of the *Mr Right* team copied in. Jas had texted him when he landed back in London to apologise for how she'd left things and he was perfectly polite, but just said they'd talk 'when you're properly back', and that for now 'we should probably have a bit of space'. How could she argue with that?

A few afternoons later, Jas was filming a group-date with Gabriella, Charlotte, Georgia, Nysha, Mackenzie and Kat. Dylan was taking them to the north of the island where they'd spend the afternoon learning Spanish before having a tapas dinner. Jas tried to throw herself into the scenario – by now all the girls in the group had grown extremely fond of Dylan and the chemistry between them all was palpable. But while they knocked back cava and shared paella in between attempts at broken Spanish, Jas slipped away to make a phone call.

'I was wondering when you were going to call,' said the familiar voice.

'Wow, Lila, not even a hello?'

'Hello. Jas, I'm sorry for upsetting you the other night, okay? I didn't mean to. But you're blowing this Richard thing out of proportion.'

Out of proportion? Jas had to bite her tongue. She took a deep breath before answering, to make sure she kept calm.

'Lila, you need to listen to me. I'm sure Richard is being charming to you. That's what he's like when he wants something. But can't you see that he's using you to get to me? He's furious with me about this divorce and he wants to hurt me. I know it sounds extreme but, honestly, it's what he's like. Or what he's become.'

'So, the only reason why your husband – my brother-in-law – could possibly be nice to me is to get to you? It's not because we're family, not because he's my friend and wants to help me? It's all about *you*, is that what you're saying?'

'You're twisting my words.'

'Am I?' Lila was shouting now. 'You *always* do this. You always make it about *you*. I've said I'm sorry and you're still not listening to me.'

'You don't know him like I do. He's a rat. He's manipulative and vicious. He wants to hurt me. He sees this divorce as a personal attack on him and his manhood or some such bollocks. Can't you see? We're fighting already … that's just what he wants!'

'You are unbelievable. You can't bear it that someone else is happy, can you? You're the one who's been on at me for months to grow up, get a proper job, all of that. Now I've done it and, just because Richard's involved, you hate it.'

'That's not what I mean at all! But I don't see how you can be friends with him. Have you forgotten what our marriage was like?'

Lila sighed down the phone. 'No, Jas. But until recently I only heard your version of events. There are two sides to every story.' Jas couldn't begin to think where to go with this.

Lila sighed. 'Look, I better go.'

'Wait a minute. What's this Connor Scott tells me about you texting him for a hook-up to get some coke? Is this Richard's influence as well?' A lump formed in Jas's throat. She felt her previous closeness to her baby sister slipping away as they spoke.

'You're kidding, right? I'm twenty-five. I'm not a kid any more. How dare you ring me up and try to tell me how to live my life? What makes *you* so special? You're just jealous because you have no one. You couldn't possibly make Richard happy, and now he's having a bit of fun with me and you can't stand it. Well, guess what? Not everything is about you, Jas. You say you're asking him for a divorce but I don't see you taking any action recently. Sounds like maybe you don't want to let him go after all. Or you don't want him but you don't want anyone else to have him either, is that it?'

'What are you talking about? You know how much I want a divorce. These things take time. The court case is next month. I can't control how long the legal stuff takes.'

'Whatever.'

'Lila, please don't do anything you're going to regret.' Jas was emotional now.

'Bye, Jas.' The line went dead. Jas wiped away her tears, pulling herself together so as not to draw attention to herself. Lila had always had a sharp tongue but there had been a new venom in her voice just now that had sent chills down Jas's spine. It brought back a feeling she hadn't experienced in a long time, not since she'd lain awake at night willing Richard to come home when it was painfully obvious he was out with another woman. Now as then, Jas had a strong feeling that something wasn't right, that something terrible was about to happen – and her husband and sister were going to be at the heart of it.

Chapter 30

It was the night of the sixth rose ceremony. The previous week Dylan had sent home Carmel and Kat, though Charlotte couldn't say she was wholly surprised. They'd each only had one alone-date with him throughout the whole process while the others had had several by now. With only seven women left, the atmosphere around the pool was tenser than ever. Dylan and the women sat together on the terrace, sipping wine and talking, Dylan inviting each girl in turn for a brief alone-chat as had become the custom on ceremony nights. Each girl got three minutes or so with him. Charlotte was first. As they walked into the villa, hand in hand, she could feel six pairs of eyes burning into her.

'How are you feeling?' Dylan asked as they cosied up on a sofa, smiling into each other's eyes.

Charlotte held on to his hand. There was no doubt about it, she was falling hard for him and would be crushed if he sent her home.

Dylan looked into her eyes. 'Can I be honest with you?' he asked.

'Of course, Dylan, you can tell me anything.' Charlotte felt the cameras circle them. Even after several weeks it still made her uncomfortable to be having an intimate conversation like this in front of two cameramen. She didn't think she'd ever get used to it.

'I really like you,' Dylan continued. 'We have so much in common and I can't stop thinking about Barcelona.'

Charlotte blushed. 'Me too.'

'But I get the sense that you're holding back and you're not fully ready to commit. Like, no matter what I do there's a barrier between us. Am I crazy?'

'No, you're not crazy. This is a difficult situation for me. There are six other women here all desperate for you. No matter how close I think we're getting, I know you've grown close to other girls too. I knew what I was getting into but I guess I just didn't realise how hard it would be. And ... I have fallen for you, Dylan.'

He edged closer. Her pulse raced. 'I've fallen for you, too,' he said softly. 'But I need to know if you're really into this.'

'I am. But ... I've been hurt before ...' Her voice trailed off. It was true. Charlotte felt that she couldn't compete with all the other confident, beautiful women here and was terrified of having her heart broken. *Please don't hurt me*, she wanted to say, but before she could utter another word she and Dylan were kissing and, at that moment, nothing else mattered.

It felt like hours had gone by but Charlotte knew it must only have been a minute. Dylan was an amazing kisser, keeping his hands wrapped gently around her waist. She knew she wasn't the first woman he'd locked lips with here, but it was her first kiss with him and she was going to savour every last second.

'Excuse me, Dylan?'

Charlotte and Dylan broke apart to see Gabriella gazing at them. How long had she been standing there?

Dylan cleared his throat. 'Hey, Gabby.'

'Sorry to interrupt. Could I talk to you? Charlotte, the girls are waiting for you over there. Your prosecco must be warm by now.'

What could Charlotte say to that? She was pissed off with Gabriella for ruining their moment, and had every right to be, but the last thing Charlotte wanted to do was cause a scene in front of Dylan. He did at least look embarrassed by the interruption.

'Oh, okay, I'll see you back there, Dylan.' As she reluctantly left them together Gabriella grinned at her.

Back at the sofas Charlotte sat down next to Melody, telling her about her first kiss with Dylan.

'I really like him,' she whispered.

Melody raised her eyebrows and glanced over to Dylan and Gabriella, who were returning from their alone-chat. Gabriella looked incredibly smug. She sat down on a sofa and started whispering to Mackenzie, her partner in crime it seemed. Georgia was once part of the Mean Girls gang but since coming on to Dylan so brazenly and staying in the competition when everyone thought she'd leave, she seemed to have been booted out of that crew entirely. She sat alone, sipping wine and twirling a lock of long hair around her finger. No one talked to her and Charlotte still felt sorry for her.

'Alex, can I speak with you?' Dylan asked, and he and Alex sauntered off hand in hand, making Charlotte's heart sink. Alex was so beautiful and confident, Charlotte couldn't imagine any man not falling at her feet. She suspected there was strong chemistry between Alex and Dylan.

'Take no notice,' Melody said quietly when she noticed Charlotte's distress. 'He has to flirt with everyone, remember?'

Charlotte topped up her glass and Melody's. 'So how do I know if he's genuine with me or not? He could be spinning the same lines to all of us. Clearly he's into Alex, too, and the rest.' She glanced at Gabriella and Mackenzie who were still whispering to each other and giggling. Georgia turned around sharply.

'It's rude to whisper,' she snapped, but the Mean Girls only laughed harder. It really was like being in school again.

'Georgia, come sit with us,' Charlotte offered, ignoring Melody's frown.

'I wouldn't get too close to her, you might catch something.' This from Mackenzie. Charlotte had never warmed to her, fake boobs always out on display and thrust in Dylan's direction. And she didn't make any effort with the rest of the household. Georgia ignored the snide comment and went to sit with Charlotte and Melody, appreciating the offer. Gabriella stared intently at the three of them, making Charlotte uncomfortable. That look was so intense it was creepy.

'How's it going with you and Dylan?' Gabriella said, not taking her gaze off Charlotte. The others all stopped talking.

'It's going great,' replied Charlotte.

Gabriella narrowed her eyes. 'That was only your first kiss though, right?'

'Yes.'

'Why do you think he waited so long? Nysha got it on with him in the second week.' Nysha looked at the floor, embarrassed. 'And almost everyone else,' Gabriella continued. 'It's weird, isn't it? He could barely keep his hands off me on our first alone-date.'

Charlotte had opened her mouth to reply when Alex and Dylan returned to the group. 'What did we miss?' asked Alex.

No sooner had Dylan sat down than Mackenzie shot to her feet. 'My turn!' She smiled sweetly, stretching out her hand to him. Charlotte had to admit that Mackenzie was most men's dream woman: long blonde hair, big eyes, big boobs. Dylan didn't need asking twice.

'Gabriella, can we grab you for a quick piece-to-camera?' asked Lyndsey.

'I'm going to the toilet,' muttered Charlotte. She stalked off to the bathroom, hoping to shrug off her bad mood before Dylan returned. Charlotte knew the key to dealing with women like Gabriella was to ignore them – they only wanted a reaction – but rising above Gabby's not-so-subtle comments wasn't easy. In fact, Charlotte was getting more and more irate. She'd understood that there would be some challenging characters in a show like this, but the fakeness of Gabriella, and the way Dylan was falling for it, was sickening to see.

Charlotte took a few deep breaths in the bathroom to calm herself down. *Don't let her get to you, don't let her get to you.*

She made her way back down to rejoin the group. As she walked past the terrace, Gabriella was being interviewed in one corner. Charlotte normally would have walked straight by, but what she overheard Gabriella saying stopped her dead in her tracks.

'The chemistry between me and Dylan gets hotter and hotter every time we're together,' she boasted. 'The way he is around me, I know he's not like that with everyone else. And you know all about our night in the hot tub. Well, that speaks for itself.' She giggled coyly. 'The truth is, Dylan is mine. I am head over heels in love with him and I know he feels the same way about me. Obviously, he didn't actually say it, I know he can't, but his look told me everything I need to know. Dylan and I are going to be together. I know it.'

'Thanks, Gabby,' said Lyndsey from behind the camera. Charlotte scuttled off before she was spotted.

'He's taken Georgia away for a chat and they've been gone a lot longer than three minutes,' Melody said when Charlotte sat back down.

'What do you think they're talking about?' she asked.

'Maybe they're not talking,' said Alex, with a stony expression on her face.

Dylan reappeared alone, looking forlorn. The women glanced at each other. 'I'm just going to come out and say it,' he announced to the group, looking disheartened. 'It

242

wasn't going to work out with Georgia. I've said goodbye to her. She's packing her things now. I think we should get on with the rose ceremony.'

Gasps came from the group. Charlotte had to admit she was happy there was one less woman in the competition, but to send someone home even before the rose ceremony? That was serious.

Jas appeared then. 'Ladies, let's all line up by the garden, please. Dylan, when you're ready.'

An assistant rolled out the white-clothed table with just four roses resting on it. The six remaining women lined up in two rows of three, all taking deep breaths to calm their nerves. What on earth had happened in the space of one evening to make Dylan decide to send Georgia home so abruptly? Had she come on too strong?

They stood silently as Dylan picked up the first rose. 'Tonight has been tough for all of us. We're getting to a difficult stage of the competition. Emotions are running high. But every week I need to think more and more seriously about who I want to be with. Tonight I found out some information about Georgia that made me realise she was not the girl for me. With only two more weeks to go I have to keep in this competition the women I think I can see myself with. Alex, will you accept this first rose?'

She beamed and walked up to him. 'Of course I will,' she said, giving him a hug.

He picked up the second rose. Charlotte breathed a sigh of relief that her name was called then and hugged Dylan tightly as she accepted. Nysha made it through too. Then, Dylan took a deep breath and read out Mackenzie's name, but when she ran up to him, he did not pick up a rose. 'Mackenzie, I have to say goodbye to you.'

'Why me?' she shouted.

'You told me some uncomfortable truths about Georgia tonight that made me question her authenticity. She's still been keeping in touch with Gary. There's no way I can keep her in, knowing that her feelings for me aren't genuine. But the way you told me, with such pleasure, made me look at you differently too. I don't know if you're the woman for me. I'm sorry.'

Mackenzie stormed off, crying. The other contestants whispered to one another. Was Georgia really still in touch with Gary after what had happened?

Gabriella and Melody both stood waiting. There was only one rose left. Everyone was glancing at each other, even the crew behind the cameras.

Dylan took a deep breath. 'Gabriella. Will you accept my final rose of the evening?'

She practically fell over herself, she was so giddy with relief. 'Yes, Dylan, of course!'

Charlotte was gutted. Melody was easily her best friend in the competition. Ever the gracious loser, Melody hugged everyone goodbye.

Charlotte hugged her back tightly. 'I'll really miss you.'

'Well, we'll just have to meet up back in London in a couple of weeks, won't we?'

'I'd love that.'

Melody leant in and whispered in Charlotte's ear, 'You got this, babe. Go get him.'

'I wish you were staying.'

Upstairs, she helped Melody put the last of her belongings together. 'Oh, wait,' she said. 'I left that lipstick I borrowed off you by the pool, let me go get it.' As Charlotte dashed back out, she came across Gabriella and Mackenzie whispering together on the staircase, though they didn't see her.

'You said just Georgia would leave if we told him that – why me too?' hissed Mackenzie, clearly still upset at being sent home. 'You told him too, didn't you, Gabs?'

'Of course I did,' Gabriella whispered, hugging her. 'Darling, I have no idea why he didn't get rid of me too, I'm sure he wanted to. I told him everything about Georgia and Gary, word for word like we agreed. I'm delighted she's gone but so sad you're going too!'

They moved off in the direction of the bedrooms and Charlotte raced away so they wouldn't see her. What a weird conversation.

Lipstick retrieved, Charlotte reached her and Melody's bedroom door where she ran straight into Gabriella. Charlotte froze, awkwardly.

'Saving the best for last.' Gabriella smiled, clutching her rose to her chest.

Chapter 31

Richard was heading home for a rare early night after an exceptionally brutal week in the office when he received an unexpected, but welcome, phone call.

'I'm sorry for phoning on a Friday night.'

'No, it's fine, Lila. I was just on my way home. You sound upset. Is everything okay?'

'Urgh, just my stupid sister. You know I told you how she kicked off about us hanging out? As you said she would.'

Richard's mouth curled into a smile, but he tried to sound serious. 'Yes. Oh, gosh, she hasn't had another go at you, has she?'

'Worse. Now she's told Meg *and* my parents, and they've all phoned me saying how insensitive and thoughtless I am.'

'Oh, Lila, that's dreadful.'

Her voice started to break. 'Why does everyone insist on treating me like a child? You know, not one person has actually congratulated me on my new job? Not one member of my family has asked how I'm feeling.'

'It's not fair at all. What can I do to help? How about a night out, my treat? Come and meet me at St Paul's. I'll take you for champagne and you can bitch and rant the night away. No judgement.'

Lila laughed. 'I'm sure you've a million other better things to do.'

'Nonsense. I hate hearing you so upset. Meet me at Madison's in forty minutes. You hungry? I'll reserve a table. Don't you worry about a thing.'

'Okay. Thanks, Richard. You're a real friend.'

'My pleasure.'

He hung up feeling very pleased with himself. Jas would be beside herself by now. He could just imagine her prissy face screwed up in rage. So much for his quiet night in. However, Richard suspected this would be much more satisfying.

Two hours, three vodka and tonics and two bowls of salmon linguine later, Richard beckoned the waitress over.

'Another round?' he asked Lila, but she shook her head.

Richard's double vodka arrived, this time without the tonic and he knocked half of it back in one go. Lila eyed him suspiciously.

'You've barely touched your food. Everything okay?'

Richard sniffed and rubbed his nose. 'Yeah, fine, fine.'

They were seated in the bustling restaurant, teeming with City boys and girls out to play after a gruelling week's work. Richard's table had a stunning view of the London skyline. He had insisted on a big night out, no expense spared.

247

'After this we should head over to Nelson's. It's much more fun.'

Nelson's was a swanky members-only bar that had just opened in the heart of the City and entrance to it was hard to secure. Not when you were a high-flying trader with money to burn, though. Lila raised her eyebrows. 'I'm impressed. Thanks for this, Richard. I really needed to let off steam.'

He rested a clammy hand on top of hers. Lila looked ravishing tonight in tight-fitting black leather trousers and chunky black heels, her lips painted hot pink. It looked like she'd raided Jas's wardrobe again as he recognised the flimsy white top from his wife's Instagram page. Richard looked at Jas's profile several times a week. What had started out as idle curiosity had turned into another addiction. One night recently he scrolled all the way back to her first post, dissecting each picture for clues as to where she was and who she was with. Not that he'd ever tell Lila that.

'Hey, no need to thank me,' he said softly. 'It's so unfair the way your family treat you like you're an outsider. Jas was always jealous of you.'

'That's not true.'

'Come on, you know you've got the looks of the family. Jas could barely contain her jealousy every time she saw you. Always talking about you. It was weird.'

Lila shifted in her seat and pulled her hand away. 'That doesn't sound like Jas. I know we've had our differences lately but I don't think she's that jealous of me.'

Richard realised he had pushed that one too far. 'No, no, I just mean she never gave you enough credit, that's all. Listen, let's get out of here. I fancy a change of scene.'

Nelson's was tucked away in a dark, secluded street that made it seem more exclusive and decadent. Richard held the cab door open for Lila but there was only so far that the cab could go before they had to get out and walk the rest of the way to the bar. The entrance was a black door with no sign on it. The only indication that the club was here were the paparazzi loitering outside, hopeful of catching a glimpse of an A-lister stumbling out. Once buzzed in, a dark and narrow staircase led downstairs to the dimly lit club, which was decked out with leather-covered sofas and wall panels. Lila nudged Richard when she spotted a famous pop star and her entourage at one table, and a gang of British actors at another.

Richard had managed to get them a tiny booth in the corner where they were squashed in together. A waitress brought over a bottle of champagne in an ice bucket and four shots of tequila.

He handed a shot to Lila. 'Patrón? Only the best.'

She giggled as they shot back both in succession. Richard sunk another one straight after. He was going for it, tonight.

'You know, I've really enjoyed the last few weeks, Lila,' he said. 'I mean, I've known you for years, obviously, but only as my sister-in-law, never as my friend.'

'I know what you mean. I hope we can stay friends after the divorce.'

Richard bristled slightly at the D-word. It was a reminder of Jas winning and it made his blood boil.

'It's such a shame things couldn't have worked out with you and Jas,' Lila went on. 'It would be great to have you around more.'

Richard was getting bored with this subject. 'I'm sure we will sort things out. Anyway, let's talk about you. Been on any more dates recently?'

Lila side stepped that question entirely. 'Really? So, you do want to get back together with her? Richard, that's ace. Maybe if you begged her to come back she *might* consider it.'

'Begged *her*? Darling, remember who you're talking to.' Richard was getting agitated. He decided to make another move and stroked Lila's thigh. 'Have I told you how gorgeous you look tonight?'

Lila wriggled so that his hand fell off her thigh. She completely ignored his last comment. 'Well, you'd probably have to beg a bit, Richard. I know there are two sides to every story but it *was* you who cheated, wasn't it? She'd need a whole lot of convincing to call off the divorce now anyway.'

Richard snatched back his hand and folded his arms crossly. 'I wouldn't beg that bitch back if she was the last woman on earth,' he spat.

'Oi! Jas might not be my favourite person at the moment but please don't call my sister that. You're getting really defensive.'

This was not how Richard had expected the night to go. Clearly slagging off her sister wasn't getting him into Lila's good books. How much more did he have to put up with before she finally gave it up? He should've taken his chance at Jas's flat while he had it.

'You're right. I'm sorry. It's just the booze talking. This divorce is hard on both of us, I guess. It's not how I expected my life to go. Look, I can barely hear myself talk in here. Do you fancy going back to my place? It's much more intimate.' He stroked Lila's thigh again. 'We can talk properly.'

'Whoa, Richard, bad idea.'

'What's wrong?'

'I just … I don't think this is working any more. Us hanging out like this. It's been really fun and it's been nice to catch up with you again, but I'm starting to feel bad about Jas now.'

'But I thought you hated your sister? She treats you like a child, you always tell me that?'

'She's still my sister.' Lila was getting defensive again. 'And I remember how miserable you made her.'

'Miserable?' He wiped his nose, poured himself a glass of champagne and knocked it back. All this preparatory work and he wasn't getting anywhere. He was angry. And steaming drunk. 'You know I've had just about enough of you Whiteleys,' he shouted, his speech lulling a little from the booze. 'The lot of you, you're so bloody ignorant. You've been taking advantage of everything I've given you without giving a shit about your sister until now. That shows your real slutty personality, doesn't it? And now all of a sudden she's your best mate again? What the fuck is that about? You've just been using me, haven't you? You're a little prick-tease. Just like your sister. Your whole family are leeches. Jasmine wouldn't even be down here in London if it weren't for me, let alone living in fucking Hoxton. And you're just a waste of space, too.'

Lila was not only incredulous, she looked mildly frightened by Richard's outburst and physically backed away. 'Richard, calm down, you're making a scene and being really horrible,' she protested.

'I didn't hear you taking her side so much when you got me back to her flat,' he sneered. 'Or when I was plying you with coke. That's hundreds of quid down the drain for nothing. That's your family all over though, isn't it? Cheap, money-grabbing whores.'

People were starting to look now and Lila flushed with embarrassment and unease.

Richard reached for the bottle of champagne to refill his glass when he brushed past the fourth shot of black-coloured tequila and it spilt all over Lila's white top. He smirked as she let out a cry.

'You wanker!' she said, running towards the women's toilets.

Fuck this, Richard thought. Beckoning the waitress over for the bill and reaching for his wallet, he paused. Why the hell should he cough up yet again for a prick-tease slut? She'd left her bag on the seat. She could foot the bill for once. Richard smirked again, delighted that he'd ordered the most expensive tequila. Wobbling slightly, he slipped out of the bar. That would serve Lila right. He was done with all the Whiteley women.

Chapter 32

'So, you know what you need to do, Jasmine?'

'Yes, Ralph. I've got all that. But I'm worried this still isn't enough to convince the judge that Richard should grant me a divorce.' Jas was talking through the finer details of her hearing, now just a few weeks away. Her solicitor Ralph was explaining that her claim was to be 'irretrievable breakdown of the marriage due to unreasonable behaviour', that her evidence against her husband would be cross-examined, and that she could be given a verdict straight away, or anything up to a few weeks later. There was even the possibility of a second hearing, which filled Jas with dread.

'Oh, God. I don't want it dragged out any longer than it has to be. What about the hearing itself, how long will we be in court for?'

'I expect no more than one day. The courts have better things to do, quite frankly. But Mr Butler certainly isn't willing to let this go easily.'

'Tell me about it,' muttered Jas. 'I want this over with as quickly as possible. Do you think we have enough evidence to win?'

'I wouldn't like to answer that.'

This didn't fill Jas with much hope, but maybe Ralph was just managing her expectations.

'Okay, thanks, Ralph. I better go. It's the penultimate rose ceremony and someone is about to be sent home.' Ralph knew all about Jas's job, though she doubted very much that he was a fan of romantic reality TV.

She was heading back into the villa when a tearful Nysha ran past her and up to her bedroom.

'What happened?' asked Jas when she got out to the terrace. 'Did I miss something? Is Nysha going home?'

Monica nodded.

'Aw, I liked her. After getting down to the final four it must be painful.' Jas gazed up at Nysha's closed door, feeling disappointed on her behalf, as well as gutted to have missed the live action. 'Is she okay? Should someone go and check on her?'

Jas lightly knocked on Nysha's door and opened it to find her flinging her belongings together in preparation for the last flight that night. Charlotte followed her into the room shortly after that and gave Nysha a long hug. After seven weeks of living in the same house, the two of them had grown close.

'I really thought I had a chance,' said Nysha, her big brown eyes filled with tears.

'I thought you were happy to be going home?' Charlotte said quietly.

'It'll be nice to see your family again, won't it?' offered Jas.

'That's true,' sniffed Nysha. 'I'm going to miss you, Charlotte, but I'm not sure I could take another week of the bitchiness between Gabby and Alex. Dylan's a fool if he doesn't pick you at the end of this.'

Charlotte silently helped Nysha pack up the rest of her belongings, but Jas noticed her blush at Nysha's last comment.

The next morning Dylan dashed to the airport to await the arrival of his mother and Ruby. He hadn't seen his daughter in almost two months and was at the airport two hours early, he was so excited. Later that day, he'd introduce her to Charlotte, Gabby and Alex before a week of alone-dates with the final three women. The following Saturday, he would decide on who was the perfect match for Mr Right.

The entire crew fell in love with Ruby straight away. She'd inherited her dad's brown eyes and sunny demeanour, and laughed and smiled constantly. Dylan spent the morning with her, letting her run around the crew's villa and be showered with attention by everyone. She was a real sweetie.

Meanwhile, in Villa Rosa's office, Jas and Monica broke away from the crew for a quiet cup of coffee together.

'Our final three,' mused Jas. 'Who would've thought Gabriella Bellamy-Hughes would have made it this far?'

'Great villain for TV, though,' Monica said, as she always said when Gabby's name was brought up. It was true. Nice girls didn't often come first in the world of showbiz.

'Can you believe we're going into our final week?' Jas asked.

'No. It's flown by. I'm really going to miss this place. Who do you think Dylan will choose? It's gotta be Alex, right? She's so stunning even I've got a girl-crush on her.'

'Oh, I hope it's Charlotte, she's such a babe.' As one of the youngest in the competition, even younger than Lila, Jas had a fondness for Charlotte. Jas still hadn't spoken to Lila since their fight and was instead directing her big-sisterly energies towards Charlotte, listening to her gush about how much she was falling for Dylan and how alone she felt since Melody had left. Now, with Nysha gone as well, Charlotte was bound to feel even more insecure, up against Gabby and Alex, who were by far the two strongest and most confident women in the whole series.

'How are you feeling about going home? You still haven't spoken to Luke, have you?'

Jas shook her head. By now she'd told Monica all about her two nights with Luke weeks ago. Although she missed him being around, she was so embarrassed about the way it had ended she was almost glad that he was out of sight so she could avoid dealing with the situation for as long as possible. It wasn't exactly the most mature approach, but her priority had to be finishing the show.

Thankfully, they were all so busy with the series – filming and finalising dates by day, and either editing footage with Lyndsey or hanging out with Charlotte or Monica at night – she had kept herself suitably distracted.

'I did some digging, you know,' Monica said. 'I spoke to the girls in the office back home and apparently Luke's on holiday now with his family for his dad's sixtieth birthday.'

Jas wondered if the pretty brunette had gone with them, or if she was still on the scene at all. Yet another thing Luke and she hadn't talked about. Jas wondered if she would be his girlfriend now if she had been more upfront with him from the start.

'Why don't you call him?' Monica suggested.

Jas shook her head. 'If he wanted to speak to me, he would. I'll be back in just over a week anyway. I think talking to him in person is best.'

'Good plan. And we've got our wrap party on the twenty-ninth of September.' It was the day they were all flying home. 'He's bound to come to that and will be desperate to see you by then. I'll text him to make sure he knows the date. It will all work out, babe.'

Jas loved Monica's optimism. 'Come on then, let's get back to work.' They were about to head over to Villa Valencia so that Dylan could introduce Ruby to his finalists. First Jas pulled him aside for an on-camera interview.

'You're clearly delighted to have Ruby here,' she began. 'How important is it that whoever Miss Right is, she really bonds with your daughter?'

'It's incredibly important,' Dylan replied. 'Ruby is everything to me, my entire world, and I want to share that with the woman of my dreams. And I know the woman of my dreams is in that other villa.'

'So you have strong feelings for all of them?'

'I never thought it was possible to be strongly attracted to three women at the same time. They're all so amazing and my feelings are really developing from like to love.'

'Is there a frontrunner to win at this stage?'

'I think there's one woman who has stolen my heart, yes. But we'll have to see how the next week goes.'

Dylan would be arriving any minute and Charlotte couldn't wait to meet his daughter and his mother, Diana. She and Alex sat on the terrace filled with anticipation. Charlotte was wearing a cute yellow playsuit and Alex denim shorts and a white t-shirt. Gabriella flounced down to join them, typically overdressed in white trousers and platforms. Had she never run around after a toddler before?

'Going somewhere special?' teased Alex when she took in Gabriella's attire. 'You do know we're going down to the beach, not to Ascot races?'

Gabriella simply smiled and sat down on the other side of the terrace. Charlotte didn't attempt to make conversation with her. She knew by now that being sociable with her rivals was not Gabriella's strong point.

'Hello, hello?' Dylan's booming voice echoed through the villa as he walked in, two cameras following him and the most adorable little girl holding his hand. At the sight of him, Gabby shot to her feet, smiling widely. He kissed all three women on the cheek and then bent down to his daughter's level.

'And this little princess is Ruby. Want to say hello to Daddy's friends, sweetie?'

Charlotte bent down and beamed at the four-year-old. 'Hi, Ruby! Wow, your daddy didn't tell me how tall you were!'

Even frosty Gabriella softened in the presence of Ruby, who was so playful that within minutes she'd insisted on the three women accompanying her while she explored the pool area and gardens of the villa. She held onto Charlotte's and Alex's hands as she did so, with Gabriella not leaving Dylan's side.

'I wanna go swimming!' Ruby announced, insisting that her new friends join her.

Diana gently nudged Charlotte. 'She likes you,' she said, smiling and nodding towards Ruby.

'Oh, it's hard not to fall in love with her,' said Charlotte.

'You seem very comfortable around children.' Diana was a softly spoken woman in her late fifties who wasn't anything like as boisterous as her son or granddaughter, but was clearly devoted to both of them and couldn't stop smiling now that they were all back together.

'I've got a Godson in London I'm very close to,' Charlotte replied.

'And you want kids of your own?'

Dylan sprang over and kissed his mother on her forehead. 'Mum, stop giving Charlotte the third degree!' Diana held her hands up in protest and Charlotte laughed, instantly warming to her. Meeting Dylan's family had only increased her feelings for him. But, much to her surprise, she wasn't the only one bonding with Ruby. On the other side of the pool, Gabriella had the little girl on her lap and was plaiting her hair. Dylan went over to join them.

Charlotte didn't have Gabriella down for the sort of woman who enjoyed mucking around with kids. For someone so cold, she certainly knew how to turn on the charm when she needed to.

Dylan decided to spend the entire next day with his mother and Ruby, the day after that with Charlotte, the next with Alex and the final one with Gabriella, before making his final decision.

On their date, Dylan and Charlotte took a trip to the north of the island while Diana and Ruby went to explore the old town. They strolled hand in hand through quaint cobbled streets, went snorkelling in the sea and drank white wine while eating fish caught locally. Charlotte was blissfully happy in Dylan's company. Conversation flowed easily and their mutual love of fitness meant they had a lot in common, though Charlotte realised their connection went deeper than that: they also shared the same values, hopes, dreams and ambitions.

Charlotte, however, could never set aside the fact that she was competing with two other beautiful women, both just as smitten with Dylan and vying for his attention while equally desperate to win the show so they could have their shot at fame. And there was always a small part of Charlotte that questioned Dylan's own authenticity. How well did she really know him, after all? Would he become someone else she'd got wrong? She was always so naïve when it came to men.

During lunch in the town square, they gazed out onto the peaceful sea – a world away from the busy and boisterous party areas of the rest of Ibiza.

'It's so beautiful here,' said Charlotte, who by now wasn't fazed by the cameras circling them. 'I had no idea that Ibiza was like this. I thought it was all super clubs and boat parties.'

'Me too,' laughed Dylan. 'Who knew there was so much more to see? I have to say, I'm going to really miss it.'

'Well, you won't get any sympathy from me. You're off to the Maldives in a couple of months.'

They both smiled but there was an awkward silence then. Of course, Dylan couldn't reveal yet who he'd be taking with him on the winning trip, even if he did know by now. Charlotte hoped she hadn't sounded desperate.

'Charlotte, there's something I need to talk to you about.'

'Go on.'

'I hope you know how much I care for you.'

'And I care for you too, Dylan.'

'And we've talked about this before, but I can't escape the fact that I feel you're holding something back from me. Like you're not giving me your full self. Is there something you're not telling me?'

'No, of course not. Like I said, I've just been hurt so many times before. I suppose I'm still questioning your feelings too ...'

Dylan edged closer to her and held her face in his hands.

'You never need to question my feelings for you,' he said, before leaning in for a long kiss. Charlotte melted into him. There was no going back now.

After their romantic day together Dylan walked her up to her room at Villa Valencia and kissed her again at the door, this time with more passion, holding her close.

'Invite me in,' he said as he softly trailed his lips over her neck. Charlotte was burning with desire for him by this point, and going into her bedroom alone would be torture, but she'd made the mistake before of sleeping with men too soon, let alone the fact that the villa was crawling with cameras. This was sure to be shown on TV and, while there were no cameras in the bedrooms, it wouldn't take a genius to work out what they'd be doing if she led him in right now. What if he didn't pick her on Friday night? She'd not only have had her heart broken, she'd be the laughing stock of the nation.

'It's not a good idea,' she said. 'Not tonight.'

Dylan groaned and kissed her again, this time scooping her up and turning towards her door, but Charlotte wriggled free. She'd love to wake up with Dylan tomorrow, but him leaving her then to spend a romantic day with Alex was too painful to think about.

'Stop!' she laughed, even though the fact that he wanted her so badly was a huge turn-on. 'Not tonight,' she repeated.

'Okay,' Dylan replied, backing away. 'I can respect that. See you soon, Charlotte. I'll be thinking about you.'

'Goodnight, Dylan.' He blew her another kiss as he turned to go back to the guest villa.

Charlotte couldn't stop smiling as she turned her door handle, only to be startled by a voice close behind her. It made her jump.

'Hi, Charlotte.'

'Alex! You scared me. What are you doing up so late?' *And how on earth didn't I see you before?*

'I'm just off to bed. How was your day with Dylan?'

'Um, yeah, really great.'

'I wondered if I could borrow your straighteners? Mine started making a buzzing sound then stopped working.'

'Sure. You, er, want them now?'

'Is that okay? I'm getting up super early tomorrow for my date with Dylan and want to look my best.'

'Yeah, 'course.' Charlotte walked into her room with Alex close behind her and fetched her GHD straighteners.

'Here you go.'

'Thanks! You never know, tomorrow might be my lucky day. Again.' And, with a wink, Alex sauntered out.

The words preyed on Charlotte's mind as she got ready for bed. Alex had just not-so-subtly implied that she and Dylan had already hooked up. Charlotte felt a pang of jealousy at the thought, though she was even more relieved now that she hadn't brought Dylan into her room. He'd been quite insistent. Had he tried the same tactic with Alex, then? It certainly sounded like it from what she'd just said. Then again, Alex could just be teasing Charlotte. She told herself Dylan wasn't the sort of man to sleep around. But it was hard to be sure.

Chapter 33

The next two days were hell for Charlotte. Knowing that Dylan would be having alone-time with Alex and Gabriella, she tried to keep her mind off them all by busying herself as much as possible. She Skyped her parents as well as Maya and Rafi, went for long runs and swam lengths around the pool, took herself off to the beach and found yoga classes in Ibiza Town.

Things only got harder for her when she returned from dinner with a couple of crew members the next night and was at the door of her room when she heard Alex and Dylan laughing together. They were arriving back from their day out and heading into the cinema room with a bottle of wine.

Charlotte obsessed about that all night, convinced not only that they'd be having sex, but that Alex would be crowned the winner and then be jetting off to the Maldives with Dylan for their romantic 'mini-moon' in a few weeks' time.

*

On Thursday morning, Charlotte woke up early to go for a run. As she searched in her beach bag for her headphones she found a small, squidgy toy – a stuffed pig that belonged to Ruby. Charlotte remembered putting it in her bag after they'd been at the pool together a few days ago and she was clearing up. She'd forgotten all about it but figured the little girl would surely be missing it, so decided to drop it outside the guest accommodation where Dylan stayed as she went out for her run. It was barely 7 a.m., he definitely wouldn't be up this early.

Dylan's own private villa was right next to the girls', with just a thin path separating them. As Charlotte sauntered down it there was silence except for the sound of birdsong. It really was a beautiful spot. Charlotte was going to miss it but she concentrated on the thought of being home, back with her family and friends. Two months was a long time to be away. Approaching Dylan's door where she planned to drop the toy, Charlotte was deep in thought about what presents to bring home for Rafi when she stopped dead in her tracks. Then she thought better of it, not wanting an encounter, and stepped smartly behind a tall shrub. For who should be creeping out of Dylan's villa at 7 a.m., barefoot and wearing a black mini dress, hair dishevelled and last night's make-up still caked around her eyes, but Gabriella.

Charlotte held her breath and hoped Gabriella hadn't seen her dive for cover. The tall, skinny redhead looked around to check if anyone was watching her take the very blatant walk of shame. With her silver high heels held in one hand and black evening clutch bag in the other, she scuttled back into Villa Valencia. Charlotte threw the toy pig towards the door and ran away as fast as she could, also hoping no one had seen her. She raced down to her usual track and ran through the shock of what she'd seen, her eyes prickling with red-hot tears. So, Gabby had spent the night with Dylan. Was it just last night or were they secretly shagging every night? And for how long? All this week Charlotte was convinced Alex was the one to beat, but was Dylan really sleeping with both of them?

Charlotte tried to run off her anxieties but needed to talk things through, so sought out the one other person in Ibiza she could trust. Jas.

She found her in Villa Rosa working on her laptop, though she immediately ran over to Charlotte when she saw that she'd been crying and gave her a hug.

'You don't want to be with a man like that anyway,' Jas insisted when Charlotte filled her in.

'It's so gross,' she replied. 'God knows who else he's been sleeping with, especially from what I saw of the other contestants. Mackenzie, Georgia ... and who knows who else!' Charlotte didn't want to be judgemental but she was growing sick of being so nice all the time. 'Surely you know everything that's gone on, Jas? You film it all.'

'You know there are no cameras in the bedrooms, babe, I don't know what goes on in there. And you know that even if I did know, I'm not allowed to tell you.' That was true. Charlotte knew she and Jas had grown close over the past weeks but Jas had every other contestant's best interest at heart too and had all their trust, not to mention abiding

266

by the rules of the show that stated she wasn't allowed to tell contestants anything so secret as who might or might not be sleeping with each other.

'I feel so stupid,' Charlotte continued. 'I know he's been kissing us all but, honestly, it didn't even occur to me before this week that he was actually having sex with any of us. I didn't think he was like that.'

Jas said nothing, which Charlotte only took for further proof that Dylan *had* been sleeping around. She figured that even if Jas was allowed to say anything, she would be too polite. And she wouldn't want to upset Charlotte.

'Listen, honey, I know it's hard. But just remember that, no matter what you feel for Dylan, you've only known him eight weeks. That's all. And clearly, if this *is* how he is, then he isn't the man for you. If it's shown on TV that he's been sleeping with a bunch of women, he's the one who will be judged and you'll always be the lady who turned him down.'

'That's true.'

'And you're down to the finals, which means loads of air-time so who knows what will come of that? I know fame isn't what you came here for, and you hate attention, but everyone will love you. Don't think about him, think about you and what this will do for your career.'

'Thanks, Jas.' But Charlotte really couldn't care less about being famous. She just didn't want her heart broken on national TV.

Even though it was only the following night, it felt like a lifetime to Charlotte before the final rose ceremony. By this point she only wanted it over with so she could go home and see her family.

Even though she'd been nervous before every previous rose ceremony, she was always excited about the prospect of seeing Dylan again and before the ceremony, or indeed any date with him, she'd spent ages getting ready, a smile plastered on her face. Now, she couldn't feel any further from that. Those images of Alex swishing out of her room talking about how 'lucky' she was going to get, then of her and Dylan sloping off to the cinema room, and the sight of Gabriella emerging from his villa that morning, were all scorched into Charlotte's mind.

As it was the very last ceremony, the three finalists were told to wear their most glamorous gown. Charlotte's outfit was a floor-length slinky Topshop Unique dress, which she paired with gold heels and red lipstick, her hair elegantly straightened. If she was losing, she was determined to look fabulous doing so. As she arrived for the champagne ceremony, as expected Gabriella was wearing a long, golden and dramatic designer number that probably cost a small fortune. Even Charlotte had to admit she looked beautiful in the gown, which made her pale skin glisten. Alex was dressed in a short, bright pink shift dress with leather trimming, and platforms that showed off her bronzed legs.

It was a few minutes before the winner was to be announced and Charlotte had popped to the toilet to freshen up her lipstick. As she emerged, she walked straight into Dylan.

'Hey,' he said. 'Wow, you look sensational, Charlotte.'

'Thanks.' They stood in awkward silence. Dylan was just as distant with Charlotte as she'd planned to be with him. Where usually he'd greet her with a huge hug and talk was easy, now there was a definite air of tension between them. Why was *he* being funny with her? It made Charlotte angry. She was the one who should by rights be giving him the silent treatment. But anything was better than this awful tension, so she broke the silence.

'So, how was your day? Get up to much?'

'Er, yeah, Mum and Ruby and I went down to the beach with Gabby.'

'Oh.' The mention of that name was like a stab to Charlotte's heart.

'What about you, what have you been up to?'

'Oh, nothing much. I went for a run. Hung out with Jas a bit.

'Ruby was asking about you today.'

'Oh, yeah?'

'I think she missed you.'

'She doesn't even know me.'

'I think I missed you, too.' Dylan took Charlotte's hand but she pulled it away.

'Speaking of Ruby, I dropped off her toy outside your door yesterday morning. You know, the stuffed pink pig? I must have taken it by accident after we were in the pool the other day.'

'That was you? I thought it was one of the crew. Thank you. That must've been early, what time was it? Why didn't you knock and come in?'

'About seven. I saw that you had company.' Charlotte hadn't intended to bring this up, let alone snap at him like that. As soon as she did Dylan blushed. He looked ashamed, and quite right, too.

'Charlotte, let me explain …'

She shook her head. She didn't want to get into this. Charlotte hated confrontation.

'You don't need to explain Dylan. You're a single man. You can do what you like.'

'You're really angry with me. This isn't how I wanted our night to go. Can I just explain?' But he didn't sound that sorry or, frankly, as if he cared that much. Something in his tone sounded like he was pissed off with *her*, which only made Charlotte angrier.

'I think I should go back out so we can get this over with. Why put either of us through any more?'

This was it: Dylan's last chance to beg her to stay, to say how sorry he was, that the night with Gabriella was a mistake and Charlotte was the one he loved.

But instead he shook his head. 'I'm confused.'

It wasn't good enough. 'You know what, I'll make it easy for you.' And with that, Charlotte walked away, back out to the lights and the cameras.

The three women lined up, looking straight ahead as crew members set up the cameras to their perfect shots. All three contestants had already packed their bags. Two of them would be on a plane back to London that night. The winner would leave with Dylan and his family first thing tomorrow.

Dylan finally emerged, holding his last rose, and began his closing speech. While he spoke, he looked at Charlotte.

'This is the hardest decision I've ever had to make. I came into this competition thinking it would be easy. That there would be a clear frontrunner. I mean, how could I possibly fall for three such amazing women? Well, you're in the final because I can see myself with all or any of you. Charlotte, you have the biggest heart of anyone I've met. And you don't even know how beautiful you are, inside and out.' She met his gaze at this, fiercely resisting a strong urge to run over and kiss him. Was this his way of making everything okay?

He turned to Alex then. 'And, Alex, you astound me. I've learnt more from you than anyone else here. But ...' He faltered for a moment.

'I've also come to realise that some people have surprised me in bad ways. After all, how well can you truly know someone after only eight weeks?'

What did he mean by that?

'And as much as I have strong feelings for all of you, there's one person who has really shone out.' With that, he knelt down on one knee in front of the person nobody had expected to win.

'Gabby, will you accept this rose and be my girlfriend?'

She flung her arms around him. 'Oh, my darling, yes, yes, yes!'

Even the crew were shocked. Charlotte made eyes at Jas, who mouthed 'What?' to her. But Charlotte wasn't that surprised. Not now.

Alex stormed out, pushing a camera aside as she did so. Monica went running after her. Gabriella burst into tears and rested her head on Dylan's shoulder. He looked over at Charlotte, though she had no idea why. He'd just made his choice, Gabriella was the one he wanted to be with. Remembering the cameras and keeping her composure, she gave Gabriella a hug, though all she felt was a bony, cold back.

'Congratulations, Gabby. I hope you two are very happy.'

Gabriella turned around, arms raised to embrace her, but said in Charlotte's ear, 'You gave it your best shot but did you really think you had a chance?' Then she pulled away, giving Charlotte a look of pure hatred before smiling sweetly at Dylan.

Charlotte was utterly taken aback. She smiled politely and gave Dylan a quick hug, but as she made to walk away he grabbed her hand. Their eyes met for a fraction of a second before Gabriella noticed and batted his hand away, pulling Dylan towards her and posing for the cameras surrounding them.

Charlotte went to change for her flight, leaving the winning couple to their big moment. What a fool she felt. She'd promised herself before she came into this whole experience that she wouldn't have her heart broken – and that was exactly what had happened. She'd really thought she had a chance with Dylan and, even tonight, retained a sliver of hope that everything would be okay. She could feel the tears rising. Ken the cameraman followed her as she walked back to her room, managing not to break down until the door was safely closed behind her.

Chapter 34

Jas landed back at Gatwick the following morning. All the way through the flight she'd thought about how heartbroken Charlotte had looked the previous night when they had hugged goodbye at the airport. But Jas had bigger things to worry about. Filming over, she needed to get her own tattered personal life back in order. Burrell had arranged for company cars to take her and Monica home. Leaving the terminal, Monica and Jas parted ways with a hug.

'See you tonight for the crew's wrap party?' Monica asked.

'Wouldn't miss it,' Jas replied.

'Are Meg and Lila still coming?'

'Meg, yes, she's driving down as we speak. Lila, who knows?'

'You've still not spoken?'

Jas shook her head. She'd not spoken to either of her sisters over the last two weeks, just had a few texts from Meg arranging her visit to London, but Jas had been so busy she hadn't thought much about it. Now she was home she'd arrange to see Lila properly. She couldn't stand the thought of Richard getting close to her youngest sister but it didn't bother her nearly as much as the thought of not being on speaking terms with her. And she couldn't wait to see Meg and get all the gossip over their weekend together.

Jas hoped Lila might even still be at her flat when she got home but she opened the door to a silent – and spotless – home. *No break-ins or damaged furniture. Well done, Lila.*

Jas dragged her suitcase to her room and threw on her favourite pink and grey pyjamas. Then she padded to the kitchen and made a steaming cup of tea. Making a brew was the first thing she did after any holiday she'd been on. She was glad to be home and had a good few hours ahead of binge-worthy telly before Meg arrived for their night out. Ibiza might have been sunny, sandy and utterly glamorous, but Jas was delighted to be home. Even if she did have a divorce hearing looming in two weeks.

Jas had been away for two months but it felt like a lifetime. So much had happened. She'd flown to Ibiza, confused about her feelings for Luke, and had now returned more confused than ever. Jas's head was telling her to let it go and just be friends with him for the time being. She'd only known him for six months after all, how attached could she really be? And if Richard found out she'd slept with another man while they were still married, albeit separated, could that affect the divorce? But letting Luke go so easily didn't feel right at all. Monica had invited him to the crew's wrap party tonight and Jas hoped he'd be there so she could explain, talk to him rationally.

Jas's door buzzer was pressed at 5 p.m., just as she was freshly out of the shower and blow-drying her hair. She was deeply tanned from her trip and had laid out one of her favourite dresses on the bed; the bottom half was a cream-coloured pencil skirt and the top was peach with thin straps and a low neckline. It was a purchase from Meg's boutique the last time Jas went up to Manchester. Still wrapped in a towel, she bounded downstairs. 'Hiii!' She hugged her sister tightly for a few seconds.

'Sorry I'm so late, the traffic was horrendous.'

'You're here now.' Jas took Meg's holdall and ushered her inside and into the living room. 'We've got about an hour before we need to leave. Is that enough time for you to get showered and ready?' Jas realised she was rattling out orders and stopped herself.

'You okay, Meg? You look pale.'

'Just tired from the drive.'

'Sit right here, I'll open a bottle of prosecco.'

'I'm okay with just a cuppa right now, if that's okay? I've caught you midway through getting ready. Go and put something on and then let's chat.'

'Gotcha. Wait there.' Jas ran off and reappeared in an old Britney Spears t-shirt, a souvenir from seeing her play at the O2 with her sisters almost a decade ago. She busied herself making tea for Meg, talking about Ibiza and then doing her make-up while sitting on the sofa, using a hand-mirror.

'Don't you want to start getting ready? What are you wearing? Raid my wardrobe if you like. If you can find anything Lila hasn't poached, that is. If she thinks for one second I'm going to forget that my Maje floral top is missing, she has another think coming!'

'Actually, Jas, I'm absolutely exhausted. Do you mind if I don't come tonight? I just don't feel like myself. I don't want to drag you down.'

'Oh, babe, of course. Don't come if you're feeling rotten. I've got loads of time to catch up with you. Can I get you anything?'

'Thanks, love. Just my luck to get sick before a much-needed night out. I think I just need to rest.'

Jas gave her a hug. 'You're here, that's the main thing. Now all we need is to get Lila out of her grotty squat. I'm going to go and throw my dress on.'

Meg followed Jas and watched as she wriggled into her dress, did up her black strappy heels and finished her look with a slick of lipgloss.

'Lila's moved out of that flat, you know. She's living back at Mum and Dad's.'

'Oh, is she?' Jas was hurt that she didn't even know where her sister was living. Then she smiled. 'Wait, does that mean she's not taking on the job at awful Richard's office?'

Meg sat down at the end of the bed. 'Nope. Says she's done with London now.'

'Oh, for God's sake.' Jas thought her sister was just being dramatic again.

'Richard tried it on with her a couple of weeks ago.'

'What!'

'Yep. Took her to some club, got completely shit-faced and tried to get her back to his flat. When she turned him down he launched into a massive tirade, slagging her off and saying we were all cheap money-grabbing whores. *Then* he buggered off and left her with a £200 bar tab.'

Jas slumped down onto the bed next to Meg, shaking her head in disbelief. 'What an utter arsehole.'

'Yep. I went round to Mum and Dad's and she told me all about it. She feels really scared by the whole thing, Jas. It's made her want to leave London. Mum and Dad don't know what's really been going on, she just turned up there a couple of days ago with her bags, saying she was done with the place. She's worried about seeing you, though. Thought you'd never forgive her for hanging out with him.' Meg burst into tears. 'God, what's wrong with me? I'm an emotional wreck these days.'

Jas gave her a hug. She *was* annoyed with Lila for hanging out with Richard. And not just that, but also siding with him against Jas. But while Lila was certainly old and bright enough to know better, picturing a drunk, sleazy Richard with his hands all over her little sister made Jas's blood boil.

'I mean, isn't that like incest anyway, trying it on with her? Seriously, what is wrong with that guy?'

'Lila reckons he's unhinged. Says she's never known anyone act so creepy and intense.'

'I need to phone her.' Jas dialled but Lila's mobile went straight to answerphone. She dialled her parents' landline next but no answer from there either. 'Shit! Where are they?' She paced furiously up and down the room.

'Calm down. They've probably just popped to the pictures or out for dinner.'

'How was she yesterday?'

'Pleased to be home. She feels guilty and very silly. I think mainly she wants to forget about it. She's worried about how you're going to react. She asked me not to tell you, but how could I not?'

It was true. Meg and Jas had never kept secrets from each other.

Jas's phone bleeped, alerting her that the Addison Lee car she'd ordered was here to collect her. 'Well, I can't go out now.'

'Of course you can. It's a big night for you and you deserve it.'

'I'm not in the mood. I want to speak to Lila and I should look after you.'

'I'm fine. Lila is fine. You staying home while I snooze in front of *Coronation Street* isn't going to change anything. Call Lila again from the cab and if you don't speak to her tonight, you will tomorrow.'

The cab beeped angrily outside. Jas didn't feel right about going out but Meg insisted she did and so, reluctantly, Jas got in the cab, promising she wouldn't be late home. As the black SUV trawled though the London traffic, Jas impatiently tried to ring her younger sister, but continued to be put straight through to Lila's voicemail. Then Jas's phone rang with an incoming call and she answered immediately, hoping it would be Lila.

'Jasmine, I'm sorry for ringing on a Saturday, but I'm on holiday at the start of next week, so wanted to give you the news as soon as possible.'

'Oh, hello, Ralph. No worries. What's up?'

'Bad news, I'm afraid. Your court hearing has been postponed until November.'

'What? How? Why? But … I've waited so long. They can't do this!'

'I'm afraid they can. It's a judicial restriction. This is a very busy time of year and the judge had to go to another case. The next available date I could get was the twentieth of November. It's only six weeks or so.'

Easy for him to say. Six weeks felt like a lifetime to Jas. She felt sick to her stomach that she'd ever let Richard touch her; the fact she was still married to him made her feel physically ill.

'As I've said before, this is low priority in terms of the family courts. It's completely standard for a contested divorce hearing to take this long. I warned you, Jasmine.'

'Twentieth of November,' she said glumly, wondering how things could get any worse for her.

At the party that night Jas stayed close to the bar, knocking back shots of tequila and ringing Lila incessantly, but each time it went to voicemail. Fortunately, the party was so lively no one seemed to notice how drunk she was getting. The entire entertainment floor of Channel 6 seemed to have shown up but Jas shied away from making small talk with anyone.

She was in a foul mood. She felt helpless, useless and pathetic. She should have been there for Lila. Her own childish pride had stopped her from reaching out since their last argument. If she'd spoken to her sister sooner maybe none of this would have happened. How could Jas ever have married such a creep? She'd known Richard was a sleaze, but trying it on with her sister just to get at his wife seemed insane. She really hoped that he would be out of their lives before too long.

Jas looked around. Her vision was decidedly blurry but there was no sign of Luke. Whatever logic was left in Jas's head, it told her that phoning him was a good idea. It rang out. Jas phoned again. And again. After the fourth attempt she gave up, not wishing to embarrass herself any further. He obviously had no desire to speak to her. Just another thing in Jas's life she'd messed up. She wobbled to the bar when she felt a familiar hand on the small of her back. She looked up to see Luke's dark eyes staring down at her.

'Whoa, you all right there? Looks like you're struggling a bit, Whiteley.'

'Luke! You're here.'

'I sure am. How about a strong black coffee for you, eh? Or a glass of water? I'm having a Diet Coke.'

'White wine, please.'

'Let's start with water.' Luke ordered from the bartender as Jas propped herself onto one of the stools. When the water came she turned her nose up and ordered a large white wine. Luke eyed her suspiciously.

'Sorry I missed all your calls just now. I was parking the car. Figured you were here anyway.'

'Parking the car? You're not drinking?'

'Nope. I'm playing rugby tomorrow with the lads so wanted to keep a clear head.'

Jas rolled her eyes. Mr bloody Perfect.

'I thought we should talk about what happened in Ibiza,' started Luke. 'I'm sorry for driving off like that but, as you can imagine, it came as a shock. I needed some time to figure out how I felt about all this.' Jas glugged her wine, half listening to him, half thinking how much she hated Richard. 'Jas?'

'Huh?'

'Were you listening to me? I was saying we should grab a coffee and talk about all this. If you want to.'

'Sure, let's go.' Jas knocked back almost a full glass of wine, after which she was so hammered she stood up only to fall directly back down again. Luke caught her.

'I didn't mean right now this second. Jesus, how much have you had to drink?'

She pushed him aside. 'Oh, piss off!' This made a few heads turn.

Monica appeared and quickly steadied her. 'Babe, I think you should call it a night, yeah? Why don't I ring for a cab?'

'I'll take her, I've got my car. I know her address.'

'Thanks, Luke.'

He led Jas outside. She shook her arm free. 'Bloody men. You all think you know best.'

'Okay,' Luke said, patiently. 'Come on, let's get you home. My car's just here.'

The drive made Jas feel sick so she kept her eyes closed and they sat in silence until Luke pulled up outside her building.

'Want to come inside for a coffee?' she slurred.

'I don't think that's the best idea.'

Jas threw her hands in the air dramatically. 'Fine, let's talk here.'

'Maybe tomorrow would be better, when you've slept this off?'

'Stop condescending me! That's all you men do, isn't it? If I'm not being patronised by you, it's by Burrell. You want to control everything all the time, don't you? You can't stand it when things don't go your way.'

Luke looked at her in disbelief. 'I don't believe this. Look who's throwing a tantrum about not getting *her* own way. Fine, let's talk now. You should've told me you were married.'

'No shit.'

'It's going to be like that, is it? God, you're a nightmare. I thought we could try to sort things out but if this is what it's like being with you, forget it. I've had enough crazy women in my time.'

Jas was furious now. She knew she was throwing a full-on tantrum that she would no doubt regret tomorrow, but she'd never expected mild-mannered Luke to hit back with that. Her, crazy?

'That's your thing, isn't it, Luke? I guess your ex and I have that in common. Crazy me, being married without telling you, and crazy her for aborting your baby. What a pair we are! I'm certainly more sympathetic to her now.'

She had no idea where that last sentence had come from but as soon as the words left her lips, Jas held her hand over her mouth in horror.

'Get out.'

'I didn't mean that. I can't believe I said that.'

Luke looked straight ahead. 'I said get out,' he repeated.

'I didn't mean that. I'm drunk, I'm emotional, I found out something tonight that ... well, come on, Luke.'

'Jas, I can't do this with you. The lies, the games, the tantrums. I'm not into all this drama.'

'Neither am I!'

'Really? I think you are. I don't think we're right for each other.'

Jas didn't know what to say to that. She glumly stepped out of the car, feeling disgusted by her own behaviour. What was wrong with her? No sooner had she closed the passenger door than Luke sped off. It was the second time that losing her temper had left her feeling wretched. But one thing was clear to her: this time she'd taken it too far.

Chapter 35

Jas was off work for the next few weeks while *Mr Right* was in deep editing mode. The last thing she needed was more time alone to spend moping around her flat, regretting her behaviour with Luke. The day after her blow-out argument with him she packed her bags and drove back up to Manchester with Meg, to stay with her parents and spend time with them, Meg and Lila. It had been months since Jas had been up there and all she wanted now was to see her family.

Helen and Graham Whiteley had lived in the same house for over thirty years, ever since Helen was pregnant with Meg. It was in a quiet suburban street on the outskirts of the city. It wasn't big; there were always two sisters sharing a room at one time, but it was home and always would be. Helen had decorated it beautifully and she and Graham kept the small garden immaculate.

Meg pulled her Ford Ka into the driveway and Helen rushed out when she heard the sound of the engine.

'Hello girls! Jas, come here and give your mum a big kiss. Graham, help Jas with her bags.'

'I've got it Mum, it's okay.'

Graham, a sixty-six-year-old retired project manager for the local council, ushered Meg and Jas through into the living room, insisting he would take in any bags.

'Hi, Dad.'

'Hello, love. Come in, come in. Good to see you. Meg, is Oscar coming?'

Having lived in a household of four women for twenty-five years, Graham was delighted when Meg married Oscar two years ago and had insisted they watch sport together every weekend. The girls always teased him.

'He's on his way, Dad, don't worry. We know how much you love your favourite child!'

Helen ordered Graham to go and make a pot of tea. 'Jasmine, it has been months. Let me look at you. Oh, you look beautiful. Very tanned. I hope you were using sun lotion over in Ibiza? But you're looking very skinny, too. We need to feed you.'

'I'm fine, Mum.'

'Meg, is your sister eating? She looks very skinny.'

'Yes, Mum, she's fine.'

If there was one thing Helen loved, it was fussing over her family. She was an amazing cook and as soon as Jas walked through the house she was greeted with the sweet waft of something baking and her mouth watered.

'What have you been making?'

'Chocolate muffins. We thought as the whole family is here we could chill out for a bit together then go for a walk and after that I'll do a nice roast chicken. How does that sound?'

Jas felt instantly relaxed. Compared to her own flat, where there was generally nothing in the fridge except wine and cheese, coming to her parents' house was like staying in a hotel. It was peaceful, cosy, and the supply of food was endless.

'Meg, you look ever so pale, are you okay?'

'To be honest, Mum, I've got a bit of a headache that hasn't gone away. I feel utterly exhausted.'

Jas looked at her sister with concern. 'Still? You must be coming down with something. Why don't you go and have a lie-down?'

'A lie-down is a very good idea,' put in Helen. 'Go and lie down on our bed and I'll come up with some peppermint tea. I wonder if it's the same thing Lila has. She's not been herself since she's been back.'

'I was just about to ask you,' said Jas quickly. 'What's wrong with her? Is she okay?'

'Oh, I don't know,' said Helen. 'I think she's exhausted, quite frankly. Living the big life in London, always out, never sleeping. It's good for her to be home.'

'Generation Snowflake!' called Graham from the kitchen. 'In my day we didn't get exhaustion. They're too entitled, this generation. You spoil them, Helen!'

Helen batted this away as Meg and Jas smiled at each other. Nothing changed in this house. Jas got up. 'I might go and check on Lila then, see how she's doing.'

'Tell her to get out of bed and come and say hello to her family!' called Graham.

Since the girls had moved out, Helen had redecorated their rooms. She loved having a project. Jas threw her bags into the room she'd shared with Meg for years. Long gone were the two single beds. In their place was a double bed with a turquoise quilt and matching cushions. Everything else was white.

Jas gently knocked on Lila's door and, not hearing an answer, let herself in. Lila's room had been painted magnolia. The curtains were drawn and it smelt awfully musty. The window clearly hadn't been opened in days. Jas could see a crumpled figure under the bedsheets, snoring softly.

'Lila?' Jas rubbed her sister's shoulders and waited for her to open her eyes before pulling open the curtains.

'Ow!' Lila squinted, pulling the pillow over her eyes.

'Come on, little one, you need some light and fresh air in here. I brought you a cup of tea. And one of Mum's muffins.'

Lila removed the pillow and eyed her sister suspiciously. 'Chocolate muffin?'

'Uh-huh.'

Lila sat up in bed and rubbed her eyes. She was so petite and looked so much younger than her twenty-five years.

'Did Meg tell you?' asked Lila, sheepishly.

Jas nodded. 'I'm so sorry for not being there for you, not listening to you ... for everything. I feel responsible.'

'You? *I'm* so, so sorry! I'm the awful one here. You've nothing to apologise for, this is all my stupid fault.'

'No, this is all *his* fault, not ours,' Jas corrected her. 'But I feel responsible for letting him into our lives in the first place and then getting between us.'

'You couldn't have known what he'd turn out like. And you can't be there for me all the time, Jas. As much as you want to protect me, I'm a grown woman and I need to make my own choices. I should have known better.'

'Like I said, he is manipulative.'

'You tried to warn me. You were only looking out for me and trying to protect me so please don't feel bad about anything. All those terrible things I said to you ...'

'Forget about it.'

'I didn't mean any of it, sis. I was angry at the world. Richard made me think that I was entitled to all these things but it's bullshit. I don't deserve anything.'

'But you're okay, right? He didn't hurt you, did he?'

'No, no, nothing like that.' Lila went through her entire recent history with Richard, from bumping into him in Print Room to their heavy nights out. She even came clean about the after-party back at Jas's flat, tearing up with shame as she did so.

Jas rubbed Lila's back softly. Her sister felt bad enough, and Jas knew she was sorry.

Lila pulled her knees to her chest. 'I just feel so *stupid*. I really fell for it. The glam treatment, the compliments. He made me feel so special and then, in the space of one night, so completely worthless. I guess it triggered some stuff in me. I started to reassess everything. The next day I knew I wanted to leave London and come home. I obviously couldn't take that job at Curtis Stoddard if it meant I had to see Richard's ugly mug every day.'

'Well, I can't say I'm not happy to hear that. Any idea what you're going to do, though?'

'I'm definitely sick of working in the pub. I think I'm going to phone my manager later and quit.'

'You'll find a great job. I'll help you, promise. And I'll be there from now on. Nothing will get between us again, okay?'

'Okay. But promise me you won't tell Mum or Dad? I don't want to get into the details of what happened with Richard. I'd rather just forget about it.'

"Course not. But you have to come downstairs and make an effort. They're so glad you're home and that we're all together. Drink your tea, have a nice hot shower then come out for a walk with us. I'll change your sheets while you're in the bathroom.'

'Thank you. Promise me we'll never, ever argue again?'

'I promise.'

Jas already felt better. Being back at home made her feel instantly at ease. Her looming divorce hearing and nasty treatment of Luke hung over her like dark clouds, but at least things were mended between her and Lila, which brought Jas huge comfort. She knew that spending the next couple of weeks with the people she loved most was exactly what she needed. But could she really win her divorce in November? She wasn't sure.

Chapter 36

The next few weeks went by blissfully for Jas. Being back at home and around her family helped Lila a great deal. Jas wondered if the brush with Richard, however unsavoury, had actually turned out to be a blessing in disguise. Lila finally seemed to be growing up and making plans. She'd even started looking for a flat-share in Manchester and a 'proper' job, much to Graham's delight.

The rest of Jas's time was spent taking long walks with her family, binge-watching TV series with Lila, and checking in with the editing team in London. Jas was never fully 'off' work' and had even started brainstorming new show concepts to pitch to Harry. Much to her delight, the press department at Channel 6 had started planning the campaign around her show and the buzz about it had reached every outlet going. Lots of the weekly showbiz magazines were requesting interviews with the contestants before they'd even seen who they were. Jas scheduled a conference call with the press team to ensure she was across every single aspect of the campaign and that no spoilers would get out.

'You'll need a new wardrobe,' pointed out Jas one morning as she and Lila were scouting job recruitment websites. 'Why don't we pop into town later and hit the shops? I can help you get a whole new look on the cheap.'

'Okay, sis. Do you reckon she still has that gorgeous cream pencil dress you had your eye on last time? Buy that so I can borrow it off you.'

'Which reminds me, where's my denim jacket?'

'It's upstairs, I swear.'

'And I bought that dress, don't you remember? Only wore it a couple of times though. To the wrap ...' Jas trailed off. The wrap party for *Mr Right*. The last time she'd seen Luke. She'd done a pretty good job of not obsessing too much about him since she'd been home. Worrying about Lila and insisting to her mother that she was eating enough had kept her pretty much occupied. But the thought of that night weighed on Jas now – and not for the first time. She was still mortified by the childish way she'd acted then and in Ibiza as well. She believed that she and Luke had amazing chemistry, but her tantrums were extremely unappealing and she knew it. Now, a week after their last meeting, she still hadn't heard from him and was starting to question if that chemistry was all on her side and not on his. Surely he'd have phoned if he was missing her?

Lila noticed that Jas was staring into the distance. 'What?'

'Nothing. Come on. Let's go see Meg.'

*

Two hours later Jas was trying on clothes in her sister's boutique. The place was a shopper's dream, with so many rows of gorgeous outfits at every price point, large and well-lit changing rooms and a blue velvet sofa outside them – usually full of weary men waiting for their wives or girlfriends. Lila sat on it, texting.

'Ooh, we just got in some wonderful pastel knitwear, Jas. Here.' Meg threw an array of jumpers into the changing room and whizzed around looking for more finds.

Jas stepped out to take a look at herself in a slinky black dress that fitted perfectly. She usually steered clear of black, opting instead for pink, red, blue and white, but Luke had once said how sexy he found black on her and for some reason it had stuck in her mind.

'I have no idea where I'd wear this but I'm into it.'

'Oh, you'll have loads of chances!' said Meg. 'You and your busy social calendar. There'll be an awards do at some point. Or what about the *Mr Right* premiere?'

'Good shout. You certainly have a lot of energy, Meg! You're running around the shop like you're on speed. Only last week you were so exhausted you couldn't move.'

Meg said nothing, but smiled to herself. It didn't go unnoticed by either sister. They both circled her suspiciously.

'Megan Whiteley, what is going on, please?' asked Jas.

Meg looked at them for a moment before a huge grin appeared on her face. 'I'm pregnant!'

The three sisters screamed and hugged.

'Argh! I promised Oscar I wouldn't tell anyone until after the twelve-week scan. You know, in case there are any

292

problems. They say you should wait that long. But, oh my God, I am so happy I can't hold it in any more!'

'And you're the worst person in the world at keeping secrets,' pointed out Lila.

Jas felt terrible for not guessing sooner. She knew Meg had been trying but was too caught up in her own problems to ask how she had been getting on. 'It's incredible news. Congratulations, honey. Can someone watch the shop while we take you to lunch to celebrate?'

Meg was about to respond when the sound of Jas's ringing phone interrupted them. 'Sorry. It's Lyndsey, I better take this. Hold that thought! Lynds, hi.'

'Hi, Jas. Sorry to bother you when you're off but I think you'll want to hear this.'

'Why, what's happened?'

'You know we've been in the editing suite, cutting the show together? Some pretty interesting footage has emerged ...'

The next afternoon, Jas was in a small editing room in the Channel 6 basement together with Monica, Lyndsey and the show's editor, Raj.

'First of all we stumbled on this scene and thought it was just golden,' Raj started, handing Jas a pair of headphones. She watched a group of *Mr Right* contestants out on the terrace of their spectacular villa. The static outdoor cameras weren't the best quality – for the big scenes camera crews were brought in – but the footage was certainly clear enough for her to see and hear what was going on. It was after one of the early rose ceremonies and a few of the girls were huddled on a sofa. Kat and Gabriella were shouting at each other while the others quietly sipped their wine, watching the drama.

'You had your alone-date and then, tonight, immediately take Dylan away for a private chat,' said Kat, slurring her words slightly and speaking loudly. 'Hello! You've spent the whole afternoon with him. Loads of us still haven't had any alone-time and you slither straight in. It's rude and disrespectful.'

'I don't care about disrespecting you, sweetheart,' Gabriella replied. 'I'm here for Dylan.'

'Yeah, we all are! We all fancy him. You never let anyone else have any time with him. You always get in there.'

'I can't help it if he wants to spend time with me, too. Dylan and I are meant to be. You're clearly not his type, honey, so save yourself the bother and go home now.'

The argument escalated as Gabriella accused Kat of being cheap, Kat accused Gabriella of being a snob, and before long they were both screaming at each other and Alex stepped in to calm them down. Kat flounced off, announcing that she was going to get her alone-time whether Gabby liked it or not and was going to turn up at Dylan's villa wearing nothing but a trenchcoat and a smile. The others were left gawping, half of them shocked by how brazen she was, the other half obviously wondering if that tactic would work and wishing they'd thought of it first. Gabriella had a look of pure hatred in her eyes.

Jas removed her headphones. 'This is terrific! Ooh, I love a good fight!'

'Uh-huh. Now watch this,' Lyndsey replied, peering over her glasses and switching to another monitor. This scene was footage of the infamous football match where Georgia and Alex had had their altercation. Several cameras were trained on the game. Lyndsey fast-forwarded and paused at the point where Jas sent Gabriella off the pitch.

'Oh, yeah, I remember that,' said Jas. 'She'd just called Alex a slag under her breath so I sent her off to fetch the protein shakes for everyone at half-time.'

'Look what this camera picked up though,' said Raj. The view was of the pitch from the other side. In one corner of the screen Gabriella was visible, heading to the table where the crates of shakes stood, passing the women's handbags as she did so. In long-shot, she could be seen rummaging around in one of the bags and removing a pen, throwing it in a bin and then returning to the group carrying a crate.

'I don't get it,' said Jas. 'What are we looking at?'

'Alex's EpiPen,' Monica replied. 'Remember how she said after the match that she'd lost it even though it should be in her make-up bag as usual? The bags stayed there the whole time and the cameras didn't pick up anyone else going near them. I don't see how the pen could just have fallen out.'

'But why would Gabby steal the pen?'

'Well, check this out,' Raj answered, pointing back to the first monitor, which showed one of Gabriella's interviews after an alone-date with Dylan. They'd been for couples massages in a spa.

'I feel good,' she said confidently to camera. 'Dylan and I are in love. There are sparks flying between us. It's obvious to everyone, but of course he has to play the game. It's irritating when other people get in my way. But I think that in a situation like this you have to go after what you want. I need to keep our winning streak going.'

'I filmed that,' said Monica. 'And at the time I didn't think anything of it, but now, doesn't it seem strange?'

Jas couldn't argue. It was certainly an extreme way of talking. That Gabby had thrown away Alex's EpiPen just hours before Alex's allergic reaction was also extremely suspicious. They watched more footage, showing the girls all talking about the weird vibes they got from Gabriella, and of Gabriella and Dylan's dates. She was incredibly full-on with him and, even when he wasn't looking back at her, she was always staring at him, almost obsessively.

'How's their relationship going now?' asked Jas.

'Well,' said Monica. 'He called yesterday saying that he was having second thoughts about Gabby. That since they'd been home she was ringing him constantly, almost smothering him. He's having doubts about going to the Maldives with her.'

'Christ!' exclaimed Jas. 'This isn't good. We need a loved-up couple. Otherwise what's going to persuade viewers to apply to go on the show next year? There has to be a happy ending otherwise Burrell will hit the roof. And there will be no chance of a recommission.'

'Well, Dylan says he thinks he made the wrong choice,' said Monica, with raised eyebrows.

'Let's get him on the phone, I want to talk to him.'

*

Dylan answered on the first ring. 'Am I glad to hear from you, Jas!'

'How's it going, Dylan? You ready for your Maldives trip? It's going to be pretty amazing! We'll get some follow-up interviews with you and Gabby in a week or so.' Jas knew he would open up to her but wanted to give him the chance first before diving straight in with questions about his feelings for Gabriella.

'Yeah ... About that. Er, I don't know if you've spoken to Monica but I'll tell you what I told her ... I'm having doubts, Jas. I mean, serious doubts. About Gabby.'

Jas's heart raced. If *Mr Right* ended any other way than with Dylan in love with his winner, Burrell would think that she'd failed. 'I'm sure it's just pre-holiday nerves. What's brought all this on anyway?'

'In Ibiza she was this gorgeous, confident, sexy, together woman. I was really drawn to that. But since we've been back she's been acting really weird. She keeps asking me when we're doing our photo shoots for the magazine. I said I hadn't a clue, that she needed to speak to you guys. Then there was all this stuff about her mates getting us into clubs where we could be photographed when the show had been on TV and we could go public. I don't want to be photographed in a club, that sounds like my idea of hell!'

Jas could imagine how insufferable Gabriella would be when they actually became famous. Dylan was a lot more of a homebody. 'I'm sure she's just excited and loved-up.'

'I don't know. I was starting to think that she was in this purely to get famous rather than having true feelings for me, but then she got kind of clingy and really possessive. And, get this, she turned up at Ruby's nursery the other day to collect her. Then my mum arrived and asked Gabby what she was doing. Gabby said they were going to surprise me. But I'd told her I was out of town on business. I was visiting one of my restaurants in Essex, that's why my mum was picking Ruby up. When I phoned to confront her, Gabby said it was all part of this big surprise and of course she'd never let any harm come to Ruby. But don't you think that's fucking weird?'

Jas had to admit that turning up at Ruby's nursery and trying to take her without prior arrangement was borderline psycho. 'Dylan, I've got to say something. I know you and Gabriella had crazy chemistry in Ibiza. But we all thought you had that with Charlotte too. Everyone was convinced you'd pick her. I hope you don't mind my asking, but what went wrong there?'

Dylan let out a sigh. 'I was really falling for Charlotte. But then Gabby came to my room in floods of tears and told me about how Charlotte was with the other girls in the house.'

'The night Gabriella stayed over?'

'Yes. Nothing happened, she was just so upset and I was trying to be nice, supportive, so I held her for a bit and then she drifted off to sleep in my bed. I slept on the sofa.'

'What exactly did she say to you about Charlotte?'

'That she wasn't genuine, that she was only using me and that she'd been really spiteful to Gabby and some of the other girls.'

'Surely you didn't believe her?'

'Yes. No. I mean, she was so upset … I was confused. Charlotte had always held back from me and at that moment I wondered if maybe it was suspicious. So I tried to talk to her on the last night. But she was really cold towards me, and walked off before I could really talk to her. I had to make a decision and, well, Gabby was just there, looking so great and happy and smiley. So, I picked her.'

Jas shook her head in disbelief. Dylan had been well and truly played.

Chapter 37

Charlotte and her blue Renault Clio were stuck in traffic. She was only a couple of roads away from her parents' house but it was rush hour and the high street in Mill Hill was crammed with cars. Rain started pouring down. Typical, she thought glumly. She was on her way back from teaching her last class of the day – an intense aerobics session that usually gave her a happy rush afterwards, but ever since she'd returned from Ibiza her life had seemed bleak. It was like those two months on the island had taken place in a dream. A distant dream. If Charlotte had felt lost before Ibiza, now she felt miserable. She was still doing the same job, still living in the house she grew up in. Wasn't *Mr Right* meant to change her life for good?

As the traffic finally eased Charlotte scolded herself for being so ungrateful. She needed to haul herself out of this rut, but unfortunately that was easier said than done. Her thoughts kept turning back to Dylan. She'd been heartbroken over losing him, especially to Gabriella, even

300

though he clearly wasn't the man she'd thought he was. She was torn between longing for him and berating herself for falling, *yet again*, for someone unworthy of her. What was she doing wrong?

Minutes later Charlotte parked up outside her parents' semi-detached house. They'd already switched the Christmas tree lights on. It was barely November but Christmas was made much of in her house.

She was fantasising about mince pies and a long bath when the sight of Jas Whitely in the living room, casually talking to her mum, made her jump. The two women hugged.

'Jas, it's so good to see you!'

'I'm sorry for turning up unannounced. I did try to call you but your phone has been off.'

'Oh, sorry, the battery died this morning and I've been teaching all day.'

'Your parents have been extremely hospitable.'

'It's our pleasure, love,' said Charlotte's mum, Joy, a mixed-race woman in her early fifties. She ushered Charlotte in and told her to sit down. 'We've heard so much about you from Charley. You two sit and talk and I'll get started on dinner. Are you staying, Jasmine?'

'Oh, gosh, I'd love to but I've got to get back. Lots of paperwork. But thanks so much.'

'Well, you're always welcome if you change your mind.'

'She's so nice,' said a smiling Jas as Joy went into the kitchen and started pottering around with pots and pans. 'And I'm loving the decorations. Never too early, eh?'

'Hmm, my dad's sentiments exactly! He insists on getting the Christmas tree up early and leaves it up until approximately the end of January. It's mad but I have given up trying to argue.'

'I think it's nice. How have you been anyway?'

Charlotte shrugged. 'It's a bit of an anti-climax, coming back to this weather after living in a sun-drenched luxurious villa for two months. I did get quite homesick towards the end, though, and as soon as Dylan made his decision I couldn't wait to get out of there.'

'Have you spoken to him at all? Heard from him?'

'No. Why?'

'He asked me for your number when we were still in Ibiza, you know. He was gutted when you left, seemed more affected by it than by any other girl leaving. I knew you two had grown very close.'

Knowing that Dylan actually had her phone number and still hadn't been in touch only made Charlotte feel worse. 'Oh, well, I guess he's happy with Gabby then.'

'Actually, Charlotte, that's what I came to talk to you about. From the minute you left, Dylan said in his interviews that he felt terrible about the way it had ended. No offence, but I figured he'd kind of just get over it and settle down with Gabby. He had chosen her, after all.'

Was this Jas's way of trying to make Charlotte feel better? She was doing a pretty bad job so far.

'But,' Jas continued, 'it seems he still hasn't got over you. In fact, quite the opposite.'

'What are you talking about?'

'He's been in touch with Monica frequently over the last couple of weeks. Charlotte, he wants you back.'

'Are you serious?'

'I spoke to him myself, at length. We all have. He says he misses you terribly and that he's certain he made the wrong decision by picking Gabby. Turns out the doubts he had as soon as you left won't go away. I think he's truly in love with you. Aaaaand ... he wants another chance with you. *If* you'll agree.'

Charlotte's heart rate immediately picked up.

'We want to get you and Dylan back to Ibiza and film an alternative ending where he changes his mind in the final rose ceremony and picks you. And it would be great if you could act surprised and wear the same clothes so it looks seamless on film, et cetera. But first I had to come and talk to you, to see if you'd even consider being with him now.'

Charlotte's hands flew up to cover her mouth. She couldn't believe it! But she had a track record of making bad decisions. Wouldn't this just be another one? Was this all just a play to garner more ratings?

'Wait a minute, Jas. He was shagging half the villa.'

Jas shook her head. 'Nope. He swears not. I already told you, kissing the contestants was a prerequisite. I had said to him he must flirt with everyone.'

'What about slipping into the cinema room with Alex? Or that session in the hot tub on Gabby's date? She was bragging about their night of passion.'

'They only kissed. He and Alex were more mates than anything else. I know it may not have seemed like it at the time to you, but we could all see there was zero romantic chemistry between them. She was probably hamming it up to make you feel bad. In all the footage I've got, he was only ever smitten by you and Gabby.'

'But I saw her myself, leaving his villa at the crack of dawn, still in her clothes from the night before.'

Jas cleared her throat. 'This is where it gets complicated. Did you, er, ever notice anything strange about Gabriella?'

'You're joking, right? Everything she did was strange!'

'Such as?'

'Such as distancing herself from everyone in the villa apart from the other Mean Girls, being a total snob towards most of us, dressing in what was basically a wedding dress to have a barbecue with Dylan for their alone-date. She made me uncomfortable every time she stepped in the room. I know we were all competing for him, even though I hate saying that, but she was properly obsessed. Oh, and there was this bizarre conversation between her and Mackenzie I overheard the night she and Georgia left.' Charlotte described the conversation to Jas.

'None of that is a total surprise,' Jas replied. She took a deep breath and relayed, word for word, what Dylan had told her about the night Gabriella stayed at his villa.

'So, you see, Gabriella told him all those awful things about you in order to manipulate him. She's crafty. As for Dylan, well, I genuinely believe that not only is he a good guy, but his feelings for you are the real deal.'

Charlotte wasn't so sure. She liked Jas but wouldn't she say anything to get a dramatic ending for her series? Charlotte wasn't about to be used to boost the show's ratings. 'He still chose Gabby over me.'

'He didn't believe her at first, but was already torn between his feelings for you and for her. When he tried to talk to you at the finale you brushed him off, so he thought

304

you weren't interested in him. He picked her in reaction to that and has been doubting his decision ever since. Her behaviour to him has only confirmed his belief that he should have picked you. He told us that, ever since the show ended, Gabriella has been acting bizarrely. The more we've watched and analysed her footage, the more certain we've become that she is seriously mixed up.'

Charlotte thought back to the night of the final rose ceremony, when Dylan had indeed tried to pull her aside and talk. 'But – but – I was only brushing him off because I thought he was sleeping with her and Alex! He didn't deny it either!'

'But did he admit it?'

'Well, no, but—'

Charlotte's mind raced. Had Gabby been eliminating the competition – or trying to – one by one? Was Dylan genuine after all?

'You really think he's into me?'

'Yes.'

'It's not just for the show?'

'No, honey. But while you think about that, I need to ask you some more things about Gabriella. Like, who did she argue with the most?'

'That's easy. Alex. One hundred per cent. Oh, and Kat. They had a massive fight the night before the football match.'

'The night before Kat got sick?'

'I guess so. And then the whole thing with Alex's face. No one could ever forget that.'

'Charlotte, do you think Gabriella is capable of poisoning Kat and Alex out of spite?'

'I was just asking myself the same thing.'

Chapter 38

Jas got an Uber back to her flat later that evening, phoning Lyndsey and Monica from the car and then bracing herself for the next thing she needed to do: email Luke and arrange a meeting about the show for the very next day. If what they all suspected about Gabriella was true, then they were dealing with two serious possible charges against her, maybe even attempted murder.

Despite everything going on with the show, Richard and Lila, the distance between Jas and Luke over the past few weeks had only convinced her that she wasn't over him. Every time her mind wandered, it was to thoughts of him. Frustratingly, he wasn't on Instagram or Twitter, and his Facebook page hadn't been updated in weeks, thus offering no clues as to his personal life. He hadn't called and Jas was determined that she wasn't going to make the first move. The last thing she wanted was to embarrass herself further by seeming desperate.

The next day, back at Channel 6, the thought of seeing him, even if it was for work, evoked mixed feelings in her. On the one hand, she was excited. Maybe he'd be pleased to see her too? And maybe the distance between them would have given him time to reflect and, most importantly, forgive. On the other hand, Jas was dreading it. Embarrassment at the way she'd acted still made her cringe and she couldn't deal with the prospect of him being cold with her when she still had feelings for him. When she'd emailed him to arrange their meeting his response was short and businesslike. But the future of *Mr Right*, and quite possibly her own career, was at stake now, so she was determined to put her personal feelings aside and concentrate on the matter at hand.

The twelfth floor where the legal department was situated was much more sterile-looking than the one where Jas worked. There, vases of flowers, books and magazines were strewn all over desks and they brainstormed using whiteboards with colourful, messy handwriting. Here on the twelfth, items on desks were sparse, save for a few black folders neatly lined up.

Jas wandered through the banks of desks and spotted Luke at his computer with his headphones on, though he stood up when she reached his desk and gave her a nod.

'Let's go into the conference room.'

Jas followed him in, feeling instantly unsettled. This was so formal. 'How've you been?' she asked as they sat down.

'Good. Busy, but good. And you?'

A few minutes of small talk followed. Luke told Jas he'd been to the Lake District with his family for a long weekend and had been playing rugby in between working. He avoided eye contact with her as he spoke, instead glancing around the room or down at his phone frequently, which she found incredibly annoying. When talk turned to the weather, Jas couldn't bear the awkwardness any more.

'Let's just get down to things, yeah?' she said sharply. 'We have a big problem with Gabriella Bellamy-Hughes. Dylan's gone off her entirely and wants to get back with Charlotte. We're going to go back and film another ending where he realises he was in love with Charlotte all along and plans a big gesture to get her back. Burrell loves it and has signed us off flying them back to Spain.'

'Okay.'

'Problem is, we've uncovered some serious stuff about Gabby. I'm pretty sure it was her who was behind Kat's food poisoning and Alex's allergic reaction. They were the ones arguing the most with her and we have footage of what looks like Gabby stealing Alex's EpiPen out of her bag. What do we do next?'

Luke held his head in his hands. 'Jas, if what you're saying about Alex is true, it's GBH. Christ, attempted murder even. And under foreign jurisdiction. We need to launch a full-on investigation.'

'This won't affect the show, will it?' She knew it wasn't the most selfless reaction but, after coming this far, she couldn't bear the thought of the show being in jeopardy.

'Just keep going with filming the new ending and everything else we'll keep behind closed doors for now. I'll deal with it,' he told her.

Once again, Jas felt entirely reassured by Luke. She gazed at him and their eyes met and held for a few seconds, then Luke looked away. Jas couldn't bear it any longer.

'We can't go on like this,' she said. 'Aren't we ever going to talk about what happened?'

Luke scratched his head. 'What do you want to talk about?'

'Us. How it ended.'

'There is no us, Jas. Look, I didn't really want to get into this now but I've started seeing someone else. It's early days, but like I said to you last time, I think it's better we stay just friends.'

Luke's words were like a slap in the face. She didn't know what she'd been expecting – for him to run into her arms? Tell her everything was okay? – but certainly not this. It wasn't just the fact that he was seeing someone else; the coldness in his voice cut her deep. Suddenly, Jas's mind flashed back to memories of when she'd confront Richard about his bad behaviour and, instead of arguing with her or shouting back, he'd reply slowly and collectedly, with such chilliness in his voice it was worse than if he'd started shouting. Jas rarely cried, in fact she hadn't since her argument with Lila and before that not for months, but now she started to well up with emotion. What was happening to her? With the worst timing possible, everything bad in her life was rising to the surface and threatening her hard-won security. Luke must have seen something in her face change. He looked concerned. 'Jas? It's not that I didn't care about you but I just don't know if we would work.'

'You're right. It's best we leave it.' Jas had to get out before the tears started. She wasn't going to embarrass herself any further. She tried to sound breezy but it came out as defensive. Fists clenched, she stepped quickly out of the room and over to the lifts, thankfully managing to keep the tears in, though it was a struggle. *Deep breaths, deep breaths*, she told herself, urging the lift to hurry up.

Luke appeared behind her and lightly touched her arm. 'Are you okay?' he said softly. Jas pursed her lips. Didn't he know that the worst thing someone can ask you when you're on the verge of tears is, *'Are you okay?'*

'Have I upset you?'

She shook her head.

'You know that no matter what's happened with us, you can still talk to me. I'm always here for you.' Jas couldn't remember the last time anyone had said that to her.

'Want to go get a cuppa?'

The lift appeared and Jas nodded. She hadn't confided in anyone else about Lila and Richard and was overcome with a desire to get everything off her chest.

In the deli next to the office, with its red-and-white checked tablecloths and Italian waiters shouting orders to each other, Jas found a table at the back. Luke brought over two steaming cups of tea. Jas hadn't known just how much she needed to talk or how much she'd been keeping locked away. She told Luke about her marriage to Richard, how young and in love she'd been and how they'd grown apart anyway but that his drug use and affairs had ultimately ruined the relationship for good. She told him how Richard had been preventing her from divorcing him, revelling in the control he had over her by doing so. Luke listened intently as the words flooded out of Jas, either nodding, shaking his head or raising his eyebrows at the more shocking aspects of her story.

'Why didn't you tell me any of this at the start, Jas? I would have understood.'

'At first I didn't know how to begin. I did try to tell you once at my place. Then I felt so guilty ...'

'That's why you broke it off?'

'Yes. And after that I went to Ibiza and I didn't know what would happen.'

'And Richard, he's not been in touch since?'

'Well, that's another thing.' Jas took a deep breath and proceeded to tell Luke about Richard's verbal attack on Lila. 'How could I possibly stay married to someone like that?'

Luke came around the table and gave Jas a hug, holding her tightly to his chest. 'I can't believe you've kept all this to yourself,' he said softly. Jas was so exhausted she didn't want to say another word, so closed her eyes and let him hold her for a few minutes of blissful silence in the otherwise noisy café where everyone else was too busy to notice them. She felt as if the chaotic world was moving hurriedly around her but, just then, she was in her own perfect place with Luke. It was exactly what she needed. Someone to be there and listen to her without judging.

'Do you think you've got enough to go on with the judge?' he finally asked.

'I hope so. Statements from friends and family, emails and messages – conversations about his behaviour with my sisters and friends, which they will back up.'

'Who's your solicitor?'

'Ralph Mackover. He's good, I think.'

Luke nodded slowly, tapping a finger on the tabletop, deep in concentration. 'When's the hearing?'

'Next Thursday.'

Luke's phone bleeped. 'Shit, I've got a meeting with the bosses. Will you be okay? I can try to cancel.'

'No, no, don't be silly. I feel loads better after letting it all out. You won't tell anyone about this, will you?'

''Course not. It's going to be all right, Jas.' They shared another hug but were interrupted by his phone ringing furiously.

'Go. You'll be late.' After planting a kiss on her forehead, which made Jas's stomach flip with excitement, Luke left.

Chapter 39

As Charlotte sat back in the car Channel 6 had booked to take her to Stansted airport, speeding along the motorway, she felt a distinct sense of déjà vu. Just a few months ago, she was making this exact same trip, en route to Ibiza, a bundle of nerves and excitement about what would lie ahead. How much had changed since then. Charlotte had fallen in love and had her heart broken. She'd made friends in Jasmine, Melody and Kat, and, unwittingly, enemies in Gabriella, Mackenzie and even Alex, who had grown extremely competitive in the run-up to the final.

Now Charlotte was heading back to Ibiza and, once again, she didn't know what to expect. Ever since Jas's visit to reveal that Dylan wanted to film an alternative ending where he picked her instead of Gabriella, she'd flipped between joy and anxiety. She'd grown so close to Dylan over the past two months and had truly fallen for him, but she'd been burnt and vowed she would never let herself be let down by a man again. Enough was enough. Could she really trust him?

And if there was one thing she knew about *Mr Right*, it was to expect the unexpected. Was a romantic reunion really what Charlotte was being flown over for, or was she being set up? And what about Gabriella? Jas had revealed just how unhinged she seemed to be, and Charlotte didn't relish the prospect of potentially seeing her again. Was she being flown out too just for Dylan to break up with her on camera?

Charlotte wondered if she was making a huge mistake. But it was too late now. She'd agreed, the plane ticket was booked and in a couple of hours she'd be greeted at Ibiza airport by Monica and Jasmine and driven back to Villa Valencia.

The car pulled into the terminal and Charlotte rolled her pink suitcase over to the check-in desk and produced her passport.

'All right, Miss Truss, it's Gate 54 for Barcelona and they're already boarding.'

'Oh, no, sorry, it's Ibiza I'm flying to, not Barcelona.'

'Um, nope, it's most definitely Barcelona. Miss Charlotte Jane Truss? I have you down for one priority seat to Barcelona.'

Charlotte pulled her phone out of her bag. 'There has to be a mistake. It was booked by Jasmine Whiteley at Channel 6? Is there any record of that?'

'Yes, Miss Truss. It was all booked by the travel desk at Channel 6. I can assure you there is no mistake. Do you need help with your bag?'

An impatient queue was forming behind Charlotte so she obediently took her ticket and rolled her cabin bag towards the security gate. Feeling baffled, she texted Jas to ask what was going on.

'Surprise! See you in Barcelona in a couple of hours. Don't miss your flight!' was the response. Charlotte had a dozen other questions but was kept busy passing through security.

A two-hour plane ride later, she was feeling excited. Charlotte passed quickly through security and immigration at the other end and found not only Ken the lead cameraman filming her arrival, but a driver holding up a card with her name on it.

'Just pretend we're not here, Charley!' called Ken from behind the camera.

'What's going on?' she called to him as the driver carried her bag and led her to a waiting limousine. Inside was champagne, and a note which read: 'Welcome to your city of love. Dylan is waiting for you.'

'Where are we going?' Charlotte asked the driver, but she got no response so sat back in the luxurious limo. They pulled into the W Hotel on the beach, an area that wasn't nearly as busy as when Charlotte and Dylan had come here in the summer, but despite the chill in the air the sky was still bright blue and beautiful. The clerk at reception had been expecting Charlotte and handed her the keys to a suite that took Charlotte's breath away. The floor-to-ceiling windows looked out onto the beach, a fruit basket and bottle of wine stood on the mahogany desk and there was a four-poster bed with a box laid on it. Charlotte opened it to see the most beautiful floor-length red gown. The bodice was dotted with sequins and the skirt made of wispy chiffon. A note accompanied it:

Dear Charlotte,

Welcome to Barcelona. I have brought you back to the city where I fell in love with you. I hope you like this dress (I can't take all the credit, Jasmine picked it out). This is just one of the gifts I have for you. I don't want to play games any more, but I still need to settle one score to make sure we are a match made in heaven. A car will pick you up at 6 p.m. in the lobby.

Love, Dylan xxx

Charlotte felt like she was in a fairy tale. She didn't know what tonight would hold but one thing was certain: she couldn't wait to see him again.

Charlotte made a visit to the gym for a quick workout, swim and sauna then spent the afternoon getting ready. She scrubbed, exfoliated and polished her body and covered her skin in buttery body cream. She usually straightened her dark hair, which now hung below her shoulders, but this time styled it so it was tousled and, she hoped, sexy. Make-up was a smoky brown and gold eye, heaps of bronzer and highlighter in all the areas Melody had taught her for a perfect, glowing look, and a slick of lipgloss. The dress fitted perfectly – *nice one, Jas* – and floating around her hotel suite in the gown, Charlotte felt like Julia Roberts in *Pretty Woman*. She took and sent several selfies to Maya who demanded constant updates, then she was good to go.

At 6 p.m. sharp she stood nervously in the lobby, wondering what was going to happen next. The same driver who had met her earlier appeared and held the passenger door open for her.

'Okay, you *have* to tell me where we're going this time,' she pleaded after several minutes of silent driving.

The driver only laughed and put his index finger to his lips.

'Pleeeeease! I can't take the suspense!'

The rest of the drive was spent in silence until he spoke for the first time. 'Your boyfriend, he is very grand.'

Charlotte gasped. Ahead of her she saw the unmistakable structure of Camp Nou, the football stadium where she and Dylan had gone on their glorious Barcelona date. Were they going to watch a match? Charlotte was hardly dressed for that!

A cameraman filmed her stepping out of the car, wide-eyed and beaming. A staff member of the stadium greeted her and led her down a deserted corridor. This wasn't the same route she'd taken last time to get to the seats. But Charlotte soon saw the glimmer of green grass ahead of her and realised she was being led straight to the pitch. The floodlights were on, cameras were everywhere and the crew of *Mr Right* were standing to one side, all smiling. In the middle, clutching a bouquet of red roses and dressed in a black suit that made him so handsome he took Charlotte's breath away, was Dylan.

She couldn't help it, she ran right into his arms and he kissed her as the crew clapped and whistled. 'Is this a dream?' she laughed, looking up at the magnificent stadium.

'The minute I let you go I realised how much I wanted you. Can you ever forgive me?'

'Is it over with Gabby?'

Dylan nodded firmly. 'A thousand times, yes. I don't know what I was thinking. There was so much going on towards the end and she told me all these things about you, horrible things. I didn't believe her but when I tried to talk to you, you were so distant ...'

'I know. But I thought you were having sex with her and Alex and that was all you wanted from me. When I came by that morning to drop off Ruby's toy, I saw Gabby coming out of your villa and I just assumed she'd spent the night.'

'She did spend the night. In my bed. While I slept on the sofa. She was crying and seemed so upset. I was only trying to be kind and supportive. I swear to you, nothing with any of those women went any further than kissing.'

Charlotte looked over his shoulder to see Jas and Monica nodding and giving her the thumbs-up.

'It was you all along ... you were the one for Mr Right and then he stupidly got it wrong! Now all I want is to make it up to you.'

To Charlotte's shock, Dylan knelt down on one knee and reached into his jacket pocket.

'Charlotte? Will you—'

Was he seriously proposing to her after knowing her for only a few months? 'No, Dylan, get up!' Charlotte hissed, a look of panic on her face, which turned to confusion

– and then relief. He reached into his jacket pocket and pulled out, not a ring, but plane tickets.

'Will you come to the Maldives with me and be my girlfriend?'

Charlotte threw her hands to her face, which was red with embarrassment. 'A thousand times yes,' she laughed, as Dylan hoisted her up in his arms.

'You didn't really think I was going to propose after just a few months, did, you?' he laughed, as the crew cheered and clapped again. 'Don't you think we've had enough drama already?'

Charlotte coiled her arms around his neck. 'I didn't know what to think! This whole day feels like a dream.'

'Well, how about you just let me try to be the best boyfriend I can be and we'll take it from there?'

'Sounds perfect.'

Jas couldn't have been happier for Dylan and Charlotte. They really did make an adorable couple and it wasn't just about ratings or a good final episode – although that was very welcome. Seeing them have their happy ending made Jas feel good.

Charlotte raced over to give her a huge hug. 'Thank you for all of this. And the dress, especially! Wow!'

'My absolute pleasure. Didn't I tell you that coming on this show would be a good idea? It will start airing on the third of January and I've got a feeling both your lives will change dramatically – for the better!'

'We'll see. I just hope Dylan really is the guy I think he is.'

'He is! You've got your happy ending, Charlotte, and no one deserves it more than you.'

'What happens now?'

'The limo is waiting to take you both for a romantic candle-lit dinner.' Jas hugged her goodbye and promised to call her when they were back in the UK. Jas didn't mention that in Charlotte's hotel suite the bed would be decorated with red rose petals for when she and Dylan hopefully went back there.

'Oh, wait, one more thing. What's happened to Gabriella?' asked Charlotte.

Jas took a deep breath. 'Dylan broke up with her. Off-camera. I'm sure he'll tell you about it but it did *not* go well. She started throwing plates at him, apparently, could have done some real damage if he hadn't swerved out of the way. She was wailing that he'd embarrassed her, ruined her life and she'd never trust anyone again.'

'Yikes. I suppose it can't be very nice to think you'd won his heart and then be dumped weeks later.'

Jas smiled. Even after what Gabriella had done, and how she'd tried to sabotage Charlotte's own relationship with Dylan, Charlotte could still feel sympathy for her. 'I wouldn't feel too sorry for her if I were you. She poisoned two of the contestants, remember? Alex could have died without her EpiPen. Gabriella's been formally charged and has admitted the whole thing.'

'To poisoning Alex?'

'Yes, she put almond oil in Alex's smoothie during the match but Alex didn't drink it until the coach ride home. She didn't think of it at the time, she was so convinced that Georgia was behind it by tampering with her face cream.'

'Wow!'

'Yep. And Gabby deliberately undercooked Kat's breakfast so she'd get food poisoning. It wasn't the shrimps from the buffet at all. She's insane, Charley. She's hoping that her confession will get her off lightly but I can't be so sure. She has some serious mental issues, that's for certain. And they should have been picked up in our vetting at the beginning of the process, so we've had to launch another investigation into why they weren't spotted.'

'I can't believe it.'

'Yes, well, it's nothing for you to worry about, sweetheart. Go on, Dylan's waiting for you.'

Charlotte hugged her tightly again. 'Thank you for everything, Jas.'

Chapter 40

The night before the divorce hearing Jas barely slept. She was nervous about the outcome, nervous that she'd screw things up and was particularly dreading being anywhere near Richard again. Lila, Meg, Oscar, Graham and Helen all came down to London to support her at the hearing. Lila, in particular, insisted that she was eager to look Richard straight in the eye so he knew she wasn't intimidated by him. Lila's written statement to the court had detailed how Jas would regularly phone her, Meg and their parents in tears over her crumbling marriage to Richard when he'd stood her up or stayed out all night.

During the hearing, the whole family were cross-examined by Richard's po-faced female lawyer about their statements and they kept their cool entirely. Jas could see Richard seething. To him, it was all about power, especially when it came to Jas and Lila. They weren't letting him keep any of it.

Celia Butler took to the stand to claim Jas had never understood the huge demands of Richard's job and how hard he worked to support their lifestyle. Friends of his then described the romantic gesture made on Jas's birthday last December when Richard had gallantly bought them both a new house, out of the city, to try to fix their marriage, only to be shot down by a 'cold', 'heartless' and 'ruthlessly ambitious' Jas. She rolled her eyes. Why was it every time a woman showed any desire to succeed in her career, or life in general, without the aid of a man, she was deemed 'ruthlessly ambitious'?

A few hours in, things weren't looking good. Jas slumped in her seat. She looked over to Celia, straightening Richard's tie as if he were a schoolchild in uniform. Richard's father, Harold, hadn't even bothered to turn up. Jas realised that, no matter what the outcome today, she was richer than her husband in so many ways.

Her lawyer, Ralph Mackover, had slipped out and now returned. He spoke to Jas as he sat down next to her. 'Don't worry, Jasmine. I know things are going Richard's way now but the rest of your witnesses are outside. Once they've had their say we should be in a *very* good position. Fantastic job, getting them to speak, by the way. Afterwards you'll have to tell me how you did it.'

Jas had no idea what he was talking about. How she'd done what? *New witnesses?*

Now, the judge spoke. She was a large, very stern-looking woman in her sixties who Jas would not want to get on the wrong side of. When she spoke, she did so slowly in Queen's English, peering over her thick-rimmed glasses.

'Shall we call your additional witnesses in, Ms Whiteley? I'd like to get this over with as quickly as possible. Beth Harrods, please.'

Jas had never heard of a Beth Harrods and didn't recognise the short woman who came in then. Richard whispered something to his lawyer and looked angry.

'Ms Harrods, please can you state your relationship to Mr Butler?' asked Ralph.

'I'm an accountant at Curtis Stoddard.'

'Where Mr Butler works?'

'Yes.'

'And what is your role there, specifically?'

'I put through Mr Butler's expenses. In fact, all the expenses for his team.'

'And you have provided copies of some of these expense sheets and claimed receipts, is that correct?'

'That's confidential!' Richard shouted to his lawyer, who told him to calm down. From a folder, Ralph brandished a clear plastic wallet crammed with signed-off expense sheets and receipts from clubs in the City and Soho. The receipts clearly displayed the early hours of the morning in which the purchases of a great deal of alcohol were made. They'd been signed off by Richard's bosses and were all made using a company credit card. While such expenses weren't illegal, they were certainly unusual and it was hard to say why a magnum of champagne paid for at The Box at 1 a.m. on a Friday morning could be for a 'client meeting'. It didn't help Richard's case – and only illustrated Jas's. There were also receipts from Agent Provocateur. Jas certainly hadn't received any gifts from Richard bought there in a number of years so it only supported her claim that he had a mistress.

Jas was stunned by this new development. Then, to her amazement, another female employee at Curtis Stoddard took to the witness stand, claiming that not only had she slept with Richard at the Christmas party but he had also offered her cocaine and she'd witnessed him taking it in his office where they'd had sex.

Two more female employees appeared in turn, maintaining that Richard's drug use and womanising were notorious in the office. Even when his lawyer sternly cross-examined them, they held their own. The last witness was dismissed.

After that the judge cleared her throat. 'I think I've heard all I need to hear. Mr Butler, Ms Whiteley, I'm sure you know that listening to couples arguing about divorce is not a top priority for the family court. Hopefully you will both think hard before entering into any future marriage, and consider all its potential consequences. But I'm afraid, Mr Butler, that in this case there is clear evidence that the marital breakdown can be ascribed solely to you. I wholeheartedly endorse Ms Whiteley's application to divorce you on the grounds of unreasonable behaviour and adultery.'

Jas let out an almighty sigh of relief. She'd won! She really was going to get her divorce and Richard couldn't stop it any more! Richard stared at her, seeming unable to believe what he had just heard. His lawyer nudged his shoulder and led him out.

'Excellent result!' Ralph Mackover was smiling broadly as he and Jas went in search of her family. 'I'll get things rolling now, Jasmine. It won't be too long before you're officially single again.'

'But, Ralph, where on earth did all these women come from?'

'I assumed that was your work? You knew them, didn't you?'

'I've never seen any of them before in my life.'

Jas was about to probe Ralph further but now they were in the waiting area her family were hugging her and talking over each other to ask questions. 'How are you feeling?' 'How did you do it?' 'How did you get them all to speak for you?' 'Did you see Richard's face?'

'It's over now, love,' said Graham softly as he hugged his daughter tight. Jas realised that during this whole ordeal she'd given little thought to how it was affecting her parents. They were always a pillar of support to her, but it must have been hard for them to witness their daughter go through a bitter break-up and divorce.

'I'm sure it must feel confusing now but you've got to remember, Jasmine, take this as one big lesson. You'll bounce back in no time.'

'Love you, Dad. Thank you.'

Helen joined them and gave Jas several kisses. 'We're so proud of how gracefully you've handled all this,' she said. 'With such dignity and maturity.' Jas blushed, thinking about the awful way she'd spoken to Luke not so long ago.

'I don't know about that, Mum.'

'Anyway, it's time for you to move on now that nasty man is out of your hair once and for all. You can start to rebuild your life, love. Oh, it's so exciting!'

Jas felt another wave of affection for her parents.

'Now, I don't know about you but I could use a stiff drink,' announced Graham, patting Oscar on the back. 'I saw a promising-looking boozer just across the road. I'll lead the way, first round's on me!'

Meg, Helen and Lila continued to talk over each other excitedly about the day's dramatic events. Jas went along with them quietly, letting it all sink in. She was overcome with gratitude to all those women for risking their jobs – their careers even – to help her. But hearing from people she didn't know about just how terrible Richard's behaviour was, and seeing one of the – probably many – women he had had sex with, in his office, while married to Jas, had made her feel queasy. Just how little could she have meant to him, for him to do such a thing? Not to mention how he'd treated Lila.

Outside, as Graham and Oscar marched towards the pub, Jas noticed the first mystery woman from the accounts department who'd spoken out against Richard. She had a cigarette in her mouth and was fumbling around in her handbag for a lighter, which she then dropped on the ground. Jas raced over to pick it up for her.

'Beth? I wanted to thank you for what you did in there. Your colleagues, too. I don't know if I'd have won without your statements.'

Beth inhaled deeply on her cigarette, exhaling to the side so as not to blow smoke in Jas's face. 'I'm just sorry I

327

didn't say something sooner. We all knew. Everyone knows what goes on and no one says anything. It's terrible that you had to put up with that for so long from your own husband.'

'If you don't mind my asking, what made you come forward now?'

'Well, you know our bosses said they'd fire anyone who spoke out in support of you?'

'I did not know that! You know that's illegal, right?'

'We were all scared of losing our jobs so we kept quiet at first. And it's not just your ex-husband who acts like that, believe me. Then, when Luke came to see us all, everything worked out.'

Jas did a double take. 'Luke? You don't mean Luke Hawkins?'

'The one and only. Oh, you've got a good one there, Jasmine. Hang onto him. He had practically every woman in the building fussing over him!'

'I'm sorry, Beth, I don't understand. What did Luke do?'

'You don't know? He had meetings with any woman who worked with Richard and said he was helping you with your divorce case. We just assumed he was your boyfriend. You're really not together? He explained our rights to us and gave us all legal advice. Said he'd personally see to it that we were represented if we wanted to sue Curtis Stoddard for unfair dismissal. That's why the four of us came forward. We all decided it was the right thing to do. He even gave us contacts for other jobs. We're all going to resign together. I can't believe you haven't snapped

Luke up already, Jasmine. You'd better hurry up before someone else does.'

Jas ran into the pub where Graham was already at the bar handing out drinks. 'There you are! Come on, Jasmine, place your order.'

'Dad, Mum, I'm sorry but there's something I have to do. Start without me?'

'But we were going to go to Di Martino's on Great Portland Street for dinner,' Lila protested.

'Perfect. I'll meet you there.' Jas quickly kissed each family member in turn and knocked back some of Lila's wine for courage, apologising again. She raced to the Tube station, calling Luke's mobile as she did but it was switched off. She called his office number. The legal assistant, Phoebe, answered.

'Oh, hi, Jas. Luke's not in, he's got the day off today. Said something about painting the flat so you might find him at home.'

Shit. Jas had never been to his house. She knew it was Archway. Could she just about get away with blagging the street name from Phoebe over the phone? Jas could find it on Google Maps and then she'd have to knock on every door 'til she found him.

'Oh dammit, you don't happen to know the street name do you, lovely? He always orders the cabs when we've gone there and I'd recognise the door in an instant but ...'

'Jas, I'm sorry, you know I can't give out an address of an employee.'

'Phoebe, please. Please, please, I swear on my life I won't tell anyone. It's an emergency. Come on, you know me. I swear I wouldn't ask you unless it was important. I'll get you on the guest list to 360 any night you want.' She'd just have to call in another favour from Connor Scott, but it was worth it. Phoebe whispered the address.

Jas thanked her and ran into the Tube station and jumped on a Northern line train to Luke's flat. Everything made sense to her now. She'd been holding back all this time but couldn't manage it any more. Not only was she allowed finally to divorce Richard, and was therefore a free agent, but finding out what Luke had done to save her was the clincher. Beth was right: why hadn't she snapped up this amazing man? Luke might have said he was seeing someone else but didn't he also say it was early days? And what he'd done for Jas surely meant that he had feelings for her too.

The train didn't move fast enough. Jas raced out of the station and would have run all the way to Luke's flat if she hadn't been wearing heels and already completely out of breath. She laughed to herself as she pictured the scene: it was going to be just like in those cheesy rom-coms ... she'd turn up at his flat and jump straight into his arms. All she needed now was for it to rain and then it really would be like the dramatic end to a Hollywood chick flick!

Eyes glued to Google Maps, she ran around the corner to Luke's flat and, as she looked up, her smile faded instantly. Luke was standing there, looking typically gorgeous in dark jeans and a black coat with the collar turned up. But he was with the same pretty and petite brunette Jas had seen him with on the Tube that summer. They were standing on the steps outside his flat, hugging and looking like the perfect Instagram couple. It was too late. Someone *had* already snapped him up. It clearly wasn't early days with his girlfriend at all. Jas ran back around the corner before she was spotted. She felt like the world's biggest idiot. Then it started to rain.

Half an hour in the back seat of a Toyota Prius later, Jas stepped out of the Uber and into Di Martino's restaurant in central London. It was Friday night and the place was completely rammed, but her family had secured a table at the back and were already tucking into their garlic prawns and tricolore salad starters.

Greetings over, Lila pulled Jas down into the seat next to her, with Meg on the other side. 'Are you completely insane? Where the hell have you been?'

'Making a complete fool of myself, Lila, that's where.' Jas poured herself a generous glass of white wine.

Meg rubbed her back. 'Here, we ordered you some garlic bread. I can't imagine you've had anything to eat today with all the stress of the hearing.'

It was true, but Jas had no appetite. Her sisters were both staring at her so there was no way to avoid talking about it.

'I went to see Luke, to tell him that I wanted to be with him. It was he who convinced all those women to come forward. We owe him everything.' She told her sisters exactly what the employee at Curtis Stoddard had told her outside the court.

'So, I went to his flat,' she continued. 'I had this grand, crazy notion of turning up at the doorstep, flinging myself into his arms and then everything would be okay.'

'Wow, Jas, I can't believe he would do that for you,' said Meg.

'He must be crazy about you, there's no other explanation for it!' exclaimed Lila, before Jas quietened her down.

'Shh! And no, you're wrong. He was standing there hugging his girlfriend. I legged it before he saw me and I made an even bigger prat of myself.'

'Oh, no,' exhaled Lila and Meg at the same time, hugging Jas from each side. 'I'm so sorry, babe,' said Meg.

'I really screwed things up this time, girls,' said Jas glumly, before excusing herself to go to the toilet. Maybe it was all the emotion of the day, maybe it was the large glass of wine she'd drunk on an empty stomach, but the second she locked the cubicle door she started crying.

Chapter 41

The next two days were miserable for Jas. Her parents drove Lila back to Manchester the morning after the hearing while Meg and Oscar set off at the same time in their own car. Both Meg and Lila offered to stay and keep Jas company in her flat but she insisted they go back, not wanting to be any sort of a burden.

Unfortunately, not even an hour after they'd left Jas started to feel lonely and wished she'd accepted Lila's offer to stay with her. She spent the entire weekend between her bed and the sofa, sleeping or trying to distract herself with thriller films. Definitely not anything romantic, Jas decided as she flicked through Netflix and Amazon Prime.

Not that the films were that much of a distraction. Being alone with her thoughts made Jas play through every moment she'd had with Luke since they'd met, over and over again, obsessing about all the mistakes she'd made. Why didn't she just tell him about her marriage straight away like Monica told her to? Even if she had told him after they'd slept together in Ibiza, it probably would have been fine, but the way it came out, in that drunken screaming fit in the middle of the night, was *so* not good. Not to mention the horrendous and childish way she had spoken to him at the *Mr Right* wrap party. Every time Jas thought of that she cringed inwardly. No wonder he'd chosen the pretty brunette over her. No doubt she was far less trouble and far less dramatic. Jas couldn't help thinking of them together: laughing, happy, and on their way to falling in love.

Jas could kick herself. She'd had the greatest guy in the world and been awful to him. Twice. And she'd stupidly thought all it would take was showing up on his doorstep to make everything all right again. What was she thinking?

By Monday morning Jas's low mood hadn't lifted, but she felt better for showering, finally, and getting ready for work. What she needed now, more than anything else, was a distraction.

On the way in she kept seeing things that reminded her of Luke: a man brushing past her wearing the same aftershave; a northern accent taking a phone call on the street. Jas scolded herself. *For God's sake, pull yourself together!* There was no alternative: she had to get on with her life.

Jas got through the day of meetings, clearing emails and watching back edited footage of the show, so busy that she barely checked her phone or lost herself in thoughts of Luke. There was a lot going on, including a press plan to finalise with the PR department and a huge launch party ahead of the first episode. She had barely even thought

334

about the next stages of her divorce, now hopefully just a few signatures away. Ralph had already emailed Jas to set up a call to discuss things. Jas had never been so thankful that she was busy. She hoped to go for the entire day without running into Luke. But, that afternoon, he appeared at her desk.

'Hey!' She was surprised to see him and clearly it showed.

Luke was wearing black trousers and a pale blue shirt, looking devastatingly handsome as always. But there was something different about him today. His eyes darted quickly instead of looking at Jas straight on. He was fidgeting. Was he ... nervous?

'I was hoping I'd catch you,' he said briskly.

Jas nodded and tapped her fingers on her phone screen. 'Yep, I'm here. Where I always am.' This was so awkward.

'So, how did the hearing go on Friday?'

Jas hit her head with her palm. For the past two days, she'd been so consumed with her feelings for Luke that she still hadn't even thanked him yet for what he'd done for her.

'Oh my God. It went great, but only thanks to you. That woman ... all those women ... They told me what you did. How you went there to talk to them and persuade them to come forward. Thank you so, so much, Luke.'

He shifted uncomfortably.

'I can't believe you did that. I honestly don't know how to thank you.'

'I couldn't just stand by and let him get away with it,' said Luke, looking fully at Jas finally. 'I didn't want to see you hurt. No matter what happened with us in the past.'

The past. There was a yawning silence. Jas broke it.

'I came to your house, you know. To say thank you.' *And that I was falling in love with you.*

'When?'

'Friday afternoon. Straight after the hearing. Left my family in the pub not knowing where I was running off to. You can imagine how that went down.'

They both smiled and Jas was glad she'd broken the tension.

'So, what, you just stood outside my door?' asked Luke quietly. He edged closer to Jas now and having him within kissing distance was almost too much for her to bear.

'I was being dramatic,' she said breezily. 'I got all the way to your Tube station then figured I'd see you at work anyway on Monday and could thank you then. And I've been meaning to come and see you today but it's been so busy. Anyway, I felt a bit bad for ditching the family so I turned around and went back to them. I was sure you would be hanging out with your girlfriend anyway and I didn't want to disturb you on your day off.'

Luke opened his mouth to speak when an almighty, booming voice sounded from down the corridor.

'HAWKINS. My office, NOW!'

Luke turned around and Jas looked over to see Harry hurtling down the corridor towards them, with his assistant and a stern-looking woman Jas identified as Luke's boss in the legal department, running behind.

Harry shouted again and motioned for Luke to follow him into his office across the floor. 'That fucking imbecile host we have on the Friday-night chat show has only gone

336

and been arrested for being drunk behind the wheel and crashing into a pub. The fucking irony! He'd been drinking with several other Channel 6 presenters and we've got press and police on every phone line. It's a legal mind-fuck. Emergency meeting in my office, NOW!'

Luke was clearly annoyed and tried to stall Harry by nodding at him. 'Right there, boss.' He turned back to Jas. 'Listen, I ...'

'NOW!' Harry roared back.

'Go, Luke. Burrell looks like he's about to have a heart attack.'

'Shit! Okay. Can I call you later?'

Jas nodded, restraining a smile. Luke wanted to talk to her. About what? Jas longed to hear what he was about to say. She so wanted to talk to him too and finally tell him how she felt. She'd have to wait, though.

At 7 p.m. Luke was still locked in Harry's office and Jas assumed they'd be there all night. She was knackered. Satisfied she'd had a full and productive day, she swept her bag off her messy desk, thinking only about what she was going to pick up from the Tesco Express near her road for dinner.

An hour later and with a plastic bag full of ricotta and spinach tortellini, a pack of tomatoes, cucumber, salad leaves, sparkling water and a bottle of white wine, Jas walked into her flat and slammed the door shut. A quick salad and two-minute-to-cook pasta was her idea of food heaven. To hell with cooking a complicated meal for one.

She dumped the plastic bag on the counter in the kitchen and poured herself a generous white wine spritzer, kicking off her loafers and padding into her living room. Then she screamed so loudly the wine glass dropped from her hand, shattering into dozens of pieces, its contents spilling onto her feet and the floor. Sitting on the sofa, holding a glass of brandy, was Richard.

Chapter 42

'Hello, Jasmine.'

She held her right hand over her chest. Her heart was beating furiously at the shock of seeing her soon-to-be-ex-husband sitting comfortably on the sofa as if he was still living with her. 'What the fuck are you doing here? How did you get in?'

'Oh, you still keep your spare keys in the same little pot by the microwave, darling. I helped myself to them when Lila asked me over. Thought they might come in handy one day.' He finished off the brandy and wiped his running nose. He looked like he hadn't slept for days, and Jas knew that this could well be true.

'She did tell you about the little party we had back here, didn't she? Lots of fun. I like what you've done with the bedroom.'

Jas shivered at the thought of Richard in her home. Jas reached for her bag and rummaged around for her phone. It wasn't there.

Richard got to his feet, his eyes bulging, and wiped his nose again.

'I would sit down if I were you, Jasmine. We've got lots to talk about.'

'No way. Get out of here, Richard.' But he came towards her, making her back away into the kitchen.

'I lost my job today. Because of all this.'

'You can't blame our divorce for you losing your job, Richard. Plenty of people split up and still manage to stay employed.' But she'd never seen her husband look like this. She knew the drugs were getting heavy, but she'd had no idea things were so out of control. The person she was looking at now was not her husband, not the Richard she once knew.

'Please, sit down and let's just talk about it,' she said softly, reasoning that talking to him rather than shouting was the best way forward. Then the entryphone buzzed.

'Don't move,' Richard said.

'Why don't I just go and get rid of them quickly?' Jas could easily run to the door but didn't want to make any sudden movements around Richard just yet, still hoping she could talk him down.

'They say I've brought shame on Curtis Stoddard,' Richard continued, pouring himself another brandy from the near-empty bottle by the sink. 'This nonsense has been going on for long enough now. It's high time I moved back in, don't you think?'

Had he completely lost it? He was clearly off his face.

'We'll call off the divorce,' he told her. 'You'll say it was all one big mistake and you've changed your mind. I'll get my job back and then everything will be normal.'

Jas shook her head furiously. 'No, Richard.'

The buzzer sounded again, an angry shrill sound that only seemed to antagonise Richard further.

'Dammit, Jas!' This time he banged the empty bottle so hard on the sink it smashed in two, so that he held one jagged shard of glass in his hand. He held it close to his other wrist and tears came to his eyes. 'Everything has turned to shit. I might as well fucking end it right here.'

A fist started banging on the door, followed by a voice outside in the corridor. 'Jas? Jas, are you okay?'

Luke.

'Don't move,' Richard said to her again, quietly. He dashed the tears from his red, bloodshot eyes and the sweat from his upper lip. 'Is this your boyfriend come to rescue you? How nice.'

Jas thought quickly. She couldn't risk staying with him here, not in this mood and armed with broken glass. She bolted for the door, Richard right behind her, and flung it open. 'Luke, watch out!' she called.

Richard was coming towards them with the glass raised in his hand, but Luke grabbed Jas and swung them both to one side. Richard tripped and fell to the ground. Luke instinctively kicked the broken bottle out of the way. Richard, out of control now, came at him with both fists flailing and swung at him. Richard was strong, but he was no match for Luke. After a short tussle he punched Richard once so hard he fell to the ground and lay still, breathing but unconscious.

Jas and Luke stood above the crumpled figure, both of them suffering from shock and trying to process what had just happened.

'Your ex?' asked Luke.

Jas nodded. 'I – I don't know what happened. I've never seen him like this, ever.'

'He's dangerous and he needs help,' Luke said firmly, and called the police. Then he turned to Jas. They stared at each other for a few seconds before she ran into his arms.

'I came to talk to you when Burrell finally let us go,' Luke said as he hugged her tight. 'You'd left your phone on your desk so I figured you'd come home without noticing.' He took Jas's phone out of his trouser pocket. 'Good thing I came when I did. Now, please tell me that's the only mental ex I have to deal with and there are no more murky secrets?'

Jas couldn't help but laugh and start crying at the same time. Everything was catching up with her. 'On Friday, I did come to your house. I saw you and that girl on your doorstep and ran away. And that's my very last secret. Promise.'

He lifted her chin and made her look straight at him. 'Yeah, I pretty much worked that out. I had just broken up with Laura, Jas. We weren't serious. It was only ever a few dates. I told her I couldn't see her while I was in love with you.'

'What?'

'You heard me, Whiteley.' And then they were kissing. Not in the ferocious, passionate, lustful way they had in Ibiza, but long, comforting kisses, with Luke's arms wrapped so tightly around her that Jas felt there was no one else in the world. She had never felt more secure or happy in her life.

One month later

'Happy birthday to youuuuuuu!'

Jas covered her face with her hands in embarrassment as the chorus rang out, sung by her friends and family. Nearby diners turned around to start clapping. A ginormous, elaborate chocolate birthday cake with butter icing and lit sparklers for decoration had just been wheeled in on a dessert cart.

Luke leant in and kissed her cheek. 'Happy birthday, darling.'

'You could have made less of a fuss,' she laughed, shifting closer as he wrapped an arm around her.

'What, now I've finally got you all to myself? This is just the start. Make a wish.'

Jas had thought she was just going for a quiet birthday dinner with Luke to celebrate her twenty-ninth, but when she arrived at the cool and upmarket Hakkasan restaurant in the West End, a seven-strong group yelled 'Surprise!' Unlike this time last year, she was delighted by the ambush. Seated at the table with Luke were Lila, Meg, Oscar, Monica, and Michael and Kimberley, his siblings, whom

Jas had met two weeks previously and fallen completely in love with. Michael was essentially an older version of Luke: polite, charming and handsome; Kim, fast-talking, constantly on her phone, wearing bold lipstick, had instantly reminded Jas of Lila and she wasn't at all surprised to see them already becoming firm friends.

Jas blew out her candles to a round of applause and a waiter started cutting generous slices of cake and distributing them around the table.

'Had any offers on the flat yet, Jas?' asked Oscar, wiping chocolate from the side of his mouth. As he was an estate agent, Jas had asked his advice before she'd put her flat on the market last month.

'Tons already! I can't believe it.'

'Oh, it's a great property,' continued Oscar. 'You'll make a good profit on it.'

'And, most importantly, get a fresh start,' put in Meg.

'Exactly,' replied Jas. 'After the whole nightmare with Richard I couldn't face living there again. Too many awful memories.'

'Any word on when his case comes up?' asked Meg.

Jas shook her head. 'But he was denied bail and is locked up on remand and out of harm's way. I really hope they send him to rehab and he gets the help he needs.'

Luke kissed her again.

Lila started clapping like an excited child. 'Let's do presents, let's do presents!' Then she was distracted by Kim and they both started taking selfies.

'Mine first,' said Meg. She handed a box to Jas and a soft package as well. Jas opened them up to find a bottle of pink gin and the stunning black dress she'd been eyeing up in Meg's boutique the last time she'd been to Manchester.

'Babe, I love them, thank you!'

'We might as well celebrate one of us being able to wear slinky outfits and get pissed!' Meg smiled at Oscar, who affectionately rubbed her very distinct pregnancy bump. Meg liked to moan about not being able to drink but Jas knew it meant nothing to her. She was thrilled by the prospect of being a mother and Jas couldn't be happier for them.

Her phone bleeped with a stream of WhatsApp messages from Dylan and Charlotte, beaming to the camera from a sandy beach. She showed Monica. 'It's their last day in the Maldives. Look at them!'

'Just call us Cupid,' nodded Monica. 'How happy they are. Which brings us nicely to my present.'

'You already got me a clutch bag!'

'Well, I've got something else for you. Technically, it's from Burrell.' Monica reached under the table and with a flourish produced a bottle of champagne with a blue ribbon tied around it and a card, which Jas read aloud.

'"Congratulations on what we know will be the show of the year, Whiteley. I've commissioned the second series so don't come in too hung-over on Monday. There's a lot of work to do."'

'Wow! A second series before the first has even been on air!' Everyone congratulated Jas and Monica, who hugged over the table.

'That's how much he believes in us, babe,' Monica said.

'I never doubted it for a second,' said Luke. 'Now it's my turn! I've got one more gift for you.'

'No! You already organised this whole dinner,' protested Jas. 'And gave me several presents this morning,' she whispered, thinking back to their marathon sex session followed by Luke whipping up a birthday breakfast of scrambled eggs, fruit, black coffee and a glass of champagne, before sending her off on a spa day in Sloane Square with Lila and Meg. He really was the perfect guy.

'Well, I can take it back if you want.' He smiled, placing a small blue box on the table.

Jas gasped as she opened it to find a thin gold ring set with three tiny emeralds. It was elegant, understated and completely beautiful.

'Oh my God!' screeched Kim and Lila in unison.

'Calm down,' said Luke. 'It's not *that* sort of ring.' He turned to Jas. 'I just thought, now that your old relationship is well and truly in the past, you might like to wear a piece of jewellery to celebrate your new one.'

Jas threw her arms around him as the whole table jibed them to 'get a room'. As Jas looked around at her loved ones, while being held in the arms of her dream man, she thought how lucky she was. She might just have spent the year from hell, but now she knew she was on a winning streak. Game over.